THE SWAN

The Lovers Duet

Book 2

ELLIE MASTERS

MASTER OF ROMANTIC SUSPENSE

JEM Publishing

This book is dedicated to my one and only—my amazing and wonderful husband.

Without your care and support, my writing would not have made it this far.

You pushed me when I needed to be pushed.

You supported me when I felt discouraged.

You believed in me when I didn't believe in myself.

If it weren't for you, this book never would have come to life.

The LIGHTER SIDE

Ellie Masters is the lighter side of the Jet & Ellie Masters writing duo! You will find Contemporary Romance, Military Romance, Romantic Suspense, Billionaire Romance, and Rock Star Romance in Ellie's Works.

YOU CAN FIND ELLIE'S BOOKS HERE:

ELLIEMASTERS.COM/BOOKS

Shop Ellie Masters Romantic Suspense and Steamy Contemporary Romance by series.

Angel Fire Rock Romance

Guardian HRS: Alpha Team

Guardian HRS: Bravo Team

Guardian HRS: Charlie Team

Guardian HRS: Delta Team

Cerberus Personal Security

The LaRouge Triplets

The One I Want Series

Angel's Peak Series

Billionaire Boy's Club

The Lovers

Changing Roles

SUGGESTED READING ORDER

START HERE

Rockstar Romance

The Angel Fire Rock Romance Series

EACH BOOK IN THIS SERIES CAN BE READ AS A STANDALONE AND IS ABOUT A DIFFERENT COUPLE WITH AN **HEA**.

IT IS RECOMMENDED THEY ARE READ IN ORDER.

Heart's Insanity

Ashes to New

Heart's Desire

Heart's Collide

Hearts Divided

Hearts Entwined

Forest's FALL

Hearts The Last Beat

CONTINUE HERE...

Military Romance

Guardian Hostage Rescue Specialists

Rescuing Melissa

(Get a FREE copy of Rescuing Melissa when you join Ellie's Newsletter)

Alpha Team

Rescuing Zoe

Rescuing Moira

Rescuing Eve

Rescuing Lily

Rescuing Jinx

Rescuing Maria

Bravo Team

Rescuing Angie

Rescuing Isabelle

Rescuing Carmen

Rescuing Rosalie

Rescuing Kaye

Cara's Protector

Rescuing Barbi

Charlie Team

Rescuing Rebel

Rescuing Stitch

Rescuing Mia

Jenna's Protector

Rescuing Sophia

Rescuing Malia

Rescuing Ally (Part 1)

Rescuing Ally (Part 2)

Delta Team

Rescuing Ember

Rescuing Aria

STANDALONES IN THE GUARDIAN HOSTAGE RESCUE SERIES YOU CAN READ ANYTIME

Saving Abby

Saving Ariel

Saving Brie

Saving Cate

Saving Dani

Saving Jen

The LaRouge Triplets

Asher

Brody

Cage

Billionaire Romance

Billionaire Boys Club

Hawke

Richard

Contemporary Romance

Cocky Captain

Romantic Suspense

EACH BOOK IS A STANDALONE NOVEL.

The Starling

The Swan

~AND~

Science Fiction

To My Readers

This book is a work of fiction. It does not exist in the real world and should not be construed as reality. As in most romantic fiction, I've taken liberties. I've compressed the romance into a sliver of time. I've allowed these characters to develop strong bonds of trust over a matter of days.

This does not happen in real life where you, my amazing readers, live. Take more time in your romance and learn who you're giving a piece of your heart to. I urge you to move with caution. Always protect yourself.

Grab the First Book in The Guardian Hostage Rescue Specialists Series for Free

https://elliemasters.com/RescuingMelissa

ONE

PAUL: The Auction

A NOTE BEFORE YOU BEGIN
! THIS IS NOT A STANDALONE !

This is Book Two.
Every love story has a beginning.
The Swan picks up immediately after *The Starling* ends. If you
haven't met Paul and Vivianne yet—if you don't know about the
Van Gogh, the kiss in Paris, or the secret that changed everything
—stop here.
Trust me. You don't want to miss how it all began.
Read The Starling first.
Then come back.
They'll be waiting.

THIRTY MILLION DOLLARS AND A BIOWEAPON—NICHOLAS ALWAYS
did like to gift-wrap his revenge.

The second painting of the evening shines under the spot-lights—a lesser Monet that won't kill anyone, unlike *Dr. Gachet,* which waits its turn like a loaded gun.

The bid price climbs past eight million, but my mind calculates different numbers.

Ten years since Nicholas and I called each other brother.

Ten days since Vivianne crashed into my world.

Three since she uncovered my secret—and Nicholas returned to steal *Dr. Gachet,* concealing anthrax beneath Van Gogh's paint.

And just five minutes since Vivianne touched my shoulder and whispered she needed water.

The bidding draws to its close, paddles dropping one by one. Urakov shifts his weight, ready to fight for his motherland's bioweapon. The terrorists think they're buying death in a frame. Interpol thinks they're tracing arms money. Vivianne thinks we're here to recover stolen art.

They're all right, and all wrong.

Nicholas orchestrated this entire setup, and I still don't know why.

"Sold!"

Bidding ends on the second painting, and *Dr. Gachet* is brought to the podium. Vivianne has yet to return.

Where is she?

After I specifically told her to stay close.

I don't have time to track her down. *Dr. Gachet* is up, and the opening bid is placed.

Urakov takes position at the opposite end of the room, close to the podium. His back is to me and the rest of the crowd. The Russian intends to bid and reclaim what he hopes is smuggled inside, but if I let Urakov have the painting, it will be lost to the world.

Vivianne wants to return *Dr. Gachet* to the Musée d'Orsay. I will see it done.

The whole exchange smells wrong, and I can't determine Nicholas's role in either theft.

In a usual exchange, a client who needs to launder several million dollars purchases a painting. Dirty cash transfers for the commodity, becoming washed in the process. In a separate event, that process reverses. The client resells the painting, pulling out clean cash.

The painting serves as nothing more than a vehicle for moving money. Nicholas complicated that transaction by adding the anthrax.

But why?

The seller must have commissioned the theft of *Dr. Gachet* and the procurement of the anthrax. They combined the two, turning the painting into a mule for the bioweapon.

The buyers intend to exchange cash for the painting and obtain the anthrax. I have no idea what the market value of weaponized anthrax might be, but the numbers don't add up.

Whoever buys the painting will be able to sell it for nearly as much as they paid, perhaps more. The puzzle nags at me.

I've yet to place a bid, but I'm tracking those in the crowd who are actively bidding. Urakov screws with the whole process. He's too obvious and too eager. His attempts to outbid his competitors unnecessarily raise the price.

I scan the room again, looking for Vivianne. Someone here works for the terrorist cell Interpol is trying to take down, and I can't let my distraction undermine that goal.

Is Interpol even aware of the bioweapons exchange?

There was no mention of it in my talks with Agent Radcliffe. It was always about tracing the flow of money, identifying the buyer, and tracking them down. I'm not even tasked with securing *Dr. Gachet*.

The Americans and Interpol have more critical concerns than whether a painting goes missing. Their intelligence never mentioned a transaction of weapons-grade anthrax. Either they don't trust me with that information, or they don't have a clue.

Urakov's frantic bidding skyrockets the price until the bid frequency drops. Still no Vivianne.

Unlike those I'm working with, I want that painting. I'll let Urakov confiscate the anthrax and return it to his homeland, but the painting belongs to me.

As for the buyers?

There are only three men actively left in the bidding war.

Within seconds of placing my bid, someone outbids me. It isn't Urakov. The Russian shifts on the balls of his feet and rubs the back of his neck. Perhaps his countrymen's pockets aren't as deep as he thought, which works in my favor.

The price climbs, and one of the three men drops out of the bidding, leaving me in competition with two others. I take another look around, making certain I'm not missing someone.

As the price edges past twenty million, another bidder bows out, leaving me going head-to-head with Bald Willy.

Why would William Teniford IV be mixed in with terrorists?

The price climbs, and Bald Willy grows nervous. My bid stands, but another is placed before the announcer pronounces it sold—not by Bald Willy and not by either of the other men.

What the hell?

I scan the room and nearly miss placing my next bid. Annabelle LaCroix, the woman who spoke with Vivianne. In her tight-fisted grip, she swipes the screen—the bid price changes.

I respond, placing my bid, and track her thumb. Unlike me, she isn't paying attention to the crowd. She focuses on the painting and the screen behind it, signaling the current bid price.

She swipes again, and the price ticks upward. I place an answering bid.

We play the game for a time, inching the bid out of the twenties and into the thirty-million range. Merlin would raise a brow, but I'm not concerned. After all, we have the painting's twin squirreled away in the cave.

The arrogant Japanese businessman, who spent more than eighty-two million, thinks to keep it hidden, crated, and stored in a warehouse in Japan, but he owns nothing more than another Starling masterpiece.

The version I bid on now isn't worth thirty million, but the pair will bring in well over a hundred million as a set.

The woman twists toward her date, leaning close to confer in a hurried whisper. Too far to hear, and I can't read her lips, but I can guess.

Like Urakov, they are reaching the limits of their funds.

My bid sits on the screen. The auctioneer raps the gavel.

Once.

Twice.

Where the hell is Vivianne?

Sold!

I'm now the proud owner of a painting and enough anthrax to take out a small city. I've been discreet in placing my bids, but I can't be sure I haven't been watched as well.

Attendants remove *Dr. Gachet* from the podium and bring up the next piece. Annabelle LaCroix blanches and tugs on her date's sleeve. The two of them head to the back of the room, passing me.

I give a curt dip of my head in greeting but am ignored as she sweeps past with a determined expression. I can only imagine the tense conversation she will have with her partners.

Now, to find Vivianne. I turn toward the restrooms, but Urakov grabs my shoulder.

"A word."

"Not now." I glance at my shoulder, making a point to stare at his meaty hand.

Urakov lifts it and takes a step back. "We need to talk."

"In a moment." I lower my voice. "Have you seen Vivianne?"

"Your woman?"

"Yes."

"Haven't been paying attention."

Without a word, I head toward the exit. The guard sits on a stool next to the door. He stands as we approach. I wave him off.

"Où sont les toilettes?"

The man gestures down a dimly lit hall. "Avant-dernière porte à gauche."

I march down the hall. Urakov follows. I don't stop at the men's toilet but knock on the door of the women's facilities.

"Vivianne?" No response. I bang on the wood-slatted doors of the two privacy stalls. The place is empty.

Running a hand through my hair, I stare at the empty room. There is no other place she could be, and I can't think of one reason she would leave the boathouse during the auction.

"What's wrong?" Urakov stands in the doorway. I didn't realize the Russian followed me.

"Something's not right."

"That's for sure. We lost the painting."

I shake my head. "The painting is being crated as we speak. It'll be delivered within an hour of the auction closing."

"To whom?" Urakov pulls at his chin.

"To me."

"You bought it?"

"I did."

"That is not what we discussed."

I hush him and lower my voice. "Probably not the best place for this conversation."

"My property—"

"Will be returned to you." I exit the women's restroom and scan the hall.

The low lighting makes it hard to make out details. Bidding continues in the main room. The doorman mans his post, focused on the people gathered rather than on me and Urakov.

Turning the other direction, I step toward the end of the hall, noting how it continues around a sharp bend. I gesture for Urakov to follow. Around the corner, the hall ends at another thick wooden door.

I try the latch.

Locked.

"Merde!"

Something is off, and I hate where my thoughts are headed.

"Come," I say to Urakov.

"Where?"

"I don't want to lose track of that painting." If what I fear has happened is true, I can't afford to let *Dr. Gachet* out of my sight.

On our way back to the auction, heading past the restrooms, I kick a discarded bottle of water. It careens across the floor, hitting the far wall. Then I step on a piece of paper. I stoop to pick it up. The fold widens, giving me a glimpse inside.

"Merde!" My curse draws Urakov's attention.

"What?"

Unfolding the paper, I look upon a Merlin Falcon in flight. Many think Merlin's name derived from the court of King Arthur, but that isn't its origin. Merlins are fierce falcons, powerful fliers that use surprise attacks to bring down songbirds. Medieval falconers called them lady hawks, and noblewomen commonly used them to hunt. What better name for a thief?

My breathing hitches when I read the inscription. *Tu as volé l'amour de ma vie. Maintenant, c'est à ton tour de souffrir.* You stole the love of my life. Now, it's time for you to suffer.

It could only have been written by one man.

"He took her." The words grind through my teeth.

"Your Vivianne?"

"Yes."

"Who?"

I gesture back toward the auction. "The man who stole that painting. The one who stole the anthrax."

My brother took Vivianne and is playing a very dangerous game. Like a master strategist, Nicholas leaves me with few options. Without knowing where Vivianne is, I can't pursue, and with *Dr. Gachet* purchased, I can't leave the building until the end of the auction.

Nicholas backed me into the perfect dilemma. I've been effectively immobilized.

The auction is still in progress. For security purposes, none of the pieces will be removed from the room until the auction concludes. *Dr. Gachet* has returned to its spot on the wall. Fortunately, only a few paintings are left up for bid.

Once my funds clear, I'll receive text instructions for picking up the piece. After crating, the auction house will either freight ship the piece to a place designated by the buyer or release it immediately after the event.

I intend to oversee that entire process.

When the text arrives, I indicate my preference and confirm my identity with a unique code. I'm instructed to remain after the auction ends. Those who didn't purchase any items, along with those who opted to have them shipped, clear the room.

I, Urakov, and Bald Willy are the only people left.

"Hello." William Teniford approaches. "It seems we are the lucky ones."

"Indeed." I clasp hands with Bald Willy.

Willy gives a pompous bow. "William Teniford the Fourth, and you are?"

"Paul de Gaulle."

Urakov grimaces as the Englishman shakes his hand. "Urakov Tarasovich."

"A pleasure." Willy's eyes are overly eager. "This is the first time I've been fortunate to win a bid."

"Congratulations."

Willy leans forward, perhaps expecting more than the terse reply. "Which piece will you be taking home?"

Urakov clears his throat. The loud, grumbly sound silences poor Willy. Fortunately, the auctioneer arrives, cutting off further discussion about who bought what.

The tall, thin, balding man glances at the three of us with confusion. "I was only expecting two."

There is no way to avoid association with Urakov, and the Russian will not walk out without his motherland's property firmly in his hands.

"He's with me."

The auctioneer cocks his head, wise enough not to ask too many questions. "As you wish." He turns and gestures to a door at the front of the room.

Urakov clears his throat, but Willy speaks into that silence. "If you don't mind, I'd rather not step away from my purchase."

"Of course." The auctioneer directs his next words to me. "Would you like to wait in our lounge while your purchase is crated?"

"No. I'll wait with the painting."

"One moment, please." He excuses himself, speaks to one of the attendants, and returns with two locked boxes.

Willy grabs the one offered and swipes his phone over the lock. I take the other. Before Willy can engage me in ponderous conversation, I stride to the bar, order whiskey, and only then open the box to retrieve my and Vivianne's cell phones. Urakov joins me and asks for a vodka pour, which leaves William Teniford to occupy himself alone.

A few minutes later, four men arrive. Two go to *Dr. Gachet*, and the others go to a larger but insignificant piece.

"Gentlemen," the auctioneer says, "if you will follow me."

Willy follows the men as they cart off his newest acquisition. Urakov and I bracket the two men holding *Dr. Gachet* and follow them through the doorway.

My cell phone buzzes. A text from an unknown number.

She's mine.

Only one person could have sent it. Gritting my teeth, I respond.

Nicholas.

Do you know what day this is?

It's Saturday, but that is not the answer Nicholas wants. I rack my brain, wondering what significance this day holds for him.

Don't mess with me…brother.

Although not born of blood, we bonded deeply as brothers. We loved each other fiercely. Defended the other when attacked. We shared secrets and painful truths. And we fought like devils over the same women, even the one who finally came between us and destroyed our fraternal bond.

Love turned to hate on the cusp of a single moment.

Merde. I know this day. Ten years to the day, sweet Catherine died. Now Nicholas has Vivianne.

It's time you paid for your sins.

Anger boils up from deep within, churning in my gut, hungry for destruction. I haven't seen Nicholas in ten years, but the rage returns as hot and fiery as that fated night.

It's nearly too much to handle. I force myself to breathe before I react and regret what comes next.

Urakov glances over. "Everything all right?"

Hatred smolders within, and I narrow my eyes, weighing the pros and cons of all the creative ways I want to exact my revenge.

But then I face an uncomfortable truth. Nicholas is already two steps ahead.

"Everything's fine."

Dr. Gachet is mine.

I have no further interest in that painting.

I think you do. Are you interested in a trade?

A long stretch passes without a response. Bald Willy and the men he follows take a sudden right turn, but those transporting *Dr. Gachet* continue forward. Urakov scans the hall, his gaze darting to either side, forward, and back. His head is fixed on a swivel, tracking everywhere and everyone at once.

I should be doing the same. Instead, I grip the phone and wait for Nicholas's response. I tap Urakov's shoulder and gesture for him to hang back.

Go home, brother. I'll be in touch.

"Be prepared for trouble." I keep my voice low.

Urakov pats his chest. "Always."

My mind races, calculating the next moves in this dangerous game Nicholas initiated. He took Vivianne, and now he holds all the cards. The painting, once my primary concern, now seems inconsequential compared to her safety. But I can't let Nicholas know how much she means to me. That only gives him more leverage.

As we continue down the corridor, I'm acutely aware of every sound and shadow. Nicholas could have accomplices anywhere. I need to secure *Dr. Gachet* and then focus all my resources on finding Vivianne.

But how?

Nicholas is a ghost, impossible to track unless he wants to be found.

"What's the plan?" Urakov's voice is low and gravelly.

I consider my options carefully before responding. "We secure the painting. Then we need to have a very private conversation."

Urakov nods, understanding the weight of my words. He knows something has gone terribly wrong, but he's smart enough not to ask for details.

At least, not here.

We reach a secure room where *Dr. Gachet* is to be crated. I watch every move the handlers make, ensuring nothing is slipped into the crate and no switches are made.

Paranoid?

Perhaps.

But with Nicholas in play, I can't afford to take any chances.

As the crate is sealed, my phone buzzes again. I tense, expecting another message from Nicholas, but it's the auction house confirming the transaction details. I breathe out slowly, trying to calm my nerves.

"Mr. de Gaulle, your purchase is ready for transport. How would you like to proceed?"

I lock eyes with Urakov before responding. "I'll be taking it with me now."

The handler nods. "Very well, sir. If you'll follow me to complete the final paperwork."

As we walk, I lean close to Urakov. "I need you to secure transport—something discreet but heavily guarded. Can you manage that?"

A curt nod. "Consider it done."

While I handle the paperwork, my mind is elsewhere. Where did Nicholas take Vivianne? What is his endgame? And most importantly, how can I turn this situation to my advantage?

As I sign the last document, a chilling thought occurs. What if the painting isn't what Nicholas is after?

What if this entire elaborate setup—the theft, the auction, even the anthrax—was all to reach Vivianne?

My jaw clenches, anger and fear warring within me. If that's the case, I've played right into his hands. But two can play at this game. If Nicholas wants to dig up the past, he'll be reminded why I was always the more dangerous brother.

Urakov returns just as I finish. "Transport is ready."

I nod. "Let's move. We have a long night ahead of us."

As we leave the auction house, *Dr. Gachet* is secured. Vivianne's fate remains unknown. Nicholas may think he has the upper hand, but he's forgotten one crucial detail.

I always win.

TWO

Paul: The Chalet

I EXPECT TROUBLE DURING THE LOADING OF DR. GACHET INTO MY Mercedes. Fortunately, the painting is small—just under two feet by two feet—and, with packing and crating materials, it easily fits inside the generous trunk of my car.

But where to?

Do I go to the chalet like Nicholas ordered? Would I be walking into a trap? Or do I stay in Lac Léman and secure the painting at the Russian consulate?

That is the wisest choice, but that painting is my bargaining chip. Whoever hired Nicholas will expect my brother to complete the transaction. For the moment, the painting stays with me.

After a quick discussion with Urakov, the Russian agrees with the plan. If he genuinely cares about the stash of anthrax hidden inside, he should argue more strongly to secure it at the consulate, but Urakov's jaw twitches every time I mention Vivianne.

I don't head to the chalet alone. Urakov and his men follow me back up the winding mountain roads. Urakov refuses to leave my side, muttering more about how we're going to get Vivianne back than what we're going to do with the painting.

The company is welcome. It gives me time to plan.

The drive down took just under two hours. I make it back in less than ninety minutes. Not caring about the winding road and hairpin curves, the Mercedes navigates the challenging terrain with the roar of its V12 bi-turbo engine.

Urakov's men try to keep up but lag in the curves. They can't match the precision of German engineering.

Still no response from Nicholas.

My brother is likely conferring with those who hired him. If this job is like any of the others we did together in the past, Nicholas didn't fulfill his commitment when he delivered the painting to the auction house.

For Nicholas's business to be concluded, it has to reach the buyer.

I robbed Nicholas of that.

My stomach turns at the thought of transporting anthrax in the back of my car, but Urakov assures me the people who smuggled it aren't keen on exposing themselves to the deadly spores. Protective measures are in place, he insists. I take faith in their desire for self-preservation because my life hinges on it.

What I don't know—and what Urakov ponders as well—is how to remove the anthrax from the painting without damaging the protective coating.

Urakov knows the two will be together, but not how the anthrax is stored. It could be in the frame, inserted inside a hollowed-out compartment, or sandwiched between the canvas and protective backing.

"And you expect him to accept this trade?" Urakov drags his finger up the seam of his dark suit. "He won't hurt your woman?"

"I'm counting on whoever hired him calling him out."

"How's that?"

"He was hired to procure the weapon and orchestrate a sale that can't be traced. That didn't happen. The buyers have nothing. That means Nicholas failed."

"They paid for nothing. Wouldn't they start over?"

"Are you saying it's that easy to get more anthrax?" I glance at him. "One would hope your people secured that area, moved the remaining supply, or destroyed it completely."

Using DNA analysis, once the spores are released, the outbreak will be traced back to Russia, which will then be tasked with admitting that they not only never destroyed their war stock but also lost control of their supply. There's always the possibility they orchestrated the whole thing.

From my conversations with Urakov, however, the Russian government doesn't care about the loss of life. It's the humiliation and international debacle that must be avoided at all costs.

"That is... complicated."

I text Merlin and fill my father in. His replies are brief and terser than Nicholas's texts.

"We're almost there." A glance in the rearview mirror reveals no sign of Urakov's men.

I have to slow down. They know where to go, but they need access through the gates. I shake my head and ease off the gas.

By the time twin headlights flash in the rearview mirror, I pull into the drive leading to the chalet. I stop at the iron gates and wait for Urakov's men to join us. Once they're close, I open the gates and roll forward. They follow behind, the gates closing silently as our tires crunch over the fallen snow.

The snow glows under the moon's pale light, casting gray shadows across the land. Light spills from the chalet, tumbling outward to spread across a lawn slumbering beneath the snow. Smoke drifts up from two of the ten chimneys, and I can imagine Merlin pacing before a raging fire burning in the library hearth.

The conversation we will soon have will tear my heart out.

As I drive up the circular drive, a slice of light catches my eye where there should be none. The front door is open, exposing the chalet to the frigid night air. My pulse leaps.

I slam on the brakes, jerking the car to a sudden halt.

"Something's wrong." I turn to Urakov. "Stay with the painting."

The massive wrought-iron doors stand ajar. I sprint up the stone steps, racing to get inside. Urakov's men pull to a stop beside my car, and the thudding of feet pounds behind me.

Inside, set upon an easel, a blank canvas points toward the door. Scrawled across it is a message.

HIM or HER?

I stumble to a stop, press both hands to my temples, and dig my fingers into my hair.

"Nicholas!" My roar shakes the foundations of my home.

A piece of paper is pinned to the canvas.

"What is this?" Urakov thunders into the entrance and pulls to a stop.

"A message." I approach the canvas and remove the hastily written letter. Not Nicholas's hand, but the shaky tremors of Merlin's elegant script.

You may save only one. This is not a time for fun and games. Father or the girl. You choose. Old or new?

A phone number is scrawled at the bottom, and smudges of ink dot the page.

A code.

Merlin left a message.

Fly, my son.

No. I won't choose. Quick taps on my cell phone tell Nicholas precisely what I think of the choice given to me. This time, the reply comes lightning quick.

CHOOSE!

I read the message and grip the phone.

"What does he say?"

"He demands an exchange. He has my father, and I must choose between him or Vivianne."

"That man has no soul." Urakov follows his outburst with a string of curse words in Russian, then stamps his feet. "We can't let him have the anthrax, the girl, or your father."

"I know my brother. He'll know if we've tampered with the painting. I'm afraid we have little choice."

"There are always choices." Urakov levels his gaze at me. "It's your job to make good use of them."

And that is the truth.

"What will you do?"

"My goals haven't changed."

"Are we going to have an issue over this painting, my friend?"

"I know what you're capable of." Urakov steps closer. "And there is no honor in what this man has done or intends to do. Tell me how I might help."

The tension drains from my shoulders. Urakov will help—at least for now.

"First, I need to secure the chalet." I have to ensure that the cave isn't compromised. "Then, we need to make sure the painting is safe."

"You want to store it here?" Urakov arches a brow, glancing at the open door.

I don't blame him. Keeping a painting safe in a home that's recently been the site of a kidnapping might not make much sense, but I don't trust anyplace else.

"Have your men bring the painting inside. I have a vault, and you can leave them to guard it while I deal with Nicholas."

"I'll do one better than that." Urakov pulls out his cell phone.

While Urakov speaks to his contact, I debate where to store *Dr. Gachet*. Nicholas demands an exchange, but I have no intention of handing over the painting.

I won't take it to the cave.

Urakov and his men don't need to know about the cave's existence, but I have several other vaults on the premises. Nicholas knows about the cave, but we've changed the security system since his arrest a decade ago. Vivianne found her way in only because I left the door unsecured.

Dr. Gachet won't be left alone. Urakov will see to that. He's gathering reinforcements. Between the three of us, Nicholas was always the savviest with technology. I have the artistic touch, but Nicholas can ferret himself into and out of any vault. And Catherine, sweet Catherine, she was a beguiling angel.

Going up against my brother will take everything I have.

THREE

Vivianne: Bait

Other than the low drone of a generator, silence presses in. My last memory is the foul stench of whatever saturated that cloth.

Drugged and kidnapped, I wake to darkness.

I blink, but the blackness remains, as does the scratchiness of cloth over my face.

Still hooded.

My toes drum against the floor beneath my feet—concrete, from the sound of it. Whoever took me hasn't bothered to remove my shoes or strip me. The tight embrace of my gown still hugs my skin.

Small mercies.

They aren't interested in raping me—at least, not yet. I mean more to them intact than defiled. I take whatever hope I can find.

The floor is concrete. I could be anywhere—a warehouse, deep underground, an isolated prison cell. A basement. A shipping container.

I struggle, whipping my head back and forth, and the cloth

slowly works its way loose. With a final violent shake, I free myself from the offensive hood.

An old-fashioned bulb hangs from a bare wire overhead, suspended from a thick iron beam. The pool of light fades into darkness in every direction. My metal chair is the only piece of furniture in sight.

A warehouse. Abandoned, from the looks of it. The concrete is old and cracked, layers of dirt and dust coating the floor. It's chilly—not the frigid temperatures of the mountains, but the cold night air around Lac Léman. Overhead, gaps in the ceiling reveal the ragged outlines of a starry sky against the roof's darker blackness.

Still night, then.

Heavy steps approach from behind me. I stop moving, unsure whether to twist around and locate my kidnapper or continue facing away. My heart races, pounding so loud I'm sure he can hear it.

"I see you've divested yourself of the hood."

A man. Not surprising. Kidnapping tends to be a masculine-dominated sport. I expect at least one. There are probably others, although only one pair of feet approaches.

"I suppose introductions are in order." His deep baritone reverberates in the stillness of the warehouse. In another place, the low rumble might be comforting. Power threads through his words, like Paul's, but this man's voice occupies a lower register. Rolling thunder across a stormy night.

I jerk as he stops behind my chair. The scent of his cologne washes over me—sexy and sophisticated, warring with my mental image of a grizzled street criminal.

He pauses as if waiting for a response, but I have nothing to say.

"It's okay." His tone softens. "I know quite a bit about you, but I'm fairly certain the same is not true for you." A *tsk* sound.

"I'm not sure the same wouldn't be said for my brother. I'm wondering, though, if you know who he is."

He means to bait me. I don't rise to it.

Give as little information as possible, Viv.

My father taught me those lessons.

Humanize yourself if ever placed in the position of a victim.

People hurt things. They kill things. My goal is to ensure this man sees me as a person and not as a disposable thing.

"Who are you?" My voice comes out steadier than I feel.

He knows who I am and holds the advantage. Asking why I've been taken might be the more pertinent question, but the directness of that line of questioning doesn't humanize our interaction.

"Now, that's an interesting question, Miss Faulks. I've been many things to many people. An unwanted child. A survivor of the streets. I've been poorer than a street rat and richer than most men. I've been beaten and used, cherished and loved. I've been both the favored and prodigal son. I'm a brother to a man I hate and to a sister I once loved more than life itself." He pauses. "Who are you, Miss Faulks? Are you any of those? Or are you simply a spoiled, rich brat with far too much wealth and a family name you don't deserve? Who are you?"

"I'm just me."

But that's a lie. And, more importantly, he knows it.

"Just you?" A scoff. "I suppose, in the deep of night, that's all any of us are. But, for now, you're nothing but bait in a trap."

"B-bait?" The stammer betrays me.

He doesn't answer, and there's nothing humanizing about being called bait. Bait is disposable. My survival depends on changing that status.

"My father—"

"I care nothing about your father." He cuts me off. "You're not here because of him, and if you're offering yourself up for ransom, we should clear that up right now. There's a price on your head—one my brother will no doubt pay, but you're not valued by the size of your father's bank account. That's not why you're here."

"Then why?"

"Because for now, you're useful to me."

"And who are you that I'm useful to you?"

"My father once called me son. My brother calls me Nicholas. And, at one time, my sister called me something else, but you might know me best by another name."

Another name?

I wish he'd stop toying with me. He taunts me to ask the obvious, but I'm unwilling to play his game. Our conversation is doing nothing to humanize me in his eyes. If anything, I'm accomplishing the opposite of what I need.

He bends over. His breath is hot against my nape. I shiver.

"My brother made his choice, my dear. Imagine my surprise when he chose you over Merlin."

Merlin?

A legend within the art community—the mastermind behind countless art heists dating back to the French Resistance. His name is spoken with reverence, respect, and a little bit of fear. The original modern-day Robin Hood, taking back art looted by the Nazis and returning it to its rightful owners.

A cause Paul has now assumed.

It can't be…

Paul never mentioned a father. He's an orphan, but if this man speaks the truth—Merlin and Paul?

Merlin and the Starling.

Which means…

"My brother will pay." The Crow's voice booms through the cavernous warehouse.

"And what will happen to me?" The question escapes before I can stop it.

"I have no interest in you."

The words land like a death sentence. No ransom value. No leverage once Paul complies. Just... nothing.

My throat tightens. Somehow, that terrifies me more than any threat could have.

FOUR

Paul: Father or the Girl

I don't have super strength or laser eyes. I can't read minds or move objects with my thoughts, but I have something Nicholas didn't count on.

Unlike Nicholas, hatred doesn't drive me. My power comes from something stronger.

My determination to save two lives sings in my blood, and the best thief and tactician trained me. I count on Merlin to help now—which begins with ignoring his hastily scratched code.

I also have Urakov's men behind me. Not FSB soldiers, but his mob contacts. Already, those men are mobilizing. In a few hours, I'll have a small army to take Nicholas down.

All I have to do is not lose Vivianne or Merlin.

That begins by finding where Nicholas took them, except there's no way to track Vivianne. Her phone and mine were locked in the box. Only two real options exist.

Either he sequestered her someplace near Lac Léman or brought her to the chalet where he captured Merlin. The second option means Vivianne and Merlin would be close to each other.

But if Nicholas left Vivianne behind in Lac Léman, I'm two

hours away from her rescue. There simply hasn't been enough time for Nicholas to kidnap Vivianne and then drive up the mountain to grab Merlin.

The only thing I can count on is that Merlin and Vivianne are being held close to each other.

Too many variables.

Except Nicholas already made his first mistake, and I count on him making a few more. Not that I underestimate my brother, but taking Vivianne lit a firestorm within me. That blaze burns bright, and I'm willing to sacrifice much to ensure her safety.

First, I secure *Dr. Gachet* in a secondary vault in my chalet. Urakov isn't pleased with the plan, but the Russian has little say in the matter.

He could take it by force at any point, but I hold an unspoken threat over his head, and the FSB officer will do nothing that might threaten his government. Besides, somewhere along the way, Vivianne slipped between the cracks of the blocky man's hardened exterior. He's somehow smitten by her, and Urakov lives by a chivalrous code.

I intend to make use of that.

For now, we secure the chalet. Two of Urakov's men guard the vault in the cellar. The other two patrol outside to ensure no other entrances have been breached. Meanwhile, Urakov and I plot in the study.

"So, who is this man?" Urakov settles into one of the leather chairs.

We're discussing my brother, a difficult conversation without revealing too many secrets. Urakov intimates he knows I'm the Starling but is unaware of Nicholas's identity as the Crow.

Too much is at risk to let Urakov connect all the dots of my family tree. Any choice I make will have deadly effects on the two people I care most about. All because Nicholas blames me for sweet Catherine's death.

"You must have the supplies on hand to separate the painting from the anthrax." Urakov's voice pulls me from my thoughts.

"If you're asking if I can pull off the frame and separate the painting from the backing, then you're correct."

"Then why don't we do that?" He scratches his head.

"Because, if I know Nicholas—and I do—he has something in play that will reveal such tampering. The only way through this is to make the exchange. I get Vivianne to safety while your men take back the painting."

"A bold plan. And what of your father?"

I don't have an answer to that.

I turn to the cold hearth and stare at the ashes. Not long ago, Vivianne posed naked before this fire.

Now?

The thought of her cold and afraid, terrified of her future, twists something in my chest. It's time to call in reinforcements.

"How closely has your government been working with Interpol?"

"Minimally." Urakov arches a brow. "Why?"

"The extra men you have coming are still a day away—"

"Hours, my friend."

"Okay, hours, but I can have Interpol here within the hour. My task is to locate and secure *Dr. Gachet*. They won't want it turned back over to Nicholas's hands. Perhaps it's time for some deeper discussions between your government and that of France?"

"Few are aware of the terrorist attack. We've been handling this quietly."

"What about guards from your consulate in Lac Léman?"

"Tricky to pull them in. The FSB likes to take care of things quietly."

"And your other contacts?" I need Urakov to know I'm aware of his secrets. We both have damaging information on the other.

"Of course, those are the ones I called. I'm not eager to involve official channels, and as charming as your Vivianne is..." He trails off. His assistance will be limited.

"I understand."

"And I think calling Interpol is at odds with truths you must keep hidden. Their involvement would result in your identity as the Starling coming to light. I wonder how that would look?"

Interpol has already used my identity against me. I wouldn't be in this mess if it weren't for them. Having an international art thief and counterfeiter working to solve art crimes across Europe enhances their efforts, but Urakov doesn't need that knowledge.

"Fine, I won't call the Art Crime Team, but what are we to do?"

"We wait." Urakov leans back and pulls out a cigar. "Do you mind?"

A dismissive wave. Not a fan of cigars myself, but I don't find them irritating like most people.

"I suppose we simply wait."

"Or we can uncrate that painting and see if this Nicholas has marked it as you say." Urakov lights up, smoke curling toward the ceiling.

"I know that anthrax is important—"

"Recovering the weapon is my mission. But even if we separate it from this painting, I will still help you recover your sweet Vivianne."

"I appreciate that." Despite any chivalrous code Urakov might have, not for a minute do I misunderstand why he's here to help. I glance at my phone, checking for a message or missed call. The battery indicates less than half a charge.

"I need to plug in my phone. Is there anything you need?"

"Only to take a closer look at that painting." Urakov puffs on his cigar.

"Okay. Let me grab a charging cord, and we'll head down to

the vault." I can charge my phone there and wait for Nicholas to make his next move.

A few minutes later, I retrieve the painting from the vault. With Urakov's help, I carry it to a nearby table and set it down.

We left it crated for ease of future transport. Given more time, I would replace the painting with the copy stored in the cave. Except I know my brother.

Nicholas hid something in that painting that will reveal evidence of tampering.

While Urakov pries off the top of the crate, I plug my phone in to charge. Less than a second later, it buzzes with a text from my brother.

Father or the girl? Only one will survive this night.

You would kill your father?

What I choose is not the issue.

There is no reason to harm either of them.

My knuckles blanch around the phone, and I bite back a string of curse words. A glance at Urakov confirms the Russian isn't tampering with the painting. One wrong move could liberate the deadly spores.

We discussed the possibility that Nicholas might have booby-trapped the painting. Hopefully, Urakov's intelligence will win over his eagerness. To be so close has to be driving him insane.

The timer has been set, dear brother. Choose.

Do not do this.

It is already done. Choose!

And then?

Nicholas's head games demand something more sadistic than a simple exchange. I struggle to decipher his intent, but nothing comes to mind.

I'll tell you where to bring the painting.

I face a terrible dilemma, one made worse by my father's hastily scratched note. During WWII, Merlin faced a similar decision. I grew up with the stories of a great love won, lost, found again, and fiercely fought over—only to be ripped away by one wrong choice.

Brigitte was Merlin's first and only love.

They courted and were promised to one another, but then the Nazis occupied France. While Merlin joined the resistance, Brigitte's family became Nazi sympathizers. A love won by fate and lost by circumstance.

The war's end brought reconciliation and reunion, but the intervening years drove an irreparable wedge between them.

In Merlin's absence, his good friend ensured Brigitte's safety. But those were volatile times, full of fear and terror. Merlin never recaptured the essence of his first love. In the end, he was forced to make a choice.

He chose passion over love.

In an odd twist of fate, the friendship between Brigitte and Merlin's best friend became an enduring union, blessed by two wealthy families. That union cemented the Faulks name, established their power base, and catapulted them into industrial royalty.

Vivianne would have never been brought into my life if not for Merlin. He may understand Nicholas's intent and is trying to take the decision out of my hands. Ever the wise one, my father knows what Nicholas is capable of, which gives me hope.

Where is the girl?

Now, why am I not surprised?

Where is Vivianne?

Nicholas sends an address. I curse. As suspected, Nicholas drew me away from Lac Léman, placing time and distance between me and Vivianne's rescue.

And father?

You get to choose only one.

I don't believe Nicholas's hatred runs deep enough to commit patricide, but worry gnaws at the edges of my resolve. I will not be forced into choosing one over the other.

There is another way.

"Forgive me, Father."

The phone chirps in my palm.

Brother, it's a long drive. I suggest you hurry. Come alone. Your Russian friends aren't welcome.

There is no way Urakov is staying behind, but if Nicholas knows Urakov is with me, the chalet is under surveillance. I clear my throat and swallow the thick lump of anger and regret. I hand my phone to Urakov. After scrolling through our conversation, he glances up.

"I see. And what are your thoughts?"

"The house is being monitored. I must go alone."

"Obviously." A glance at the painting. "The weight of the world..."

"Pull that out of the crate. We have work to do."

My phone chirps again. Urakov glances down. His brows draw together, lips pursing into a frown.

"What is it?" My hands curl into fists at my sides.

"You must hurry." He turns the screen around.

Strapped to a metal chair, Vivianne sits inside a cistern. Water trickles from a pipe overhead, splashing her as it falls. Her eyes are wide, wild, and she pulls against the restraints with desperate jerks.

There is no doubt of Nicholas's intent.

He intends for her to drown.

FIVE

Vivianne: Drowning

I yank against the restraints. My heart races, and all I want is to curl into a ball and wait for someone to save me, but there isn't anyone.

No one knows where I am.

The psycho who kidnapped me intimates Paul will come, but what can he do?

A choked cry forces itself up and out of my throat. A strangled thing, it squeaks into the emptiness of the hellhole I find myself in. A drop of water runs down my cheek. It could be a tear or a splatter of cold water raining down on me. That bastard taped a hose to the top of the deathtrap he placed me in.

Strapped to a chair, bound at my hands and feet, I'm not going anywhere.

There's no way this is the end of the road. I, Vivianne Faulks, am not going to die in a dark warehouse, drowned in a creepy contraption meant for a horror movie. There has to be a way out, and I need to find it soon.

Already, the water rises past my ankles and moves up my

shins. It pours in a steady stream, splashing over me during its fall. It has nowhere to go. And it's frighteningly cold.

My prison slowly fills. Soon, it will reach over my head.

I struggle and try to stand, but the chair is bolted to the floor. My feet are bound to the legs, my wrists secured to the armrests. Other than the steady cascade of water, there's no other sound.

My captor left me to my fate, fading back into the darkness until he disappeared altogether.

The cold barely matters. Every natural body movement is on hold. Even my shivers seem to have paused as the reality of my fate settles in.

What should I do?

My body should be soaked in sweat, but it's impossible to tell what's sweat and what's moisture from the drops that splash on my dress. A throbbing settles behind my eyes, and my ears vibrate with a high-pitched buzz. The thumping of my heart adds to the incessant noise, sending blood surging past my ears and intensifying the buzzing roar in my head.

My fingers curl into fists, nails digging into the soft flesh of my palms. I've likely drawn blood by now, but it doesn't matter.

Nothing matters.

The rapidity of my breaths intensifies. For now, oxygen floods my lungs, moving in and out with unceasing regularity. Soon, water will take the place of air.

My breaths will slow.

Stop.

My heart…

I turn my eyes upward, once again examining the confines of my prison. There's no way out. My gut churns with tense cramps, but I can't let it overwhelm me.

Not now.

Not when I have little time left to escape this hell.

Seconds turn to minutes. Time marches on. Water fills my

prison, rising to my shins, creeping over my knees, crawling over my waist, swallowing my shoulders.

I thrash against the bindings as the inevitability of my fate approaches. But there's no rescue, and all my efforts to free myself result in the bindings around my wrists cinching down tighter than ever before.

With my circulation cut off, I no longer feel my fingers or hands, and even my feet suffer the same effects. Not that it will matter much longer. The chill water steals my heat, plunging my core temperature to a dangerous level. I've stopped shivering, and that's probably a bad sign.

The water laps at my lips, and I press them closed. Tilting my head back, I lift my nose above the encroaching water.

But that will only buy me a few minutes.

The water level rises.

I break the surface with superhuman effort, lengthening my spine and gaining a few precious millimeters. Gulping at the air, I find myself under the water again.

My heart hammers against my ribs. There's no one to hear my screams. When I can no longer hold my breath, I struggle again. Stretching and pushing against the chair, I lift my nose above the surface and fill my lungs.

Then, with barely a splash, I'm under again.

This time, there's no fighting it. Soon, oxygen deprivation will steal my thoughts, and my life will end. Every cell in my body screams for oxygen, and the urge to breathe becomes unbearable.

I need to breathe, but if my instincts override my self-control, I'll flood my lungs with water. I'm not ready to die. I want to be saved.

Rescued.

Darkness envelops me. The water closes in, filling me with the oppressiveness of my impending death. I hold my breath as long as I can, struggling to fight the aching burn.

Red splotches dance behind my lids. I squeeze them tight, unwilling to watch my eventual end as it approaches, but it doesn't matter if my eyes are open or closed. The urgent need for air makes my chest ache and my heart pound.

A splash. The water moves. Someone grabs my wrists. They tug as my vision turns black. I sink into the blackness. I open my mouth, gasping for air, only to feel the press of lips sealed against mine.

Hot, moist air floods my lungs, and my eyes pop open.

In my watery grave, an angel.

Paul cups his hand over my mouth. He pinches my nose. My lungs hurt. They hurt so much. He kicks off the floor, leaving me strapped to the chair, and heads up.

Then he returns.

His lips find mine… again. They form a seal around my mouth. Air floods out of my nose in a stream of bubbles. Then he breathes out, exhaling air into my lungs.

The next few minutes pass in a fog. Paul breathes for me, kicking to the surface before returning to feed my lungs. He does that several times and then places a finger over my lips. I understand and nod.

More splashing follows. A banging sound. Something hard slides against my skin. A sharp yank angles away from my wrist, and my left hand floats free. More kicking.

Paul gives me another breath.

Water swirls around us as his body twists. All the while, Paul continues to breathe for me. He slides what must be a knife against the bone of my ankle and saws back and forth. My lungs scream for air.

My left leg is free.

Paul pulls me against him, lifting me until my head breaches the surface. I gasp. I tug in breath after breath, filling my lungs with precious air. Then I'm coughing hard.

He ducks back under the surface. Now that I can stand and am no longer confined to that chair, the water reaches chest-high. After more tugging, that sawing sensation, he frees my right leg.

Popping back to the surface, he takes in a deep breath of his own. Then he grabs me and hugs me tight against his chest.

"Vivianne…are you…"

My arms feel like lead weights, and my body, previously shiver-free, shakes like a leaf. I wrap them around his neck and sob against his chest.

"You found me."

He sweeps back the wet tangles of my hair from my face and cups my chin.

"I was nearly too late."

"Paul—"

He hushes me, placing a finger over my lips. "Let's get you out of here. Your skin is ice-cold."

Indeed, I'm shivering again.

It takes some maneuvering, but Paul pulls me out of the tank. Water sluices off my body. My evening gown is ruined and clings to my body, but I only care about each wonderful breath surging into my lungs.

"Come, we need to get out of here."

A glance at the floor, the puddle of water beneath our feet, and the open and empty crate.

"No." I cry out as Paul pulls me away. There's only one reason that crate is here. "No!"

A shot rings out, and Paul lurches. His eyes open wide, and he glances down. Crimson spreads across his belly.

My scream rattles the rafters, and I catch him as he collapses into my arms.

A voice speaks from the darkness. "Miss Faulks, I suggest you run."

No way in hell will I leave Paul after he saved me.

Clutching him tight against my side, I support most of his weight. Together, we move to the opposite side of the cistern, away from what looks to be the only entrance, but also out of the line of the gun sight.

"What now?"

Paul grits his teeth against the pain but then takes a deep breath. Agony twists his features. With a shaky hand, he points to a metal set of stairs. "That door. If it's unlocked, we exit there."

A small service door sits at the top of the stairs. I don't know how to get Paul up the steps, and his wound needs tending.

He pulls out his leather belt, grimacing with each movement, and then yanks the wet shirt over his head.

"Did the bullet go all the way through?" He turns, and I examine his back.

Sure enough, an exit wound gapes and blood spreads outward.

"Yes."

"Good." He wads his shirt and wraps it around his side. Then he fumbles with the belt.

I understand his intent and secure the belt in place.

"Tighter." He grunts. "It needs to be tighter."

Complying with his direction, I give another glance up the metal stairs.

"How am I—"

"I can make it, but I need you to be brave. I need you to head up there and open that door. I'll be right behind you."

One glance at that landing confirms my fears.

Whoever is shooting at us will have a clean shot. I have to open the door and hold it while Paul struggles up the stairs, all the while praying the man with the gun has poor aim.

I don't think that will be the case. My value alive is easily a thousand times higher than dead. I won't be the target. Paul has come to the same conclusion. The door is metal. All I have to do is shut it before another shot hits something more vital than Paul's side.

"You ready?"

No. I will never be ready for this, but staying put isn't an option.

"As I'll ever be. You promise to be right behind me?"

"I'm only going to wait a moment. The cistern gives us cover only until the last few steps. I need to make sure you can open that door."

"Okay."

A squeeze to his hand and a kiss on his cheek. I take a fortifying breath. Cold weighs my entire body, but some circulation returns to my arms and legs. I can make it up a few stairs.

And I do.

I dash up the stairs. It's more of a drunken stagger.

Hypothermia from my immersion saps more of my strength than I realized, but I make it to the top. A pull at the lever on the door, and the rusty mechanism groans in protest. It moves.

Holy hellfire, but it moves.

I open the door and glance down. Paul sways on his feet, unsteadily climbing the steps.

But he climbs.

Faster than I think possible. I widen the opening for Paul. When his foot hits the last step, a shot rings out. The bullet whizzes through the air and hits the metal railing beside Paul's head. Sparks fly, and the bullet ricochets into the darkness.

Paul makes it up the last step and lunges for the opening. I take one hand to push him the last few inches through while grabbing the inner handle to swing the door shut. A bullet hits the other side of the metal, and Paul falls to the floor.

"Paul!" Was he hit a second time?

I search his body but find only one bullet hole. Well, technically, two—the entrance and exit wounds.

His chest heaves with the force of his breaths, and he groans as he struggles to rise.

"Shh. Take a minute."

"We don't have a minute." He clenches his jaw. "Help me up."

I pull Paul to a stand, with him hissing in pain. He leans against me, using me to support much of his weight.

He glances down a catwalk extending into the distance. Another set of stairs heads down. The only indications I have that he wants to head that direction are his body's wobble and the lean that follows.

Taking one step at a time, I struggle to reach the stairs.

SIX

Paul: Blood Pact

THE BITE OF THE BULLET BURNS HOTTER THAN I THOUGHT possible. Every movement brings excruciating pain, but there's little time to deal with it. Not when Vivianne remains at risk.

It won't take long before Nicholas discovers I switched the painting.

It was a risk, and retrieving the copy from the cave took time, but after one look at Urakov, there was no other option. The Russian wasn't willing to risk the anthrax falling back into Nicholas's hands.

I lost even more time replacing my version of *Dr. Gachet* in the frame, but I raced down the winding road to Lac Léman, taking the sharp curves at breakneck speed. I was almost too late.

Vivianne nearly drowned.

How close I pushed it. I've lost Merlin, a man whose sacrifice will follow me to my grave, but losing Vivianne would have destroyed me.

Nicholas knew what choice I would make.

Urakov has what he came for; the deadly anthrax will be returned to Mother Russia. The world will be safe from yet another senseless terrorist attack. The Musée d'Orsay will have its masterpiece back. Everybody is—or will be—happy.

That leaves me to deal with my brother. I have seconds to get Vivianne to safety. Gritting my teeth and bearing down against the pain, I stagger down the catwalk.

Behind us, the door screeches on rusty hinges. I bite back a curse.

Nicholas follows, which means…

"Brother." The word scrapes out of him, raw and dangerous. "You dare defy me? This will cost not only your life but hers as well."

Vivianne gasps, and I try to bear more of my weight but slump against her when the pain becomes too intense. I can barely breathe.

Little light penetrates the abandoned warehouse, but enough to make out vague forms. Nicholas remains in the shadows, his outline barely discernible. One beam of light reflects off the barrel of his gun.

My brother doesn't bother with stealth. No need. There's nowhere to run. The stairs at the end of the catwalk might be less than fifty feet away, but they're too far for escape. I need to stall my brother and somehow distract him.

Cool air whispers over my skin as I face the barrel of Nicholas's gun.

Is this how my life will end? Vivianne's? I steady myself on my feet, bite back against the pain, and place Vivianne firmly behind me.

"Go. Run."

She clutches at the wetness of my shirt. Ice-cold, her fingers tremble.

"Not without you."

A bullet spits out from the end of the barrel. White-hot light flashes, and a deafening crack splits the air. I push Vivianne, urging her forward. The bullet misses, whizzing far too close for comfort.

"You have nowhere to go, my brother."

"Let the girl go." I keep my voice steady. "That was the deal —the painting for the girl. Let her go."

"Do you think I'm a fool?"

"Never."

My brother is deranged.

"We made a pact, my brother. Do you remember it? Do you remember sealing our souls in blood?"

I remember.

Foolish promises made by mere boys—children who knew everything about heartache and loss, and nothing about family, love, or commitment. We clung to each other and developed strong bonds in our loneliness, but time and circumstance chipped away at the dreams of those two little boys.

"You lied to me, brother. You lied to me about Catherine. You lied about everything."

"Catherine is dead, Nicholas. You killed her."

"See, that's another lie." His coarse laughter rings hollow through the deserted warehouse. "You killed her, just as you stole her from me."

"That's not true."

Catherine was never mine—at least, not in the way Nicholas thinks. We've had this conversation time and time again, but Nicholas refuses to face the truth.

"Your carelessness put Catherine at risk. She sacrificed herself for you. Not me."

"Lies!" The word comes out in a hiss. "All lies. You wanted her but couldn't have her, so you killed her."

Heat floods my blood, and my temper barely stays in check. Arguing with my brother is pointless, except that it buys time and distance.

I keep my hand behind me and push Vivianne back. One step becomes two. Two become four.

I have fifty feet to cover and am determined to close that gap. Using my body as a shield, I'll buy Vivianne the time she needs to get to safety.

I could use a little backup. Where the hell is Urakov?

Three loud pops crack through the darkness. Nicholas's silhouette wavers. The barrel of his pistol dips, and he staggers forward.

"What?" He glances down, eyes going wide, and then his expression twists. "What have you done?"

Nicholas stumbles backward and bumps against the railing. Five more shots tear into him, jerking his torso and propelling him over the edge in an awkward cartwheel. He falls, disappearing into the darkness, until a sickening thud sounds below.

My head swivels, searching the darkness for the shooters. More than one.

A few seconds pass. I teeter on my feet. I've lost too much blood.

Gripping the railing, I fight to remain conscious.

Behind me, Vivianne wraps her arms around my chest, soft cries shaking her body. The thudding of boots on metal rings into the stillness, and then the world turns dark.

SEVEN

Vivianne: Promise

THOSE LAST MOMENTS IN THE WAREHOUSE REMAIN FOGGY. I struggle to put all the pieces into a cohesive picture. One moment, Paul's brother is standing. Next, he jerks and tumbles over the railing. I have no memory of shots being fired, but I'm told that's what happened.

Then Paul collapses. He's barely breathing.

Boots.

The stomping of scores of boots rings out of the darkness. Strong hands lift me from behind.

Tears.

Those I remember, and the choked cries that followed. My sobs pull at my chest and clog in my throat.

Light.

A sudden infusion of brilliant light pushes back the darkness. Spots dance in my vision, but Paul's pale complexion and his blood-soaked shirt cut through the haze.

We're taken to a safe place, and now I sit as the guest of an unexpected ally. Urakov sits across from me in a spacious sitting room within the Russian consulate. There, he pours tea and fixes me a plate of ladyfingers while I stare listlessly out the window.

"Miss Faulks, you must eat." He lifts the plate. His clipped English is buried beneath a heavy Russian accent.

I manage a practiced smile, the product of years of social conditioning. My hand trembles, but I take the plate.

"Thank you."

"One lump or two?" He turns to the pot of tea, pouring two steaming cups.

The civility of tea and ladyfingers is going to drive me crazy. I need a stiff pour of whiskey, brandy, or hell, even vodka.

"One, thank you." I nibble at the finger sandwich and sit back in the overstuffed chair.

A thick cotton throw wraps around me. After our arrival, I was provided a change of clothes. Light cotton pants and a long-sleeved blouse provide warmth and modesty. Urakov even gave me wool-lined slippers.

"How is Paul?"

Paul was taken to the hospital, while I was brought to the Russian consulate.

It's been several hours since our rescue. The late morning sun spills through mullioned windows and casts a triangle of yellowish light onto the dark walnut floor of the sitting room. It advances across a brilliant blue carpet, a relic of unknown significance, cutting a path to the glossy cut stone of the floor lining the hall.

As sunlight creeps into the room, it glides over burnished gold statues, completing the ostentatious display of Russian glory. I blink a few times, adjusting to the encroaching light, trying to forget about that terrible darkness, trying desperately not to scream.

"He is well. Recovering from surgery." Urakov settles deeper into his chair.

"When will I be able to see him?"

Urakov's lips press into a thin line, and he takes a long pull of his tea.

"That might be more problematic."

"I need to see him."

"I know, and he would like to see you, but there are complications."

"The Crow?"

"Has been taken care of." Urakov sets down his cup. "You do not need to worry yourself over him."

He never mentions dead, although there's no way anyone could survive that fall, not after taking that many shots.

Paul is barely clinging to life, and he only took one bullet. His injury must be more serious than I've been led to believe.

"Agent Larson will be here shortly, and a representative from your father." Urakov shifts in his seat.

"Why is my father involved?"

"After we contacted Agent Larson, they notified your father."

And my overprotective father will storm in—not to save me, but to provide damage control on anything remotely threatening the Faulks name. He will demand my immediate return to the States where I will linger until properly wed to my contracted fiancé.

"How much time do I have?"

"Not much." He pauses. "And I suspect the American consulate, along with your father—"

"I have no doubt what will happen next. I'm a civilian contractor for the FBI. With how this turned out, they'll want me as far from this case as possible. My father will want me even further." I clasp my hands in my lap. "Please, I need to see Paul."

"I'm very sorry, but I don't see how that's possible." He shakes his head.

I never get to see Paul before they force me from Geneva.

Larson arrives a few hours later, bringing with him my chauffeur, Jacques. My father's instructions can't be denied, so I return home on a private jet without discussion.

Larson debriefs me before my departure. Paul's identity as the Starling is known. They've been using him to ferret out larger prey. Larson asks how much I know, and I admit to discovering Paul's identity as the forger and thief. I keep to myself the secret of his cache and the more important revelation of Merlin being alive.

However, Merlin might not have survived the night. The Crow mentioned Paul being forced to make a choice.

All my life, I've wanted to meet the mystical Merlin, a mystery to the world. Like everyone else, I believed his name was derived from the stories of King Arthur, never understanding its true roots.

It makes sense, though.

Merlin was a predator, the Starling a mimic, and the Crow a thief.

Three men, all bound together by one man's vision—steal from those who stole from others. Return what they can.

Somewhere along the way, the Crow took a darker path. And then there is Catherine.

A woman who came between two brothers.

One day, I hope to hear the whole story.

I spend the next few weeks on lockdown at the Faulks estate. My father debriefs me, but his questions make little sense. He isn't interested in the case, the auction, or the recovery of *Dr. Gachet*.

Instead, his questions center on how Paul entered my life. He wants to know about *The Lovers* and grills me incessantly about the Starling and Merlin. Unlike Larson and Urakov, my father knows nothing about Paul being the Starling, and I will make sure it stays that way.

My father's frustration intensifies, but he believes my lies. As his paranoia deepens, my need to know something of Paul's fate increases. One day, I wander the halls of the estate until I stand before the painting that started it all.

I stop short at the empty expanse on the wall.

The Lovers no longer hangs on display.

I make my way to my father's office and knock on his door.

"Come." His voice is clipped. A command.

When I cross the threshold, he pins me with a fierce look that nearly stops me in my tracks, but I suck in a breath and ask my question.

"Father, what happened to *The Lovers*?"

"That painting is no longer your concern." He taps his pen on the legal pad before him.

"Not my concern?" I take several steps into the room, but halt at another pointed look. Intimidating at the best of times, his cold demeanor could freeze hell. "I would say it's very much my concern."

"That painting has been moved to a place of higher security."

"Which is where?"

"None of your concern."

"Father—"

"Silence." He tosses his pen down and stands. Bracing himself on the table, he leans forward. "Your foolish dream has risked too much. You've placed our family's legacy at risk."

"I risked nothing."

"You risked it all!"

"How?"

"You brought our family to Merlin's attention."

"Merlin is dead." I raise my voice. It helps suppress the lump forming in my throat.

"How can you be certain?"

Because Paul traded Merlin's life for mine.

"Why do you fear a ghost?"

"He knows Faulk's secrets, my dear." He softens his voice, but that does nothing to ease the hardness of his eyes. "The Starling carries on his work. Your little foray brought the Starling's attention to you—and, by extension, the family. I don't need to tell you how damaging that can be."

"I doubt the Starling has much interest in us. Nobody knows we have *The Lovers*."

"If you believe that, then you are a fool." He arches a brow.

"Father."

"I've indulged you long enough. It's time you stopped chasing this dream of yours. I'm moving up the wedding." He shakes his head.

"No." My chest tightens, ribs constricting around my lungs. I'm not ready for my freedom to end.

"The announcements go out tomorrow. You have six months. You'll submit your resignation to Dr. Phillips."

"You can't do this. I've worked hard to make a name for myself. Don't you see what my position can do? What it brings to the Faulks name?"

"It has brought nothing but chaos and exposed us to enemies long thought buried. You did nothing to honor our legacy. Instead, you've threatened everything we've tried to build."

I ball my hands into fists. "I'm not resigning."

"It's non-negotiable. I've already arranged the meeting. You'll meet with Dr. Phillips in the morning." He sits and picks up his pen.

"Is this how the rest of my life will go, Father? You arranging every interaction? What if I refuse to go through with the wedding?"

"That will never happen. Good day, Viv. I suggest you prepare your resignation letter."

I'm dismissed.

The rest of the day, I stomp around the mansion. None of the drivers will take me out, and I have access to none of the keys to any of the many cars. The Faulks estate sits several miles from the main road, and the nearest town is twenty miles away. I've been effectively imprisoned within my own home.

The next day brings me to Dr. Phillips's office. I storm around the cramped space, fuming over my father's decree. There's no reason to draft a resignation letter, but my father already saw to that. He even forwarded the letter on my behalf.

"I suppose I'm still reeling with the news. I can't believe it. Have you heard from him?" Dr. Phillips leans against the window, staring out at the campus lawn.

I've filled him in, telling him all the secrets I've kept from my father. Dr. Phillips isn't a man who can be bought off. His life passions revolve around the provenance of art, and he has a similar interest in the art plundered during World War II.

It's been weeks—plenty of time for Paul to recover fully. Yet, I've heard nothing, and my snort answers Dr. Phillips's question.

"What are you going to do?"

"I don't know." I shrug. "I contacted the Russian consulate. They told me no man by the name of Urakov works for them. He disappeared. Paul disappeared. And Merlin is dead."

"It's a shame. After all this time… I would have loved to have met him."

"Me, too. But how am I going to find Paul? Even those at the ACT won't give me any details. Larson is a closed book."

"What about that fellow we met in New York?"

"Agent Radcliffe?" I give another snort. "He's less than helpful. When I called, he thanked me for my service and told me how the recovery of *Dr. Gachet* wouldn't have been possible without my help. When I asked about Paul, he switched the subject and ended our conversation. I'm afraid my opportunities to work with them are ruined. That leaves me with nothing. After all my hard work…" I vent a sigh.

"It's not that bad."

"You don't understand. After this wedding, I'll be a prisoner. My duties will revolve around charity events, galas, and social hobnobbing. My father wants a quick pregnancy and hopes for his male heir. After that, I'll truly be stuck. If I leave my child to grow up under my father's influence, I'll lose everything. My position as an art expert was going to be my escape. He's taken that from me."

"I'm sorry."

I wave to the letter sitting on Dr. Phillips's desk. "Exhibit A." Walking over, I crumple the paper and toss it in the trash. "He's a monster."

A soft knock sounds on the door. A young student pops his head inside.

"Dr. Phillips, you have a delivery."

"Well, bring it in."

"Um, you need to come to the examination room." The student glances around the room, uncertain.

"Why?"

"It's a series of crates."

"Just sign for it, and I'll be there momentarily." Dr. Phillips takes in a deep breath and lets it out slowly.

"Sir, the man said you had to sign in person. He's waiting."

"Come on. Let's see what's so important that it can't wait." I shake my head, glancing at the wastebasket and the crumpled resignation my father penned. There has to be another way.

"Well, let's see what it is."

We walk down the hall and head to Dr. Phillips's examination room. This is a private lab area reserved for his use. I spent the better part of my training there, learning about the art of forgery and the methods behind revealing them as fakes.

Five large crates fill the room. A man with silver hair supervises three other men unboxing the crates. He turns, blue eyes twinkling under the harsh fluorescents overhead.

"Anthony!" I rush forward.

I would hug him, but the reserved man maintains a certain air of decorum. Instead, I grip his hands and give them a light squeeze.

"What are you doing here?" My pulse races. Anthony is alive. And knowing who the enigmatic man truly is…

He survived.

"Mademoiselle Vivianne, it is a pleasure."

"Where's Paul?"

"He could not make the trip and asked me to see to the delivery." Anthony's bushy brows twitch.

"Of what?" Although I can guess. My breath catches.

Anthony gestures to the crates—the cover of the first crashes to the ground. The men peel back Styrofoam and a layer of plastic wrap. They step aside and allow Anthony to approach. He cuts away a final layer of paper and reveals the most stunning partial nude I've ever laid eyes on: the sweeping curve of a woman's back.

My back.

"Oh my. That's magnificent." Dr. Phillips steps closer.

A river of long, flowing golden hair cascades down her back, caressing her narrow waist and kissing her hips. A roaring blaze in a fireplace silhouettes her body, the flames billowing around her nakedness. Her skin glistens with a sensual sweat and glows beneath the heat of the fire, softening her features—a single starling cartwheels in the flames.

The other men pause in opening the crates to stare at the painting.

"Who is this? What artist?"

"The Starling sends his regards." Anthony turns to me and hands me a folded piece of parchment.

My hands shake as I open the paper. Meanwhile, Anthony directs the men to uncrate the other four pieces.

My dearest Vivianne,

Love is a possession of the soul. In you, I find myself whole. You belong to me, and I belong to you. I am coming, my darling Swan.

Your Starling

I touch my neck, clutch the pendant. I haven't removed it since he placed it there. I thought it was a gift. Now I understand. It's a promise.

Paul is coming.

For me.

I turn to give Anthony a message, but the elderly man has slipped away.

"Viv, do you see this? He exposed himself to the world." Dr. Phillips stares at the paintings.

There's no reason to look at them. I know what each will reveal. One promise after another, and I have no doubt Paul will rescue me once more.

EIGHT

Vivianne: The Unveiling

THE ROLLS-ROYCE GLIDES TO A STOP BEFORE THE Metropolitan Museum of Art. My pulse drums against my ribs, a staccato rhythm matching the flashes of cameras outside. I take a deep breath, smoothing down my designer dress—a crimson sheath that hugs every curve. The silk whispers against my skin, cool and sleek.

The first exhibit of the Swan Collection is causing quite a stir in the art world, and tonight's unveiling of the remaining pieces draws the elite of society.

And since the elite are gathering, my father faces the onerous task of attending as well.

After weeks of being imprisoned in our mansion following my abrupt return from Paris, this is my first public appearance.

The tight leash my father keeps me on has only grown shorter.

"Remember." Father's voice cuts like ice. "You're here to represent the Faulks name. Nothing more."

If only my mother were here. In my imagination, she would stand beside me, her hand warm in mine, telling Father to ease up, to let me breathe. But she's been gone since I was barely old enough to remember her face—just fragments of warmth and the scent of jasmine.

Grandmother tried to fill that void, raised me with as much love as she could offer, but she never once stood up to him. Never once told her son he was wrong. I'll never understand why.

I nod, swallowing the sigh that threatens to escape. This public appearance feels both thrilling and terrifying. The air in the car is thick with Father's cologne, a scent that once meant safety but now feels suffocating.

We step out into a barrage of light and noise. The camera flashes blind me. Father's hand on my elbow is both support and restraint as he guides me through the throng of reporters. The night air carries a hint of autumn, crisp and full of promise.

"Miss Faulks! Mr. Faulks! Any comments on the Swan Collection?"

Father's grip tightens—a silent command to say nothing. We sweep past without comment, the cool air of the gallery a balm after the stuffy car ride.

Inside, the air thrums with excitement. The elite of society mingle, their chatter a constant hum beneath the staccato of my heels on polished marble. Crystal chandeliers cast a soft glow over the gathering, their light dancing off jewels and designer gowns.

As we move through the crowd, a hush falls. Conversations pause, heads turn. Father's presence commands respect, and the sea of people parts before us. The weight of their stares presses in—some admiring, some envious, all curious.

"Mr. Faulks." A portly man in an ill-fitting suit approaches, hand outstretched. "What an honor to have you here tonight."

"Harrison." Father nods curtly, barely acknowledging the man's presence. "I trust the gallery is prepared for tonight's event?"

"Of course, sir. Everything is in order. We've spared no expense." Harrison nods eagerly, sweat beading on his brow.

"See that it remains that way." Father's lips curve in a smile that doesn't reach his eyes.

We move on, leaving Harrison stammering behind us. This is Father's world—a place where his word is law, where a single nod or frown can make or break careers.

"Vivianne." Dr. Phillips hurries toward us, tie askew and face flushed. "I'm so glad you could make it. This is going to be quite the reveal."

"I wouldn't miss it for the world. Though I must admit, I'm nervous. The first piece was... breathtaking." I return his smile, willing the butterflies in my stomach to settle. "I've been dying to ask about the other paintings. What can I expect?"

Father's eyes narrow at my words. I was present at the unveiling of the first painting weeks ago, and the memory still quickens my pulse. The exquisite detailing, the play of light on skin—Paul captured every nuance of that night at the chalet.

"Oh, my dear, they're simply exquisite. You can't believe the talent of the Star—" He catches himself, eyes widening. "The artist. It's truly remarkable work." A chuckle, though there's a twinkle in his eye.

"What were you going to say, Dr. Phillips?" My father leans in.

"Nothing, nothing. Just an old man's ramblings." Dr. Phillips waves a hand dismissively, but a hint of nervousness threads through the gesture. "But trust me, these paintings... they'll take your breath away. Now, if you'll excuse me, I must get ready for the reveal."

As we move further into the gallery, the excitement is palpable. Collectors, critics, and socialites press close, vying for the best view. I scan the room, hoping for a glimpse of Paul, but he's nowhere to be seen. Does he know I'm here? Does he know what happened after I returned from Paris?

Prescott approaches, his gait as predatory as ever. He's not an unattractive man, with his golden hair and chiseled features, but his eyes—those eyes are as dark as his black soul, and they send a chill down my spine.

He immediately lays his hands on me. His touch is possessive, his smile cold.

"Vivianne, darling, there you are. You look ravishing tonight."

He's dressed impeccably in a tailored suit that screams of wealth, but it's a new wealth, not the old money of the Faulks family.

His gaze rakes over me, lingering on the curves accentuated by my dress. I suppress a shudder, forcing a smile. "Thank you, Prescott. I didn't know you'd be here tonight."

"And miss the debut of my future wife's... discovery?" The sound that passes for his laugh is hollow and cold. "I wouldn't dream of it."

His voice drops to a whisper, meant for my ears alone. "Enjoy your little games while you can, Viv. Once we're married, you'll have more... pressing duties to attend to."

My mother would have stopped this. She would have fought for me, protected me from being sold off like livestock to secure Father's business deals. But she's been dead for over twenty years, and Grandmother—sweet, gentle Grandmother Brigitte, who raised me after Mother died—she never challenged Father either.

Not once.

She'd just smooth my hair and tell me it would all work out, that my father knew best. But he doesn't know best. He only knows control.

The threat in his words is clear, and heat floods my cheeks—anger and something darker.

Before I can respond, a group of art critics approaches. Their eyes light up as they recognize me.

"Miss Faulks." An older woman with a severe bun grasps my hand. "Your work on uncovering the forgery of *The Lovers* was brilliant. Simply brilliant."

"We're all so excited to see where your career takes you." Another chimes in. "The art world needs fresh eyes like yours, especially when it comes to identifying forgeries. Although we're told your discovery of fresh new artistic talent is unparalleled. We're excited to view this new artist's work."

I smile, even as my stomach sinks. If only they knew. If only Father would allow...

"Thank you. I'm honored by your kind words. This artist's work is..." I grasp the air as if seeking words. "It's simply phenomenal."

Prescott's grip on my arm tightens painfully. "Yes, Vivianne has quite the eye. It's one of the many reasons I chose her. Though I'm sure her talents will be put to better use once we're married."

Chose. As if I were a prized racehorse or a piece of art myself. Bile rises in my throat.

Would my mother have let him speak about me this way? I don't remember if, like my grandmother, she caved to my father's will, but I believe she would have stood up for me, reminded him that I have a brilliant career ahead of me, that my work matters.

I'll never know if she would've fought for me. All I have are scattered memories—her laughter, the way she sang to me at bedtime. Grandmother loved me—I know she did—but she never fought for me. She never told her son that he was wrong to control every aspect of my life, wrong to arrange this marriage, wrong to treat me like property.

I used to ask her why she wouldn't stand up to him, but she'd look away, her eyes sad and distant. She's been gone for years, and I'm entirely alone.

The critics exchange glances, clearly uncomfortable with Prescott's possessive tone.

"Vivianne, might I have a word?" Dr. Phillips appears at my side, a welcome interruption.

I seize the opportunity to escape his grasp.

"If you'll excuse me." I flash an apologetic smile.

I follow Dr. Phillips to a quieter corner of the gallery. The sounds of the crowd fade to a dull murmur.

"Dr. Phillips, please, tell me more about these paintings. You can't leave me in suspense." My voice is low and urgent.

He hesitates, glancing around as if to ensure we're not overheard. "My dear, they are more perfect than the first. As a collection, they will rock the foundations of the art world. Beyond that, you have to understand that these paintings are unlike anything I've ever seen. They're something else entirely. Original, breathtaking, and..." He pauses, meeting my eyes. "Intimate."

I know. I was there.

"How intimate?"

"Nothing to be nervous about, my dear. It's just another exhibition. Shall we?"

A bell chimes, signaling the start of the unveiling. The crowd hushes, anticipation thick in the air. I make my way back to Father and Prescott, my pulse racing.

Dr. Phillips takes his place at the front of the room, the covered paintings looming behind him. The air feels charged, electric. The scent of excitement mingles with expensive perfumes and the earthier smell of canvas.

"Ladies and gentlemen, it is my great pleasure to present to you a collection that will, I believe, redefine contemporary art. I give you... The Swan."

With a flourish, he pulls back the curtain covering the first painting. Gasps ripple through the crowd. I lean forward, eager to see the piece I'm already familiar with—and then I freeze.

My body, rendered in exquisite detail. The brushstrokes capture every curve and shadow with breathtaking precision. I'm posed before a roaring fire, back to the viewer, head turned just enough to hint at a profile without revealing my identity.

As Dr. Phillips unveils each subsequent painting, the shock deepens.

Five pieces, each more intimate than the last, each unmistakably me. The final painting shows a woman kneeling, head bowed, in a position of supplication that makes my cheeks burn.

The crowd's reaction is a mix of awe and intrigue. Curious stares press in, but not recognition.

Paul masterfully obscured my identity while capturing my essence. The air fills with whispers, theories, and speculation about the mysterious woman in the paintings.

But it's not just the poses that capture my attention. In each painting, the woman is adorned with jewelry—familiar earrings that belonged to my grandmother, and a necklace I've never seen before.

It's the fifth and final piece that steals my breath.

The painting looms large, commanding the room with its presence, yet the closer I step, the more intricate the details become—exquisitely delicate, almost painfully precise. The firelight flickers, casting soft shadows across the canvas, drawing my attention to the ruby pendant painted around my neck. It gleams as though it's real, not just pigment on a brushstroke. The texture is so finely rendered, I swear I can feel the cool weight of the gem resting against my skin.

I've never seen this pendant before. It's not mine, and yet the earrings in the painting match it perfectly, as if the artist knows something I don't.

I lean in, eyes locked on the gem, and that's when I see it—the imperfection.

Inside the depths of the ruby, just beneath the surface where the light fractures, there's a flaw, delicate yet unmistakable.

At first glance, it's nothing more than a flicker, a ripple of light. But as I focus, it takes shape—a swan, impossibly graceful, gliding effortlessly across an invisible lake. Its neck curves elegantly, wings tucked close to its body, as though frozen in the midst of a tranquil journey within the very heart of the jewel. The water beneath it is smooth as glass, undisturbed, reflecting the firelight in rippling waves. The swan, serene and perfect, seems forever suspended in that quiet, dreamlike moment.

The firelight catches the ruby again, and for a brief moment, the swan almost appears to move, its reflection shimmering across a mirrored lake.

The detail is maddeningly perfect, so real that I could reach into the painting and touch it, feel the smooth surface of the lake, hear the silent glide of the swan's wings through the water.

How can something I've never seen feel so intimate? So connected to me, yet completely foreign? The swan stirs something deep inside, an almost visceral pull, as if it knows secrets I'm not yet ready to uncover.

"Vivianne." Dr. Phillips murmurs beside me. "Are you alright? You look pale."

I open my mouth to respond, but no words come out. My mind races back to the day I met Paul, the way his gaze lingered on my earrings.

He noticed them, memorized them, and recreated them with perfect accuracy.

But the necklace... where did that come from?

A sharp intake of breath beside me draws my attention.

Father stands rigid, his face a mask of barely contained fury.

His eyes flick between the paintings, locking onto the ruby pendant in the fifth one. His knuckles whiten around the champagne glass, the tremor in his hand betraying his calm facade. The heat of his anger is oppressive, suffocating, but Prescott's presence beside me is somehow worse.

"Quite scandalous, isn't it?" Prescott's breath is hot against my ear, making my skin prickle. His voice is low, his words meant only for me. "A woman on her knees… perfectly obedient. A preview of things to come."

I tense, my gaze flicking to the painting in question—the woman kneeling, head bowed in complete submission, her arms soft at her sides. The detail is exquisite, haunting, a reflection of vulnerability and surrender. But the way Prescott describes it, with that smug edge in his voice, makes my stomach turn.

He's not referring to the painting. His meaning is clear. It's a glimpse of what he expects from me. From our wedding night.

His hand settles on the small of my back, the touch deceptively gentle but firm, pressing against me like a silent claim. It feels like he's forcing me into the same position as the woman in the painting, kneeling at his feet, submitting to his every demand. Every instinct screams to wrench myself away from him, but I stand still, locked in place by his suffocating presence.

"Perhaps we should move up the wedding date, my dear. No need to delay the inevitable." His lips hover near my ear, his breath brushing my jaw. "Soon enough, you'll be on your knees for me, and you won't be able to refuse me." His tone sharpens, dark with promise. "I expect all the pleasures that come with an obedient wife. And I can't wait to start making those babies your father desperately wants."

Bile rises in my throat, and my hands clench into fists, nails digging into my palms. The weight of his words, his expectations, presses down on me. There's no affection in his voice, no warmth. He doesn't see me as a person—just a body, a means to an end, a symbol of wealth and power he believes he's entitled to.

But the painting—that damned painting. I look at it again, at the woman on her knees, and a strange pull tugs at the edges of my mind. I've never craved submission, but when I imagine kneeling before Paul—the one who painted me in that position, who saw me like this—my body reacts in a way that shocks me. There's something there, something unspoken, electric.

With Paul, the thought of submitting doesn't fill me with dread. It excites me, twists my insides in a way that's both terrifying and exhilarating.

I can see myself like that—kneeling before him, not because I'm forced, but because I want to. Because there's a power in the way Paul sees me, the way he's captured me in this painting, that Prescott will never understand. Paul doesn't want to break me—he wants to free me, to know me, and that thought is more intoxicating than anything Prescott can offer.

But here I am, standing next to Prescott while he speaks to me like I'm already his possession, already trapped in the gilded cage he's prepared for me.

"Move it up if you like." My voice is calm but laced with cold defiance. My pulse pounds in my ears, but I refuse to let him see how much his words affect me. "Don't mistake compliance for obedience. You may get your wife, but you'll never have me."

His fingers dig into my waist, and his smug smile falters. His gaze narrows, searching my face for any crack in my facade, but I give him nothing. I won't let him see how much I want to tear myself away from him.

"Careful, darling." His voice oozes with false charm. "In the end, you'll find resistance only makes things harder. You'll kneel, and you'll spread those legs you keep closed like a vice. You'll learn your place." He straightens, brushing a thumb across his bottom lip as if considering his next move. "In time, you'll be everything I tell you to be."

My skin crawls at the possessiveness in his tone, but I hold my ground, glaring up at him. I won't let him intimidate me, won't give him the satisfaction of seeing me cower. He may think he has control, but I refuse to be that woman in the painting for him.

If I ever kneel or submit, it will be on my terms. And it won't be to a man like Prescott.

I steal one last glance at the painting, the image of the ruby pendant and the kneeling woman burning itself into my mind. The firelight glimmers off the swan inside the pendant, and a quiet resolve forms deep inside me. Prescott may believe he's won, but he's sorely mistaken.

"Viv." Father's voice slices through the crowd like a blade.

I barely have time to react before his hand clamps around my arm, the force of his grip as unyielding as his scowl. He doesn't say another word as he pulls me away from Prescott, dragging me through the sea of guests, each step more hurried than the last.

Dread builds with every stride. We break free of the crowded room, slipping through a side door into a quiet hallway, where the noise of the exhibit is nothing but a dull hum in the distance.

He finally lets go, but the sting of his grip remains. I barely have time to catch my breath before he whirls on me.

"Is that you in the painting?"

His voice is low, but the controlled anger simmering beneath the surface makes my pulse quicken. I hesitate, avoiding his piercing gaze, but there's no escaping his interrogation.

"No." The lie feels feeble even as it leaves my lips.

"You think I'm a fool?" He steps closer, eyes burning into mine as if daring me to deny it again. "You can't lie to me. I know that pendant. You posed for that filth, didn't you?"

My throat tightens. There's no point in lying anymore or trying to deflect the truth. He already knows.

"Yes." The word is barely a whisper. "It's me."

He steps back, disgust replacing the anger on his face. "Why? Why would you do something so reckless? So stupid?"

"Because I wanted to… to feel free." My voice is small against the weight of his disapproval. "To be myself."

Mother would have understood. Somehow, I know she would. In the few memories I have of her, she was vibrant, alive in ways Father never allowed. Maybe that's why he's kept her memory locked away, never speaking of her, never letting me know who she really was.

Grandmother could have told me, should have told me, but she stayed silent. Silent about everything that mattered. And now they're both gone, and I'm facing Father's rage alone, wishing desperately for someone—anyone—to stand between us.

His eyes narrow, lips curling in cold contempt. "You're not free to do as you please. You're a Faulks. My daughter. You don't get to indulge in these whims at the cost of our family's reputation." He straightens, his voice taking on that deadly calm that always makes me feel small and insignificant. "You'll close this exhibit. Tonight."

Panic surges in my chest. "Close the exhibit? That'll make even more of a scene, Father. It's—"

He cuts me off with a sharp wave of his hand. "Close it. Immediately. I never want to see those paintings in public again." His voice drops lower, more menacing. "Have them delivered to the house. I'll deal with them myself."

My stomach knots. "Delivered? You can't—Father, Paul's work—this is his first public exhibit. It's meant to launch him. You can't just—"

"Burn them." His tone is absolute, final. "I'm going to burn those paintings. No one will see them ever again."

"You can't burn them." The defiance slips past my fear. "This exhibit is everything to Paul. It's his chance to break free and be seen for who he is. You can't take that from him."

"Paul?" Father's voice drips with disdain. "That art forger you've tangled yourself with? The one who should be grateful I haven't had him arrested?" He steps closer, towering over me, his words venomous. "You think I care about his so-called career? You've humiliated this family. You've risked everything."

I bite back the tears welling in my eyes. "I'm not going to let you destroy his future because you're afraid of a few paintings."

"Afraid?" His look could freeze hell. "This isn't a request. You don't have a choice. This is bigger than your little dalliance with Paul de Gaulle. You'll do as I say or deal with the consequences."

I take a deep breath, trying to steady my shaking hands. "You don't get to decide what's best for me, Father."

"We'll see about that." His eyes narrow, his lips pulling into a thin, cruel line. "Close the exhibit. Those paintings will be gone by morning. If you know what's good for you, you'll stop fighting me."

I'm utterly alone. No mother to shield me. No grandmother to offer hollow comfort. Just me against Father's iron will, against Prescott's predatory expectations. I don't know which loss cuts deeper—the mother I barely knew, or the grandmother who loved me but abandoned me to this fate through her silence.

My father turns sharply on his heel, his hand raised in a final gesture of dismissal.

I watch him storm down the hallway, his back stiff with rage, and for a long moment, I can't move. My body feels locked in place, the weight of his threats bearing down on me, but there's something stronger stirring inside me.

I can't let him take this from Paul.

I push off from the wall, determination hardening my resolve.

He may think he's won, but I won't let him bury me—or Paul's future.

Not without a fight.

Before I can move, my father strides toward Dr. Phillips, leaving me frozen in place. Their hushed conversation grows heated, fragments reaching my ears over the excited chatter of the crowd.

"...family heirloom..."

"...impossible..."

"...Merlin..."

The name sends a chill down my spine. Merlin, the legendary art thief. Why does my father care about Merlin?

"This exhibition ends now. Pack it up. All of it." Father's voice rises, drawing concerned looks from nearby patrons.

"But sir, the collection—" Dr. Phillips sputters in protest.

"Is over. Shut it down and deliver the paintings to my estate."

Dr. Phillips shoots me an apologetic glance as Father grabs my arm, pulling me toward the exit.

"We're leaving." His grip is painfully tight.

"Is everything alright, sir? Perhaps I should accompany you..." Prescott falls into step beside us, his face a mask of polite concern.

"Not now, Prescott. We'll be in touch." Father cuts him off with a sharp look.

The night air hits me like a slap as we exit the gallery. Reporters surge forward, sensing a story, but Father's glare holds them at bay. The limousine appears, a sleek black shadow in the night.

The ride home is tense and silent save for Father's occasional muttered curses. I stare out the window, mind whirling with questions. The city lights streak by in a dizzying kaleidoscope of color, each flash blending into the next.

What is the significance of the swan necklace? Why does it match my earrings, and how is Merlin connected to all of this?

The scent of leather and Father's cologne fills the car, familiar yet suffocating. I long to open a window, to breathe in the night air, but I dare not move. Father's anger is a living thing, filling the space between us.

"Our family's legacy is at stake." His voice is low and dangerous. "You will tell me everything you know about this... this artist."

NINE

Vivianne: The Swan Pendant

THE ROLLS-ROYCE GLIDES THROUGH THE NIGHT, ITS POWERFUL engine a mere whisper beneath us. Inside the plush interior, silence reigns, broken only by the occasional creak of fine leather as Father shifts in his seat. The privacy partition separates us from Robert, our chauffeur, cocooning us in a bubble of tension so thick it threatens to choke me.

I steal a glance at Father. His face is a mask of granite, jaw clenched tight enough to crack stone. Those steel-gray eyes, usually so cold and calculating, dart frantically between the tinted window and his phone, thumbs flying over the screen in a fury of silent communication.

"Father, please, what's going on?" My voice is small in the vast expanse of the car.

The silence that greets me is familiar. It's the same silence that's filled this house since I was three years old, since my mother died and left me with a father who doesn't know how to talk to his daughter.

My grandmother tried to bridge that gap, to soften his edges, but she never challenged him. Not once. Even as a child, I sensed something wrong in that—the way she'd avert her eyes when he snapped at me, the way her hands would flutter helplessly before she'd retreat to her gardens.

Why didn't you fight for me? The question died with her.

My father gives no response. Not even a flicker of acknowledgment. Just the incessant tapping of his thumbs against the glass.

The city lights blur past, a kaleidoscope of neon and streetlamps that does nothing to dispel the darkness gathering in my chest. As we leave the urban sprawl behind, the shadows deepen. Trees loom on either side of the road, their branches reaching out like gnarled fingers, grasping at our sleek vehicle.

Father mutters under his breath, words barely audible over the soft hum of tires on asphalt. "...protect what's ours... can't let them..." His leg bounces—an uncharacteristic display of nerves.

"Who's 'them'? What are we protecting?" The words tumble out, desperation coating each syllable. Blood rushes in my ears, pulse pounding.

He whips his head toward me, eyes blazing with an intensity that makes me recoil. "Enough, Viv. You've done quite enough already."

My throat constricts, a vise tightening around my windpipe. What have I done? The paintings flash through my mind—Paul's masterpieces, my body immortalized in oils. But how could Father know?

Father's agitation grows as the traffic thins, and we pick up speed. He raps sharply on the partition.

"Robert. Faster."

"Sir, the speed limit—"

"Damn the speed limit. Get us home. Now."

The car surges forward, pressing me back into the supple leather. Familiar landmarks whiz by, but in the darkness, lit only by our headlights, they seem alien. Unfriendly. The pristine hedgerows of our neighbors' estates. The gleaming gates of the country club. The spire of the old stone church, where generations of Faulks have been baptized, married, and buried.

We round the final bend, and the Faulks estate looms before us, a colossus of stone and glass erupting from manicured grounds. Even shrouded in night's embrace, it's an awe-inspiring sight. Windows blaze with light, warm squares carved out of the darkness. Floodlights illuminate the facade, throwing every cornice and column into sharp relief.

The grounds stretch endlessly—lush lawns, artfully placed topiaries, and gardens that would make Versailles weep with envy. A fountain burbles in the circular drive, its mist catching the light and creating a halo of droplets.

Grandmother's rose garden is somewhere in that darkness, the one place in this estate that ever felt warm. She'd take me there after my father's rages, let me bury my face in her skirts while she murmured soft reassurances.

But she never stood between us. Never told him to stop. I was too young when my mother died to remember her voice, but surely—surely—a mother would have fought for her daughter. Surely a mother wouldn't have watched silently while her child was crushed under the weight of a family name.

Home. A place I've known my entire life. When I was a kid, it was my castle, and I was its princess. Now it's my prison. I'm the damsel in distress, locked in an ivory tower.

Robert barely has time to bring the car to a stop before Father is out, striding toward the grand entrance. His Italian leather shoes crunch on the gravel, the sound sharp and urgent. I scramble after him.

The massive oak doors swing open at our approach, opened by unseen hands. We sweep into the grand foyer, its opulence hitting me anew. Crystal chandeliers drip from coffered ceilings, their light dancing off marble floors polished to a mirror sheen.

Priceless art adorns walls covered in silk damask—a Monet here, a Renoir there, casually displayed as if they were simple family portraits.

"Mr. Faulks." Mrs. Holloway, our house manager, materializes from a side door. Her usual poise is ruffled, clearly taken aback by Father's demeanor. "Is everything alright? Shall I have the kitchen prepare—"

"Not now." Father barrels past her, making a beeline for his study.

Following in Father's wake, I catch the staff's reactions. Amelia, one of the maids, flattens herself against a wall, duster clutched to her chest. Robert nearly drops a Ming vase in his haste to clear a path.

They're all afraid of him. Every single person in this house. Just like my grandmother, though she hid it behind gentle smiles and soft touches.

I used to think she was brave for staying calm in the face of his temper. Now I realize it was surrender. When she was dying, I begged her to tell me why—why she never stood up to him, why she let him control everything.

She just squeezed my hand and whispered, "Some battles can't be won, my darling."

As a young teen, I didn't understand. Now I'm trapped in an arranged marriage, and I understand all too well.

Father's study door flies open with such force that it rebounds off the wall. I slip in behind him, my presence barely registered. He makes straight for the far wall, where a massive oil painting hangs—a Turner, one I've studied countless times.

The canvas depicts the Battle of Trafalgar, Turner's masterful brushstrokes bringing the chaos of naval warfare to vivid life. Smoke billows from cannon fire, obscuring parts of the scene in hazy grays and browns. The sea churns beneath the warships, white-capped waves betraying the fury of both nature and man.

In the distance, barely visible through the smoke and sea spray, the silhouettes of other ships loom, a reminder of the battle's epic scale.

What always strikes me about this piece is Turner's use of light. Even amid destruction, golden sunlight breaks through the clouds, casting an almost ethereal glow over the scene. It's a study in contrasts—beauty amid horror, hope in the face of despair.

With surprising strength, Father lifts the frame. It swings outward on hidden hinges, revealing a wall safe I never knew existed. My breath catches.

How many other secrets does this house hold?

How many secrets did Grandmother know? She lived here her whole married life, raised Father in these halls, then raised me. Did she know about this safe? About the hidden doors and vaults?

Or was she kept as blind as I've been?

I remember her sometimes pausing in doorways, a strange look on her face, as if the house itself confused her. Once, when I was young, I found her standing in the library, hand pressed against the wood paneling.

Father's fingers fly over the safe's dial, movements practiced and precise. A soft click, and the door swings open. He reaches inside, withdrawing a wooden box. It's surprisingly plain given its hiding place—simple oak, unadorned save for a small brass lock and a delicate mother-of-pearl inlay forming the shape of a swan.

Without a word, he turns and strides out of the study, box clutched tightly to his chest. I follow, confusion mounting with each step. We move deeper into the house, past rooms I've known my entire life, until we reach a small, nondescript door I've never paid much attention to before.

Another key, another lock. Beyond lies a tiny room, barely larger than a closet. Its sole feature is a state-of-the-art safe embedded in the wall. Father punches in a code, then submits to a retinal scan. The safe clicks open.

From within, he retrieves a single key. It's old and ornate—the kind you'd expect to see in a fairy tale, not in this modern fortress of a home. With trembling hands, he unlocks the wooden box.

Inside is a ring of iron keys, each unique and bearing the patina of age. Father scoops them up, leaving the box behind. He strides out, heading for the wine cellar.

The cellar is a cavernous space, filled with rack upon rack of priceless vintages. Father moves to a seemingly unremarkable section of the wall. He slides aside a wine rack, revealing yet another hidden door.

This one requires a key from the iron ring. As it swings open, cool, musty air washes over us. Beyond lies a narrow corridor, lit by flickering sconces that spring to life as we enter.

I used to measure the house as a child, pacing off distances between rooms. Grandmother would find me counting steps in hallways, and instead of scolding me, she'd get this sad, knowing look. "Old houses have their mysteries," she'd say. But these aren't mysteries—they're deliberate deceptions. Hidden corridors carved out of space that should exist.

At the end of the hall, we face a final barrier—a sleek, modern door with an electronic keypad. Father punches in a code, his body blocking my view of the numbers. A soft beep, a hiss of hydraulics, and the door slides open.

The room beyond takes my breath away. It's a vault, yes, but calling it that feels woefully inadequate. It's a treasure trove, a museum's worth of priceless artifacts crammed into a space the size of a small apartment.

Paintings line the walls, stacked three and four deep in places. I recognize some immediately—works thought lost during the war, pieces whispered about in art history lectures. A Klimt here, a Klee there. My eyes widen as I spot what can only be Raphael's *Portrait of a Young Man*, missing since 1945.

Interspersed among the paintings are display cases filled with jewelry, ancient artifacts, and items I can't even begin to identify. Gold glints in the low light, gems sparkle, and the weight of history presses down on me.

Father moves to a central pedestal, topped with a heavy glass case. Another key, another lock opened. From within, he withdraws a small velvet box. His hands shake as he opens it, relief flooding his features as he sees its contents.

I lean in, curiosity overcoming my trepidation. Nestled on black velvet lies a necklace that steals my breath. A massive ruby, easily the size of a quail's egg, hangs from an intricate gold chain. But it's the stone that captures my attention. Within its blood-red depths, a flaw catches the light—the perfect silhouette of a swan.

"My God. It's beautiful."

"Beautiful?" Father's lips twist in a sneer. "You foolish girl. Do you have any idea what this is worth? What it means to our family?"

I shake my head, taken aback by the venom in his voice.

"Of course you don't." He spits the words. "It's priceless. Truly priceless. And not just in monetary terms. This stone... It's our legacy. And you, with your careless, idiotic dalliance in Paris, have put it all at risk."

"Father, I don't understand. What does my trip have to do with—"

"That man you've been with." He cuts me off, eyes blazing. "He's not who you think he is. He's been searching for this necklace for decades, and you, my foolish daughter, have led him right to our doorstep."

My mind reels. Paul? But he already knows... Unless... "You mean Merlin?"

Father's eyes narrow. "How do you know that name?"

I bite my tongue, cursing my slip. "Everyone in the art world knows that name. He's a master thief."

He studies me for a long moment, suspicion clear in his gaze. Finally, he nods, seemingly satisfied with my explanation. "Yes, Merlin. The most dangerous art thief in history. And now, thanks to you, he knows we have the Swan."

"How?" I manage to choke out. "How do you know all this?"

"Did you think I wouldn't have you followed? That I'd let my only heir gallivant around Europe without protection?" Father's laugh is hollow, devoid of humor.

Anger flares, hot and bright. "You had me watched? How dare you?"

"How dare I?" He roars, face flushing crimson. "How dare you be so naive. So reckless. You've put everything we've built, everything we've protected for generations, at risk for what? A pretty face and some flattery?"

Tears sting my eyes, but I blink them back furiously. I won't give him the satisfaction of seeing me cry. "It wasn't like that."

"It doesn't matter now." Father deflates suddenly, looking older and more vulnerable than I've ever seen him. "What's done is done. We need to move quickly if we're going to salvage this situation."

He turns back to the necklace, lifting it from its velvet nest. The ruby catches the light, sending crimson reflections across the vault's shadowy interior.

"This necklace has been in our family for generations." His voice takes on a strange, almost reverent tone. "It's more than just a pretty bauble. It's power. It's history. And now, thanks to your foolishness, it's in danger."

I want to argue, to defend myself, but the words die in my throat. I've never felt more like the little girl who lost her mother before she could remember her face. The teenager who watched her grandmother die without ever getting answers. I'm standing in a secret vault surrounded by stolen masterpieces, and all I can think is that I have no one.

No mother to tell me I'm not crazy for falling in love. No grandmother to at least offer the comfort of her presence, even if she won't fight my battles.

Just Father and his cold calculations, Prescott and his threats, and me—alone in a house full of hidden rooms and buried secrets.

TEN

Paul: Evidence

THE FAMILIAR CORRIDORS OF THE UNIVERSITY FEEL ALIEN AS I make my way to Dr. Phillips's office. Each step sends a ripple of pain through my abdomen, a stark reminder of the bullet that nearly ended me. I grit my teeth, forcing my breathing to remain steady.

The doctors warned me against pushing too hard, too soon, but I've never been good at following orders.

Flashbacks of my recovery flit through my mind—the stark white hospital room, the endless hours of physical therapy, the frustration of being confined to a bed when all I wanted was to find Vivianne. Her face, etched with terror as Nicholas dragged her away, haunts me. I push it aside and focus on the present.

I'm here, I'm walking, and I'm going to set things right.

As I approach Dr. Phillips's office, the usual bustling energy of the university feels muted. Hushed whispers and furtive glances follow me down the hall. I catch snippets of conversation from a group of students huddled near a bulletin board.

"Did you hear about Viv?"

"I can't believe her dad shut it all down."

"Something big must have happened."

My pulse quickens. What went down last night?

I reach Dr. Phillips's door and pause, steadying myself. The pain in my side throbs, a constant reminder of how close I came to losing everything. I knock, the sound echoing in the suddenly too-quiet hallway.

"Come in." Dr. Phillips's voice is weary.

I push open the door, and the sight that greets me sends a fresh wave of concern coursing through me. Dr. Phillips, usually the picture of academic composure, looks like he's aged a decade overnight. His normally pristine desk is a chaos of papers and coffee cups. He looks up as I enter, and his eyes widen.

"Paul." He rises from his chair. "My God, we weren't sure you'd—Are you alright?"

I nod, not trusting my voice just yet. Dr. Phillips gestures to a chair, which I sink into gratefully. The simple act of walking here has left me more drained than I care to admit.

"What happened?"

"It was chaos. Absolute chaos." Dr. Phillips runs a hand through his thinning hair. "Vivianne's father showed up at the exhibition last night, furious. I've never seen him like that. He demanded we take down everything immediately."

The necklace. It has to be about the necklace. "What did he say exactly?"

"He was ranting about family secrets, about danger. Said Vivianne had put them all at risk." Dr. Phillips shakes his head. "I tried to reason with him, but he wouldn't listen. He had security guards with him. They started taking down the paintings right there and then."

Cold dread settles in my stomach. "The paintings. Where are they now?"

"They're still in the gallery. We're preparing them for transport to the Faulks estate. Mr. Faulks was insistent that—" He hesitates.

"No." My voice is sharp. "You can't let that happen. You need to make sure those paintings stay here. Don't let anyone take them, especially not Vivianne's father."

Confusion clouds Dr. Phillips's face, but he nods. "Of course, but what's going on? Why are these paintings so important?"

I open my mouth to explain, but the words catch in my throat. How much can I tell him? How much should I tell him? The less he knows, the safer he'll be. But I need his help.

"It's complicated. Those paintings... they're more than art. They're evidence."

"Evidence? Of what?"

"Of a crime that's been decades in the making." I lean in closer, lowering my voice. "I need you to trust me. Those paintings cannot leave this university. Not yet."

He studies me for a long moment, brow furrowed. Finally, he nods. "Alright. I trust you. I'll make sure the paintings stay here. But what about Vivianne? Have you spoken to her?"

The mention of her name sends a jolt through me. "No. I haven't been able to reach her. Do you know where she is?"

"Her father took her home last night. She hasn't been answering her phone. I'm worried about her. The way her father was acting... it wasn't right." Dr. Phillips shakes his head.

My hands curl into fists, ignoring the twinge of pain the action causes. "I need to see her. To make sure she's safe."

"That might be difficult. The Faulks estate is like a fortress. And after last night, I imagine Mr. Faulks will have tightened security even further."

There has to be a way. Some event, some occasion that would force the Faulks family out into the open. And then it hits me.

"The wedding. Vivianne's engagement. When is it?"

"I'm not sure of the exact date, but they were planning to

announce it soon." Dr. Phillips blinks, taken aback by the sudden change in topic. "Why?"

"Because that's my way in." I stand, ignoring the protest from my body. "I need to go. Thank you. For everything."

"Be careful. Whatever you're involved in... it seems dangerous." He rises as well, concern etched on his face.

"It is." A grim smile. "But so am I."

With that, I leave his office, my mind already racing with plans. I have calls to make, favors to call in. I need to find out when and where that engagement announcement is happening.

And I need to be there.

ELEVEN

Paul: The Blue Room

TWO WEEKS LATER, I STAND ACROSS THE STREET FROM THE ST. Regis, one of New York's most prestigious hotels. The sun is just beginning to set, casting a golden glow over the city. Under normal circumstances, I would appreciate the beauty of the moment, but right now, all my attention is focused on the sleek black limousine pulling up to the hotel's entrance.

My pulse quickens, hammering against my ribs. The chauffeur emerges, crisp and professional in his uniform. The front passenger door swings open.

Marcus Aberdine, Faulks's bodyguard, unfolds his imposing frame from the seat. His chiseled face turns, eyes scanning the surroundings. I shrink back, melting into the crowd of onlookers. Just another face.

Marcus's gaze sweeps over and through me, seeing everything and nothing. His hand hovers near his hip—the telltale sign of a concealed weapon. Ex-military, highly trained, fiercely loyal to the Faulks family. A formidable obstacle.

The chauffeur opens the rear door. Prescott emerges first. His tailored suit screams new money. His hand extends back into the car, an outwardly gentlemanly gesture.

Vivianne's delicate fingers appear, clasping his. She emerges from the limo, a vision in ivory silk. Her golden hair cascades down her back, catching the light like spun sunshine, but it's her eyes that capture me—those deep blue pools that have haunted my dreams for weeks.

My trained eye picks up on the details others might miss. Tension in her shoulders. Tightness around her eyes. The almost imperceptible flinch when Prescott places a hand on her back.

His touch is possessive, his smile never quite reaching his eyes as he guides her onto the sidewalk.

Mr. Faulks emerges from the limousine, every inch the powerful businessman. His expensive suit and perfectly coiffed hair exude an air of authority that bends the world around him. Cold calculation glimmers in his eyes as he surveys the gathered press.

I hunch my shoulders, angling my face away from their line of sight. Just another nameless spectator, unremarkable and forgettable. But my gaze never leaves Vivianne, drinking in every detail, cataloging every subtle shift in her expression.

This tableau before me—the doting fiancé, the dutiful daughter, the protective father—is all a carefully crafted illusion.

Vivianne's gaze darts nervously across the crowd, searching. Looking for an escape, perhaps? Her gaze sweeps past me, then immediately snaps back.

Our eyes lock.

The world falls away.

Electricity crackles between us, as potent as the day we met. The slight furrow of her brow. The way her fingers twist the fabric of her dress. The rapid rise and fall of her chest.

Her lips part in a silent gasp, and she sways. Prescott's arm shoots out, steadying her.

"Are you alright, darling?" Saccharine concern laces his words.

"I'm fine." She blinks rapidly, tearing her gaze from mine. "Just a bit lightheaded."

But the tremor in her hands, the flush creeping up her neck—she felt that jolt of recognition, that surge of desire.

The promise of possibility.

They make their way into the hotel, Marcus clearing a path through the throngs of reporters and photographers. Prescott guides her, never once removing his hand from her body. Her father walks ahead, leading.

Vivianne's gaze finds mine once more. A fleeting glance, heavy with unspoken words. Then she's gone, swallowed by the revolving doors, leaving me breathless in her wake.

The St. Regis is a monument to luxury, all marble floors and crystal chandeliers. Security is tight, but nothing I can't handle. I've spent the last two weeks memorizing the layout, the staff rotations, every possible entry and exit point.

She's not safe. Not with them. Every instinct screams at me to grab her and run. But I can't. Not yet. I need to be smart about this.

I slip away from the crowd, ducking into a narrow alley behind the St. Regis. The acrid stench of garbage mingles with the sweet rot of discarded food. A cat yowls, darting between overflowing dumpsters. My eyes adjust to the dim light, scanning for my target.

There—the service entrance. A cigarette dangles from the lips of a bored-looking security guard. I check my watch. Any second now...

A crash echoes from further down the alley. The guard's head snaps up, his hand moving to his radio. He hesitates, then heads toward the sound.

Merlin's timing is impeccable. Right on cue.

I slip through the door, the rush of cool air carrying the scent of bleach and freshly laundered linens. Voices echo from around the corner. I duck into a supply closet.

Uniforms hang in neat rows. I strip quickly, the rough fabric of the borrowed clothes scratching against my skin. The bow tie gives me trouble—it's been a while since I've tied one of these. Finally, it sits straight. I clip on a name tag that says "James."

I emerge, straightening my cuffs. A harried-looking woman rushes past, barking into a headset.

"We need more champagne in the Astor Ballroom, now."

Perfect.

I grab an empty tray and stride purposefully toward the kitchen. The cacophony slams into me—pots clanging, knives chopping, orders being shouted in a mix of English and rapid-fire Spanish. Steam billows from massive pots, carrying the rich aroma of simmering sauces.

"You. New guy." A red-faced chef points at me. "Take these canapés up. And don't drop them, or it's your ass."

I nod, loading my tray. The elevator ride gives me a moment to steady my nerves. The doors open, and I step into another world.

The Astor Ballroom glitters with wealth and power. Crystal chandeliers cast rainbows across marble floors. The air is thick with expensive perfume and the low hum of cultivated voices. I weave through the crowd.

There's the mayor, laughing too loudly at his own joke. A cluster of Wall Street types, greed oozing from their pores. To the side, a trio of impeccably dressed older women—socialites, their faces frozen in forced smiles, exchanging whispered judgments behind jeweled fingers, dissecting each other's outfits and scandals like it's a sport.

The ballroom is a sea of glittering dresses and dark suits. The cream of New York society gathered to witness the joining of two powerful families.

The moment I spot Vivianne, my chest tightens. That unmistakable cascade of golden hair, pinned up in intricate waves, glows under the chandeliers like a beacon meant to ruin me. I tear my gaze away, forcing myself to stay calm.

I pivot, steering myself in the opposite direction. My path leads straight to Dr. Phillips, who's engaged in an animated conversation with another guest. I need to get a message to Vivianne, and he's my way in.

I approach with my tray. "Canapé, sir?"

Dr. Phillips turns, his hand outstretched. His fingers freeze mid-air, a flicker of recognition sparking in his eyes. The scent of his cologne—sandalwood and spice—mingles with the aroma of the delicate pastries on my tray.

He recovers swiftly, plucking a canapé from the tray. "Ah, yes. Thank you."

As he brings the morsel to his lips, I lean in, close enough to see the faint sheen of sweat on his brow.

"Tell Vivianne to meet me in the Blue Room. Ten minutes." The words are barely a whisper.

A champagne flute clinks nearby.

"Mmm, exquisite." He announces it to his companions. "Now, where was I? Ah yes, the brushwork..." He coughs, covering any reaction, then pops the canapé into his mouth, chewing thoughtfully.

I step back, melting into the crowd. The weight of the tray, the press of bodies around me, the constant hum of conversation —it all fades as I track Dr. Phillips from the corner of my eye. He gesticulates wildly, drawing his audience closer to examine some detail of the painting. Then, with practiced ease, he extricates himself.

"If you'll excuse me, I see someone I simply must greet."

He weaves through the crowd toward Vivianne. I busy myself with offering hors d'oeuvres, every nerve on high alert. Dr. Phillips reaches her, clapping Prescott on the shoulder with feigned joviality.

"Prescott! I was telling someone about that marvelous Picasso you acquired. You must come meet them."

As Prescott preens, Dr. Phillips leans close to Vivianne. His lips move, forming words I can't hear over the orchestra's swelling crescendo. Vivianne's spine stiffens, a near-imperceptible reaction, but her face remains a mask of calm, a practiced smile never wavering.

"Oh, Dr. Phillips, you do go on." Her laugh is crystal bells over the din of the party.

Satisfied, I make my way to the edge of the room. The crowd thins here, the air cooler away from the press of bodies. A service door, innocuous in its plainness, beckons. One final glance over my shoulder—no one's watching. The door handle is cool under my palm as I slip into the dimly lit corridor beyond.

The sounds of the gala fade, replaced by the low hum of air conditioning and the distant clatter of dishes. I lean against the wall.

Now, to wait. And hope.

I push off from the wall, my footsteps echoing in the empty corridor as I make my way to the Blue Room. The plush carpet muffles my steps, a stark contrast to the cold concrete of that warehouse floor. My side twinges—a phantom pain from the bullet wound, long since healed but never forgotten.

The Blue Room door looms before me, its ornate handle cool beneath my fingers. I slip inside. The room lives up to its name— sapphire wallpaper, midnight blue drapes, cerulean accents on the furniture.

Elegant and refined.

My mind floods with images of Vivianne. Strapped to that chair, water drowning her. The panic in her eyes, the desperation in her movements. The way she clung to me when I pulled her free, her body shaking with cold and fear. The relief that washed over me, knowing she was safe, only to have it shattered by the crack of a gunshot.

I pace the room, unable to stay still. My fingers trace the scar on my abdomen, a permanent reminder of Nicholas's betrayal.

My brother.

My enemy.

The ache of his presumed death mingles with the relief that he can no longer hurt us. The staccato of gunfire, his body falling into darkness—it plays on repeat in my mind.

Urakov's men were thorough.

Efficient.

Cold.

But necessary.

He protected me and Vivianne.

I check my watch. Two minutes until Vivianne is due to arrive. Will she come? Does she still feel what I feel? Or has the time apart and the pressure from her family changed things?

The soft ticking of an antique clock on the mantle counts down the seconds. I adjust my borrowed uniform and smooth back my hair. A crystal decanter catches my eye—whiskey, probably older than I am. The temptation to pour a steadying drink is strong, but I need a clear head.

One minute.

I move to the window, peering at the glittering New York skyline. Somewhere out there, Merlin is watching, waiting. My adoptive father, my mentor, the man who shaped me into who I am. Does he approve of this plan? Or does he see it as another reckless move, driven by emotion rather than logic?

The door handle turns.

I spin, my breath catching in my throat. This is it. After months apart, after all we've been through—Vivianne is here.

TWELVE

Paul: The Announcement

The door opens.

My breath catches as a sliver of light appears, widening. A figure slips through the gap, movements cautious and deliberate.

Vivianne.

She closes the door behind her, pressing her back against it. Her eyes, wide and luminous in the dim light, lock onto mine. For a heartbeat, we're frozen, drinking in the sight of each other.

Then, as if a dam has burst, we surge forward.

We collide in the center of the room, bodies crashing together. My arms encircle her waist, lifting her off her feet. Her hands clutch at my shoulders, fingers digging in to assure herself I'm real.

I bury my face in the crook of her neck, inhaling deeply. The scent of her perfume—lilacs and roses—floods my senses, achingly familiar.

"Paul." My name is a prayer on her lips.

"Vivianne." I pour weeks of longing into those three syllables.

The grandeur of the gala fades into insignificance. Her ivory gown hugs her body, and I'm drawn to her with an urgency that obliterates everything else.

She pulls back just enough to meet my gaze. Her eyes shimmer with unshed tears that catch the light.

"I thought I lost you." Her voice is husky, raw.

I cup her face, thumbs brushing away the tears that trace paths down her cheeks. Her skin is soft, warm, slightly flushed—a stark contrast to the cool elegance of her gown.

"Never." The word holds the weight of a thousand promises.

Our lips collide with a fervor that steals the air from my lungs. I devour her mouth as if it's the very essence of life, my hunger matched only by the desperation of our circumstances. The kiss is raw, primal—tasting of shared suffering and the isolation of months apart.

Her mouth is eager, urgent, as if she's been starving for this very moment. I meet her desperation with my own, our lips moving together in perfect synchrony. The months of separation, the fear, the longing—they all surface in this kiss.

Our bodies press closer, hers soft and yielding against my hard frame, like puzzle pieces clicking into place. She clings to me, hands gripping my shirt, pulling me closer, as if she can't bear even the slightest distance between us.

The silken fabric clings to her like a second skin, revealing every curve, every delicate line. The knowledge that only a thin layer of material separates us sends a surge of raw desire coursing through me. I ache to explore every inch of her, to reclaim what has always been mine.

I want to tear away the ivory gown, expose the flesh beneath, and brand it with desperate kisses. But I resist, knowing the destruction of her dress would leave her exposed when she returns to the gala. The anticipation is its own torment.

Her breath comes in quick, ragged gasps, mirroring my own. Her pulse pounds against my chest, its rhythm matching mine.

Our bodies meld, and my hands roam her back, sides, hips, reacquainting myself with every curve and line. Her fingers tangle in my hair, tugging, urging me closer, deeper into the kiss.

I trace the seam of her lips with my tongue, slow and deliberate, savoring the soft gasp that escapes her as she opens to me. Her taste floods my senses—sweet like champagne, uniquely Vivianne.

It's a taste that has haunted my dreams, and now that I have it again, I'm consumed by hunger for more. Our tongues meet, each stroke sparking a fire that burns hotter within me.

My hands drift from her hair, tracing the contours of her shoulders, her back, before settling on her hips. I pull her closer, and she melts into me with a soft moan that nearly undoes me.

I'm painfully aware of my body's response to her, the throbbing ache that grows more insistent with each passing second. I want her right here, right now, amidst the glitz and glamour of the gala. Instead, I channel my desire into our kiss, into the way my hands roam her body, memorizing every curve.

Her hips press against mine, a subtle, tantalizing movement that sends shockwaves through me. I can feel her need matching my own, and it takes every ounce of self-control not to give in to the primal urge to take her right here.

I trail kisses along her jaw, down the column of her throat, reveling in the little sounds of pleasure that escape her lips.

For a blissful eternity, nothing exists but this—the taste of her, the feel of her body pressed against mine. The world outside fades away, narrowing down to just us, just this moment.

But reality intrudes all too soon. The distant sound of laughter reminds us where we are and the danger we're in.

Reluctantly, I break the kiss, resting my forehead against hers as we both struggle to catch our breath. We cling to each other, frantically making up for lost time. Her tears mingle with the salt on our skin, erased by fervent kisses. Vows are silently made and received, promises of forever sealed in fleeting touches.

"We don't have much time." Though every fiber of my being rebels against letting her go.

"Then let's make it count." Her fingers trace the line of my jaw.

"We need to talk about the painting."

"I saw the necklace."

"Yes, in the painting. That's what I want to talk about."

"Not in the painting. I saw the real necklace."

I freeze. "You saw—Where? How?"

She glances nervously at the door. "My father has it. In a vault beneath our house. Paul, there's so much down there—paintings, jewels, things I never knew existed."

I struggle to process this information. The necklace, after all these years...

"Vivianne, that necklace—it's more important than you know."

"Tell me."

"It's a long story. One, I promise to tell you in full, but for now, you need to know this—that necklace was given to your grandmother by Merlin for safekeeping just before World War II. It was stolen when she married your grandfather."

The color drains from her face. "My grandfather? But that would mean—"

"Viv? Where the hell has that girl gotten to?" Her father's voice slices through the air, sharp and grating. It carries an edge that leaves the room tense in its wake—abrasive, demanding attention whether you want to give it or not.

Vivianne's eyes widen. Her hand flies to her mouth, stifling a gasp.

"Paul, you have to go. Now." The words are barely audible.

I nod, understanding the urgency. We both know what's at

stake if we're caught together. Vivianne's gaze darts to the door, then back to me. She takes a half-step toward me as if pulled by an invisible thread before jerking back.

I gesture toward a second exit I scouted earlier.

Vivianne squares her shoulders, composing herself with visible effort. She smooths her dress, fingers trembling slightly as they brush over the fabric. With one last longing look at me, she turns to the door.

"I'm here. I'm coming, Father." Her voice is steadier now but still tinged with tension.

She slips out, closing the door softly behind her. Through the wood, I hear her fabricate an excuse.

"I'm sorry, Father. I... I needed a moment alone. The excitement of the evening..."

"Nonsense." Mr. Faulks's tone is sharp enough to make me wince. "You've been raised better than to abandon your guests. Prescott has been looking for you."

"I apologize. It won't happen again."

"See that it doesn't." His voice lowers, but I can still make out his words. "This is an important night, Viv. The announcement of your engagement... It's time we showed the world the strength of the Faulks name."

"Yes, Father." The words sound hollow, rehearsed.

"Come, everyone's waiting. It's time for the announcement."

I wince, imagining Vivianne's fingers frantically smoothing down the hair I shamelessly ran my hands through moments ago. Their voices fade as they move away, leaving me in sudden silence. My fists clench at my sides. The revelation about her family's vault hangs heavy, another complication in our already tangled web.

I take a deep breath, forcing myself to focus. There will be time to deal with that later. For now, I need to get out of here undetected. And then... then we plan our next move.

Their footsteps fade, swallowed by the gala's ambient noise. I lean against the door, forehead pressing against the cool wood. The weight of what we're up against settles heavily on my shoulders.

But the memory of Vivianne in my arms, the taste of her still on my lips, steels my resolve. Her father, Prescott, this whole damned engagement—they're just obstacles.

And I've never met an obstacle I couldn't overcome.

I slip out of the Blue Room, straightening my borrowed uniform. The cacophony of the gala washes over me as I make my way back toward the main ballroom. Glasses clink, laughter bubbles, the orchestra swells…

I barely take three steps when a vice-like grip clamps on my shoulder. My muscles tense, ready for a fight, as I spin around.

Marcus—the bodyguard—fixes me with a steely gaze, his massive frame blocking the corridor.

"Mr. de Gaulle." His voice is low and menacing. "I'm afraid you're not on the guest list."

I force my lips into an easy smile, though my pulse races.

"Surely there's been some mistake. I have an invitation right here."

My hand slips into my jacket pocket, fingers closing around a taser—something that will buy me the seconds I need to escape.

Marcus's eyes narrow. He opens his mouth, likely to call for backup, when a sudden commotion erupts from the ballroom. We both turn instinctively toward the sound.

Mr. Faulks is at the podium, microphone in hand. His voice booms through the room, silencing the chatter.

"Ladies and gentlemen, thank you all for coming. We have a very special announcement to make tonight."

My stomach twists. No. Not now. Not like this.

"It is my great pleasure to announce the engagement of my daughter, Vivianne Faulks, to Mr. Prescott Harrington."

The world seems to slow down. Prescott slips a massive diamond ring onto Vivianne's finger. It catches the light, throwing off prisms that mock me with their beauty. Prescott leans in, pressing a kiss to Vivianne's cheek. Mr. Faulks beams, every inch the proud father.

But Vivianne... her gaze darts through the crowd, searching. She finds me, a silent plea in her eyes. The anguish there mirrors the pain lancing through my chest.

Applause erupts, shattering the moment. I use the distraction to wrench free from Marcus's grip, melting into the sea of well-wishers. Plans A through Z crumble to dust.

They moved up the engagement.

The wedding will follow soon.

This changes everything, but one thing remains constant—I will not lose her. Not to Prescott, her father, or anyone.

Vivianne's eyes find mine one last time. A promise passes between us, unspoken but binding.

This isn't over. Not by a long shot.

THIRTEEN

Vivianne: Brigitte

THE MANSION SLEEPS AROUND ME, A BEHEMOTH OF STONE AND shadow that feels more like a mausoleum than a home. My bare feet whisper against the plush carpet as I navigate halls I've known my entire life, yet tonight they feel foreign. Menacing. Moonlight spills through the towering windows, painting everything in shades of silver and doubt.

My pulse hammers against my ribs. Each step toward the west wing tightens the vise around my chest, makes my breath come shorter, faster. The air feels thick, pressing against my skin like a physical weight. Every creak of the floorboards sends a jolt of adrenaline through my system, and the hair on the back of my neck stands on end.

I shouldn't be doing this. Father would—

No. I push the thought away. I'm done being the obedient daughter who asks permission to breathe.

The west wing looms ahead, its doorway a dark mouth waiting to swallow me whole. Father sealed these rooms the day after Grandmother's funeral, as if grief could be contained behind a locked door, as if memories could be buried along with the dead.

I wasn't allowed to say goodbye to her space, to sit one last time at her vanity, or curl up in her reading chair where she used to read to me. Just like I was too young to say goodbye to Mother when she died, too small to understand that gone meant forever.

Everyone I've ever loved has been taken from me or locked away.

The brass doorknob is cold beneath my trembling fingers. I half-expect it to be locked, half-expect Father to have changed the locks or installed some security measure I don't know about. This house is full of secrets I'm not privy to, after all. Hidden safes. Concealed vaults. Lies stacked upon lies.

But the knob turns. The door yields.

Musty air rushes out to greet me, thick with dust and the ghost of Chanel No. 5—Grandmother's signature scent. It hits me like a physical blow, and for a moment, I can't breathe. Can't move. I'm six years old again, pressing my face into her cardigan, inhaling that smell of lavender and face powder and safety.

Except she wasn't safe, was she? She never stood up to her own son. Never protected me. Never fought.

I slip inside and ease the door shut behind me, my pulse thundering so loud I'm certain someone will hear it. Darkness presses in, oppressive and complete. My fingers fumble along the wall, searching for the switch. When I find it, soft lamplight blooms, and I have to bite back a gasp.

It's exactly as she left it. As if she just stepped out for tea and will return any moment to find me snooping through her things.

The room is frozen in time—her reading glasses folded on the side table, a book still marked with a ribbon at page one hundred and forty-three. Her slippers arranged neatly beside the bed. The throw blanket she crocheted draped over the armchair by the window, the one where she'd sit for hours watching the gardens.

Her gardens. The only place in this entire estate that felt warm.

My throat tightens. Grief wells up, sharp and unexpected, after all these years. I force it down, swallow it back. I'm not here to mourn. I'm here for answers.

I move to her vanity, its ornate mirror reflecting my pale face back at me. My fingers trail across the surface, leaving tracks in the dust. One by one, I ease open drawers, rifling through forgotten treasures that smell of another lifetime. A tarnished silver hairbrush with a few gray hairs still caught in its bristles. Faded ribbons in colors she favored—dusty rose, sage green. A half-empty bottle of Chanel No. 5.

Nothing. Just the detritus of a life lived small. Confined. Silent.

Frustration builds in my chest, hot and tight. There has to be something here. Something that explains why Father reacted so violently to those paintings, why that ruby necklace matters so much, why everything in this family feels like a carefully constructed lie.

A glint of gold catches my eye. Tucked beneath a silk scarf, nearly hidden, is a locket I've never seen before. My breath catches as I lift it. The metal warms in my palm, and my hands shake as I pry it open.

Two photos. One of my grandmother as a young woman— but not the grandmother I knew. This woman is radiant, her eyes bright with mischief, her smile wide and uninhibited. She's beautiful in a way that steals my breath. Alive in a way I never saw her.

The other photo shows a man I don't recognize. Dark hair, intense eyes, a smile that suggests he knows secrets worth keeping. He's devastatingly handsome in that old-fashioned way, and something about the set of his jaw reminds me of—

No. It can't be.

But the way he looks at the camera, as if seeing right through it to the person holding it... it's the same way Paul looks at me.

My search grows frantic. There has to be more. I run my hands along the underside of the vanity, feeling for anything unusual. My fingers find a slight unevenness, barely perceptible. I press, and—

Click.

A small drawer slides open, revealing a bundle of yellowed envelopes tied with a faded ribbon. My hands shake so badly I nearly drop them.

The top envelope bears a name in elegant script: *Brigitte.*

Not Grandmother. Not Mrs. Faulks. Just Brigitte. A woman's name. A person, not just a role.

My pulse slams against my ribs. The ribbon's silk frays beneath my fingers as I untie it, the delicate fibers threatening to crumble. The first letter unfolds, revealing bold, passionate handwriting that seems to pulse with urgency.

My dearest Brigitte,

I sink onto the edge of her bed, unable to stand. Unable to process what I'm seeing.

I write this under the dim light of a candle, its flame flickering like the fragile hope I cling to in these dark times. The sounds of war surround me— boots on stone, the distant rumble of artillery—and yet my thoughts are only of you.

War. Artillery. This is old. Very old.

I fear what this world is becoming, the shadows of battle growing longer with each passing day. But more than anything, I fear the day when I can no longer reach out and feel your warmth, when your laughter becomes a memory lost in the din of war. The nights are cold here, but colder still is the thought of a world without you in it.

My grandmother's laughter. I try to remember it and can't. When did she stop laughing? Was it before I was born, or did I just never notice?

I hold on to the moments we shared, the stolen kisses under the stars, your smile that has kept me alive more times than I can count. I carry your love with me, a shield against the madness that surrounds me. It is my only armor, my only strength.

Stolen kisses. My prim, proper grandmother who never raised her voice, never contradicted Father, never showed a hint of passion about anything—she had stolen kisses under the stars?

If I do not return—though I will fight like hell to make sure I do— know that every beat of my heart belongs to you, now and always. Until I can hold you again, I remain yours, in this life and the next.

Forever yours, Anthony

Anthony. The man in the locket. The fire to Grandfather Henry's steadfast earth.

A memory surfaces, sharp and vivid...

I'm six years old, curled in Grandmother's lap in the sunroom. Afternoon light streams through the windows, turning everything gold. She smells like lavender and powder, and her arms around me feel like the safest place in the world. The only safe place in a house full of Father's cold disapproval.

"Vivvy, darling, let me tell you a story of two men I once knew." Her voice is softer than usual.

I nestle closer, captivated by something different in her tone. Something almost... wistful.

"One was like fire." Her voice takes on a dreamlike quality I've never heard before. "Passionate, intense, burning so bright it almost hurt to look at him." Her fingers absently stroke my hair. "His eyes... oh, Vivvy, they held entire worlds. When he looked at me, I felt like the only person in existence."

Even at six, I can hear the longing in her voice. The loss.

"The other was steadfast as the earth, reliable and strong. A rock in stormy seas, always there, always constant."

"Like in fairy tales, Grandma? The dashing prince and the noble knight?"

"Oh, if only life were so simple, my love. Both men held pieces of my heart in such different ways." Her laugh is sad. So sad.

"But you chose Grandpa, right? He was the best one?"

A shadow crosses her face. "I chose between them. For family, for duty." Her hand cups my cheek, her eyes boring into mine with sudden intensity. "But remember, Vivvy, true love... it leaves its mark on you forever. It shapes you, changes you in ways you can't always see."

"Does it hurt?"

"Sometimes, my darling. But the pain reminds me that I once loved and loved deeply. And that's a precious thing." Her smile is bittersweet.

Now, sitting on her bed with Anthony's letter in my hands, I understand. She wasn't telling me a fairy tale. She was confessing. Warning me. Trying to give me something she never had—a choice.

But she still didn't fight for me. Still let Father control me, just like she let him control her.

My hands shake as I unfold the next letter.

My dearest Brigitte,

The war presses harder against us each day. I feel it in the air, heavy and suffocating, as though the very earth beneath my feet trembles with uncertainty. Yet, in the midst of all this chaos, you are my anchor. Every time I close my eyes, I see you—your smile, the way your hair catches the light. You've become my sanctuary, the only place my soul finds peace.

I can't reconcile this passion with the quiet woman who raised me. The woman who moved through this house like a ghost, never making waves, never demanding anything for herself.

I'm not the man I was when I left you. Each battle strips something from me, something I fear I'll never get back. But what remains, what keeps me standing, is the thought of coming home to you. Every letter you send is a lifeline, a reminder that there is still beauty and love in this world, though it often feels like a dream I may never touch again.

Did she write back? Did she send those lifelines, or did her silence begin even then?

I don't know when this war will end. I only know that when it does, I need you by my side. Hold on to me, my love, as I hold on to you. I fight not just for country or honor, but for us—always for us.

Yours eternally, Anthony

Yours eternally. But she wasn't his, was she?

The next letter unfolds in my trembling hands.

My dearest Brigitte,

I dream of you often, of the day I'll finally come back to you. It's the thought of that moment—your arms around me, your laughter filling the air —that keeps me going through all of this.

Her laughter. God, when did she stop laughing?

I've asked my best friend, Henry, to check in on you while I'm away. I trust him with my life, and I know he'll keep you safe, just as I wish I could. It brings me some comfort to know someone I trust is near you, even if I can't be.

Oh no. Oh God, no. Henry. Grandfather Henry?

My stomach drops. I know how this story ends, and suddenly I don't want to keep reading. But I can't stop. The words pull me forward like a current I'm powerless to resist.

The war feels endless, but I hold on to the hope that soon I'll be able to look into your eyes and feel like myself again. Stay strong, my love. We will have our time again, I promise you that.

With all my heart, Anthony

"Stay strong," I whisper to the empty room. "But she didn't, did she?"

The betrayal is there in the next letter before I even unfold it.

I can feel it in the quality of the paper, the urgency of the handwriting.

My dearest Brigitte,

It's been weeks since I've heard from you. I tell myself that letters can be delayed in times like these, but the silence gnaws at me. The war intensifies around us—bombs rain down like a ceaseless storm, and the fear grows thicker each day. I feel... lost without your words. I'm fighting in a fog with no direction.

My chest aches. I know this feeling. The silence of someone who should love you but doesn't respond. The desperate need for confirmation that you still matter, that you're still seen.

I need to hear from you. I need to know that your heart still beats with mine, that the world outside these trenches hasn't swallowed us whole. I've seen so much death, too much for any man to bear, but losing you would be the one blow I could not recover from.

I bite my lip hard enough to taste blood. Don't cry. Don't cry.

But I am crying. For him. For her. For all of us trapped in cycles we can't break.

Please send word soon. Tell me you're still waiting for me, that you still believe in what we have. Without you, none of this makes sense.

With all my love, Anthony

The next letter trembles in my hands.

My dearest Brigitte,

There's a strange shift in the air. I can feel it in every bone, a prelude to something I cannot yet name. I haven't received a single reply from you. I've heard from Henry, and he said he saw you not long ago. He mentioned you looked well, that you were smiling.

No. No no no.

It should have brought me comfort, but instead it twisted something inside me.

He knew. On some level, he already knew.

I try to focus on my duties, but my mind is always with you, wondering why your letters stopped, why I feel this growing distance between us. Is it me? Is it the war? Has it changed me too much? I look in the mirror and don't recognize the man staring back. I wonder if you won't recognize him either.

My throat constricts. The desperation in his words is palpable, reaching across decades to wrap around me and squeeze.

I don't know what I'm asking for. Just... some kind of sign. Something to tell me you haven't slipped away from me.

Forever yours, Anthony

But she had slipped away. Chose safety over passion. Duty over desire.

Just like she never fought for me.

The final letter isn't from Anthony. The handwriting is different—smaller, more controlled. Feminine. I recognize it from birthday cards and Christmas notes written in my childhood.

My grandmother's hand.

My dearest Anthony,

My breath catches. She wrote to him. Finally, she wrote to him.

This letter is one I never thought I'd have to write, but after months of silence, I cannot continue to keep my heart locked away from the truth. So much has changed since you left for the war, more than I could have anticipated. We've both changed, and I fear that the distance between us is now more than just miles.

Cold. It's so cold compared to his letters. So measured. So careful.

I've grown close to Henry. He's been here through all the uncertainty, through the fear, and somewhere along the way, my feelings shifted. It wasn't intentional, but I must be honest with you, as much as it pains me to say. I love him. And I've chosen him.

She chose his best friend. The man he trusted to keep her safe. The betrayal is staggering, even now, even knowing how the story ends.

I know this will hurt you. I never meant to cause you pain, but I couldn't wait any longer. I hope that one day, you'll understand, though I don't expect forgiveness. Please, take care of yourself. You are a good man, but I can no longer be yours.

Goodbye, Brigitte

Goodbye. Just... goodbye. After everything, that's all she gave him.

I stare at the letter, trying to reconcile it with the woman I knew. The woman who stroked my hair and told me stories. Who let Father control her, control me, control everything.

She made her choice for duty. For safety. For the man who was there instead of the man she loved.

And it hollowed her out. Turned her from that vibrant woman in the locket—eyes bright with mischief, smile wide and uninhibited—into the ghost who raised me. The woman who taught me, through silence and surrender, that love wasn't worth fighting for.

But the letter was never sent. It's here, with his letters, hidden in a secret drawer. She kept them all. Every single one. Even the letter she wrote to end it, she couldn't let go.

She carried this with her for her entire life. This grief. This loss. This choice she made killed something vital inside her.

Is that why she never fought for me? Because she'd already lost her own battle? Because she'd chosen safety once and knew, bone-deep, that it was the wrong choice, but couldn't bear to see me make a different one?

The weight of it presses down on me, suffocating. I sink to the floor, letters scattered around me like fallen leaves. Like all the words she never said, all the fights she never fought.

My grandmother loved someone deeply—loved him enough that losing him carved her hollow. And she still chose duty. Chose family expectations. Chose the safe path.

And it destroyed her.

I clutch the letters to my chest, and the tears come hot and fast. For Anthony. For my grandmother, who lived her entire life as a shell of who she could have been. For my mother, who I'll never know, who might have fought for me if she'd lived.

For myself. Trapped in the same cycle. Engaged to Prescott. Under Father's control. Repeating history.

No.

The word crystallizes in my mind, sharp and clear.

No. I won't do this. I won't become her—carrying regret like a stone in my chest for the rest of my life, letting fear make my choices, surrendering myself piece by piece until there's nothing left.

The ground shifts beneath me. Everything I thought I knew about my family is crumbling. The Faulks legacy isn't built on strength, honor, or tradition.

It's built on lies. Stolen love. Women who sacrificed themselves on the altar of duty and spent their lives as ghosts in their own homes.

Well, I'm done being a ghost.

Loyalty wars within me. To Father, who raised me but kept me prisoner. To Paul, who awakened something in me I can't deny—something my grandmother felt once and lost. To Grandmother herself, whose choices shaped my fate.

But maybe it's time to be loyal to myself. To the woman I could be, if I had the courage to choose differently than she did.

I gather the letters with shaking hands. There's more to uncover, more truths lurking beneath the surface. The ruby necklace. Merlin. The connection between Anthony and Paul.

But first, I need to hide these. Protect them. They're evidence of something Father desperately wants to keep buried—proof that the Faulks family's perfect image is built on betrayal and loss.

A creak echoes from the hallway. Footsteps. Heavy, deliberate.

Marcus.

Panic explodes in my chest. My breath catches, pulse slamming against my ribs. He can't find me here. Father will—

I scramble to my feet, shoving the letters back into the hidden compartment with trembling fingers. The latch sticks, refusing to close properly. My palms grow slick with sweat. The footsteps grow louder. Closer.

Come on, come on, come on—

Click. The compartment seals. I slam the drawer shut, the sound too loud in the silent room. I lunge for the armchair by the window, trying to arrange myself as if I'd been sitting there all along, just a grieving granddaughter seeking comfort in memories.

The door swings open.

Marcus fills the doorway, his bulk casting a long shadow across the floor. His eyes narrow, suspicious, sweeping over the room with precision. He's Father's man through and through—loyal, observant, dangerous.

"Miss Faulks?" His voice is flat, giving nothing away. "What are you doing in here?"

I force a smile, praying he can't hear the frantic gallop in my chest. "Couldn't sleep." I gesture vaguely at the room. "I just... I miss her sometimes."

It's not entirely a lie. I do miss her. Or maybe I miss the woman she could have been, if she'd been braver.

Marcus steps further into the room, and I resist the urge to shrink back. His gaze sweeps over the vanity, and my stomach drops. Did I close all the drawers? Is everything exactly as it was?

"Your father doesn't like anyone disturbing your grandmother's rooms."

"I know." I stand, smoothing my nightgown with hands that won't stop shaking. "I just needed... I don't know. Connection, maybe."

He studies me for a long moment, calculating, measuring,

deciding whether to report this to Father. Then his phone rings, shrill in the tense silence.

He pulls it from his pocket, frowning at the screen. "Yes?" His expression darkens as he listens. "I'll be right there." He pins me with a hard stare. "Back to your room, Miss Faulks."

I nod meekly, slipping past him. My legs feel like jelly as I hurry down the hall, expecting him to call me back at any moment. To ask what I was really doing. To notice something out of place.

Only when I'm safely behind my locked door do I allow myself to breathe.

I press my back against the door, sliding down to sit on the floor. My whole body shakes with adrenaline and grief and something that might be hope.

I know the truth now. At least part of it.

My grandmother loved deeply and chose duty, and it killed her. Made her into a shadow. A cautionary tale I'm supposed to learn from.

But I'm learning the wrong lesson, aren't I?

I'm not supposed to see that choosing duty destroyed her. I'm supposed to see that duty matters more than love. That family expectations matter more than personal happiness. That women like us don't get to choose—we surrender.

Except I'm done surrendering.

Tomorrow, I'll find a way back to those letters. I'll piece together the rest of the story. I'll figure out how that ruby necklace fits into this tragedy, why Father is so desperate to keep it hidden.

And then I'll make my choice. Not the choice my grandmother made. Not the choice Father demands.

My choice.

FOURTEEN

Vivianne: Sentinel

The breakfast room smells of fresh coffee and something sweet—cinnamon rolls, maybe, or those delicate French pastries Father insists on ordering from the bakery in the city. My stomach should growl at the scent. Instead, it twists into knots.

Across the table, Father sits like a king at court, his newspaper held high—a shield, a wall, a reminder that I'm not worth looking at. The pages rustle as he turns them, crisp and deliberate. Each snap of paper feels like a slap.

I sit woodenly in my chair, last night's discoveries pressing down on my chest like a physical weight. Anthony's letters. Grandmother's confession. The woman she could have been, burned away by duty until only ash remained.

Clara, one of our servers, glides in with a silver tray. She sets down a plate of pastries, their golden crusts gleaming with butter. The scent intensifies, rich and cloying, and my stomach rebels.

"You're not eating." Father's voice cuts through the quiet like a blade. He doesn't lower the paper.

I force myself to reach for a croissant, tearing off a small piece. It's still warm, the layers flaking apart in my fingers. I bring it to my lips but can't make myself bite down.

"Not hungry."

The paper lowers. Those steel-gray eyes lock onto mine, and I shrink, becoming smaller under his gaze. It's a trick he's mastered—making me feel like I'm six years old again, standing before him with mud on my shoes, waiting for judgment.

"You look tired." He sets his coffee cup down with a deliberate click against the saucer. "Late night?"

My pulse slams against my ribs. The croissant crumbles between my fingers, flakes falling onto the china plate like snow. Does he know? Did Marcus tell him more than I thought?

"Couldn't sleep."

"Hmm." He lifts his cup again, drinks slowly, never breaking eye contact. "Marcus mentioned finding you in your grandmother's wing. At three in the morning."

Not a question. An accusation dressed up as casual conversation.

I swallow hard, tasting bile. "I was looking for something."

"And did you find it?"

The question sounds almost pleasant. Almost. But the tension in his jaw, the way his fingers tighten around the cup's handle—

"Some old letters. From the war."

The temperature in the room drops. The air goes still and cold, like we're suddenly encased in ice.

Father sets down his cup. Folds his newspaper with precise, measured movements. Smooths it flat on the table. Each gesture is controlled, deliberate, and somehow more terrifying than if he'd thrown the cup across the room.

"I see." He steeples his fingers, elbows on the table. "And what, exactly, did you think you'd accomplish? Digging through dead people's private correspondence?"

The words land like stones. *Dead people.* As if Grandmother was just anyone. As if her heart, her choices, her pain don't matter because she's gone.

"I wanted to understand." My voice comes out smaller than I intend. Weaker. I hate how he does this—strips away every ounce of strength until I'm nothing but a scared little girl. "I wanted to know about Grandmother. About Grandpa Henry. Their story. My story. You always talk of family and legacy. I just needed help to find my place."

"Their story." He repeats the words slowly, each syllable dripping with contempt. "They were your grandparents. That's all you need to know."

"But there's more, isn't there?" Something in me rebels, pushes back even as fear churns in my gut. I lean forward, and the movement feels bold. Dangerous. "The letters talk about choices made during the war. About love and—"

"Viv."

Just my name. But the way he says it—low, warning—makes me flinch.

I don't stop. Can't stop. "There was someone else. Before Grandpa Henry. Someone named Anthony. Why did she choose Henry? What happened to—"

His hand slams down on the table. The china jumps. Coffee sloshes over the rim of his cup, spreading across the white tablecloth in a dark stain. Clara, hovering near the sideboard, goes rigid.

"These matters." Father's voice is deadly quiet now, more frightening than if he'd shouted. "Are none of your concern. They belong in the past. Where they will stay."

"But they're part of my history." The words tumble out faster now, fueled by desperation and the image of Grandmother's face in that locket—young, radiant, alive in a way I never saw her. "Don't I have a right to know where I come from? The choices that shaped our family?"

He stands. The chair scrapes against the hardwood floor, a harsh screech that makes my teeth ache. He's tall—I forget sometimes, when I'm not in the same room with him, just how tall. How he uses his height to loom, to dominate, to make everyone around him feel small.

"You're treading on dangerous ground."

"Dangerous?" I stand too, even though my legs are shaking. "Why? What are you so afraid of me finding out?"

His face goes very still. It's worse than anger—this cold, calculating blankness. "Afraid? You think I'm afraid?"

"The letters mentioned hidden treasures. Rescued art. Was our family involved in that?" The words rush out, reckless. "Is that where our fortune comes from? Is that why—"

"Enough."

But I can't stop. Won't stop. Not when I'm finally getting close to the truth. "Just tell me. Tell me what happened. Tell me why Grandmother chose—"

"ENOUGH!"

His fist comes down again, harder this time. A plate jumps off the table and shatters on the floor. Porcelain shards skitter across the hardwood. Clara makes a small sound—quickly stifled —and hurries from the room.

I'm frozen, standing with my hands braced on the table, staring at the man who raised me and realizing I don't know him at all. Have never known him.

His chest heaves. A vein throbs at his temple. When he speaks again, each word is enunciated with terrifying precision.

"Those matters are in the past. Where they belong. I will not have you dredging up ancient history. Not now. Not ever. Do you understand me?"

I sink back into my chair. My hands shake, so I hide them in my lap, fingers twisted together so tight they ache.

"I just want to understand our family."

"What you need to understand—" He leans forward, palms flat on the table, bringing his face level with mine. His breath smells like coffee and something bitter. "Is that you have an obligation. To honor the choices made by those who came before you. Choices that secured the privileges you enjoy today."

"But—"

"No." He straightens, smooths his tie. "No more foolishness. It's time you focused on your future. Not the past."

The shift in his demeanor is instant, jarring. The rage drains away, replaced by something worse—cold efficiency. He settles back into his chair, picks up his coffee cup as if the last five minutes didn't happen.

"I've been speaking with the Harringtons. We've agreed to move up the wedding date."

The world tilts. I grip the edge of the table, willing the room to stop spinning. "Move it up?"

"Three months from now should be sufficient." He drinks his coffee casually. As if he's discussing the weather. "Invitations go out next week."

"Three months?" I can't breathe. The air is too thick, too hot despite the coldness radiating from him. "But... I thought I had more time."

"Time for what, Viv?" He sets down his cup with that same deliberate click. "To continue your little art hobby? To gallivant around Europe on these so-called assignments?"

The way he says *assignments*—dripping with disdain—makes my chest tight with rage.

"My work isn't a hobby." I force the words out through clenched teeth. "I have expertise in forgery identification. I've made a name for myself internationally. It's more than a passion, it's—"

"It's a childish fantasy I've indulged far too long." He picks up his newspaper and snaps it open. Dismissing me. "The Faulks name carries weight. It's time you started living up to it."

Something snaps inside me. The fear, the careful restraint I've maintained my whole life—it cracks.

"And marrying Prescott is how I do that?" The words come out sharp, bitter. "Lie back, spread my legs, and pop out the heir you so desperately want?"

The newspaper lowers slowly. His eyes are ice.

"Don't be vulgar."

"Why not?" I laugh, and it sounds slightly unhinged even to my own ears. "That's all I am to you, isn't it? A womb to be filled. A pawn to marry off for business deals and family alliances."

"You are a Faulks." Each word is clipped, precise. "And you will behave accordingly."

"What does that even mean?" My voice rises. "Smile and stay silent while you auction me off? Pretend I don't have thoughts or dreams or—"

The door opens.

Prescott strides in, all polished charm in a thousand-dollar suit. His cologne fills the room immediately. He bends to kiss my cheek, and I force myself not to recoil as his lips graze my skin.

"Good morning, darling." Smooth as silk and just as artificial. "You look radiant as always."

I force a smile. It stretches across my face like a mask, stiff and false. "Prescott. What a lovely surprise."

He takes the seat beside me—too close, his thigh pressing against mine under the table—and reaches for my hand. I let him take it, fighting the urge to yank it away. His palm is damp. Hot.

"I hope you don't mind the intrusion." He addresses Father. Not me. Never me. "I was eager to discuss some wedding details."

"Not at all." Father's voice warms, the ice melting into something almost pleasant. Almost human. "Your timing is perfect. We were just discussing the new date."

"We were discussing our family's history, actually." The words come out petulant, childish. I don't care.

"Viv. Enough." Father's eyes narrow.

"It's quite all right, sir." Prescott's thumb strokes the back of my hand, and my skin crawls. "Family history can be... complicated."

"You know about it." I turn to face him, pulling my hand free. "Don't you? The letters. The war. All of it."

His smile never wavers, but something flickers in his eyes. Something cold and calculating that reminds me of Father. "Of course I do."

"Of course you do." I laugh again, that same slightly unhinged sound. "Why am I not surprised?"

Prescott exchanges a glance with Father. Something passes between them—an understanding, an agreement. They're united, these two men who claim to care about me.

"Viv, darling." Prescott's voice drips with condescension. "There are aspects of both our families' pasts that are... sensitive. It's best not to dig too deeply into things we can't change."

"Can't change, or don't want me to know?" My voice rises. "What are you hiding? What else have you kept from me?"

"Nothing that concerns you." Prescott's grip on my hand tightens, fingers digging into my wrist. "But our wedding—now that concerns us both. Three months. I'm thrilled we won't have to wait so long to start our life together."

He turns to me, and his blue eyes gleam with something that makes my stomach turn. "Aren't you, darling? Excited to finally be mine? In every way?"

The words hang in the air, heavy with implication. My mouth opens, but nothing comes out. The weight of their expectations, their plans for my body, my future, my life—it presses down until I can't breathe.

I manage a weak nod.

"All I want—" My voice cracks. I clear my throat, try again. "Is one straight answer."

Father stands abruptly. His chair scrapes against the floor again, harsh and final. "That's quite enough. You're tired from your late-night snooping. Perhaps you should retire to your room and rest."

"I'm not a child." I stand too, facing him across the table. Broken porcelain crunches under my feet. "I deserve to know the truth about my family."

The air between us crackles with tension. His jaw works, that vein throbbing at his temple again.

"What you deserve—" He bites off each word. "Is to show gratitude for the life you've been given. The privileges. The opportunities. All built on choices made long before you were born. Choices you have no right to question."

"Let's not get carried away. Viv is naturally curious. It's one of the things I admire about her." Prescott rises, positioning himself between us like a referee. Or a jailer.

The lie is so blatant it would be funny if it weren't so horrifying.

"But perhaps—" His hand settles on my lower back, possessive. "We could focus on more pleasant topics? The wedding, for instance. I have some lovely ideas for the venue."

I sink back into my chair, defeat washing over me in cold waves. They're a wall. An immovable force. And I'm just... me. Small. Powerless. Alone.

"Of course." The words taste like ash. "The wedding. How lovely."

Father smooths his tie, composure restored as if the last ten minutes never happened. "Finally. Some sense." He fixes me with a look designed to remind me of my place—beneath him, beneath Prescott, beneath the crushing weight of the Faulks name. "You'll learn to let Prescott take the lead. He speaks sense and understands his duty."

He settles back into his chair and picks up his coffee cup. "The venue will be here, of course. The estate. I want to minimize any... distractions."

Distractions. He means me. My movements, my breath, my existence—all carefully controlled and contained.

"Everything will come to us." He waves a hand dismissively. "Caterers. Decorators. Florists. There's no need for you to be running around making arrangements."

Running around. As if I'm a child who might wander off and get lost.

"It's all for your ease, my dear."

My ease. My prison. Same thing, apparently.

I clench my fists under the table, nails digging into my palms hard enough to leave crescents. If I say anything, I know what will come. More lectures. More icy dismissals. But if I stay silent, I'm complicit in my own burial.

They drone on—flower arrangements, guest lists, seating charts. Trivialities that matter so little when my entire life is being snuffed out. Father's words wrap around my throat like hands, squeezing, choking.

I withdraw. Pull deeper into myself while they plan my funeral disguised as a wedding.

Paul. I have to contact Paul. Warn him about the accelerated timeline. Find some way to—

"Speaking of preparations." Father's voice snaps me back. "We'll need to ensure Prescott is comfortable here. The estate will be your home after marriage. May as well begin the transition now."

My stomach drops.

"I've arranged for the West Wing to be modified." He doesn't look at me. Doesn't ask. Just states facts, decisions already made. "It will accommodate both of you. Your marital suite will be there. No sense waiting until the wedding for Prescott to move in. He may as well settle in now."

The West Wing. Our marital bed. The words echo in my skull, each one a nail in my coffin.

"That makes perfect sense, sir. Very practical." Prescott nods, completely unfazed.

Of course it does. To them.

"I'm not feeling well." I stand, and the room tilts. "I have a headache. I need to lie down."

Neither man seems particularly concerned. Father waves a dismissive hand, already turning back to Prescott.

"Go rest. We'll handle the arrangements."

Of course they will. They'll handle everything. My wedding. My life. My body.

I flee.

Back in my room, I pace, bare feet wearing tracks in the plush carpet. My thoughts spin, chaotic and desperate. I can't use my phone—it's undoubtedly monitored. Every call, every text, every search is probably reported straight to Father.

But social media. My rarely-used Instagram account that Father thinks is just vanity. He doesn't understand it, so he may not be watching it as closely.

My hands shake as I log in, craft a post that seems innocent but might—*might*—reach Paul.

"Feeling nostalgic today. Remembering that beautiful garden in Paris, with its hidden corners and secret pathways. How I long to walk those grounds again, to feel that sense of freedom and possibility. Perhaps in three months, when the roses are in full bloom? #ParisianDreams #Garden-Escapes #CountdownToAdventure"

I stare at the words. Will he understand? Will he see the

message beneath the message—three months until the wedding, a plea for help, for rescue, for anything?

I hit post before I can second-guess myself.

The walls feel closer suddenly. Suffocating. I need air. Need to move, to breathe something that isn't saturated with Father's cologne and Prescott's expectations.

I step into the hallway, intending to escape to the gardens, when voices stop me dead.

Hushed. Urgent. Coming from Father's study.

Curiosity overrides self-preservation. I move closer, pressing myself against the wall beside the door. It's slightly ajar—careless of them, or maybe they don't think I'm brave enough to eavesdrop.

"Viv is asking too many questions." Prescott's voice is low and tense.

"I'll handle my daughter." Father sounds bored. Dismissive. "You focus on your priorities."

"Yes, sir. But—" Prescott hesitates. "It might be wise to give her something small. An illusion of freedom. Quiet her until the wedding."

My blood runs cold. *An illusion of freedom.* Like I'm a pet that needs appeasing.

"I didn't ask for your opinion." The ice in Father's voice should be familiar by now, but it still makes me flinch. "Sentinel is at a turning point. It's time to finalize the family merger. We can't afford distractions."

Sentinel. The word drops into my consciousness like a stone into still water, sending ripples of dread outward. What is Sentinel? Why does it matter more than my questions, my rights, my life?

"Of course, sir." Prescott's voice drops lower. "I only meant—Viv is persistent. Already suspicious. For now, it might be easier to let her believe she's making decisions."

A pause. Long and weighted.

"I will not coddle her." Father's words are sharp, final. "She'll do as she's told. And you will ensure there's an heir as soon as possible. Sentinel takes priority over her whims."

Heir. The word makes my stomach churn. I press a hand over my mouth, fighting nausea.

Another pause. Then Prescott, his voice so low I have to strain to hear: "Since I'll be moving in... shall I take care of that before the wedding night? Or are we to wait?"

The audacity. The casual way he discusses my body, as if it's already his property. As if I'm a broodmare to be bred on command.

"She's still my daughter." Father's tone shifts—not warmth, but something close to possession. "We abide by tradition. You'll consummate the marriage on your wedding night. After that, I expect no delays."

A tense pause. Then Prescott again, and there's something dark in his voice. Something predatory.

"And if she resists?"

The question hangs in the air. I stop breathing, waiting for Father's response. Waiting to see if there's any line he won't cross, any protection he'll offer his only child.

The silence stretches.

And stretches.

And I realize with dawning horror that he's actually considering it. Weighing his options. Calculating whether tradition matters more than results.

FIFTEEN

Vivianne: The Cage

MY BREATH CATCHES, THE SOUND TOO LOUD IN MY OWN EARS. I press harder against the wall beside Father's study door, praying they can't hear the thundering in my chest. The wood is cool against my cheek, smooth and unyielding.

Waiting for his answer. Waiting to see if there's any line my father won't cross.

"You know your duty." Father's voice is flat. Businesslike. "Get it done. I don't care how. But don't take your eye off Sentinel."

My knees threaten to buckle, and I lock them, forcing myself to stay upright. Stay silent. Don't make a sound.

He doesn't care. Doesn't care if I resist, if I'm hurt, if I'm—

"Of course, sir. My apologies." Prescott's voice shifts—eager to please, like a dog that's been corrected. "Sentinel is my top priority."

"As it should be." Papers rustle. The clink of glass on glass—Father pouring a drink. "Malfor is anxious to see our families unite."

Malfor. I mouth the name silently. Who the hell is Malfor?

"Combining my family's tech expertise with your financial

resources will push Sentinel's operations forward." Prescott sounds confident now, back on solid ground. "We'll be decades ahead of any competition."

"Precisely." The sound of Father settling into his chair—leather creaking under his weight. "As the Fifth, I've managed our wealth for decades. But we need more than capital now. Your family's digital infrastructure is key. The world's shifting, and we can't afford to fall behind."

The Fifth. Fifth what? My mind spins, trying to make sense of the fragments.

"I'm ready." Pride creeps into Prescott's voice. "I've been groomed for this since I was a kid. Our cyber operations will be crucial. I've been developing a blockchain system that could revolutionize how we move funds within the organization."

A pause. When Father speaks again, his tone has sharpened. "And is your father planning to step down anytime soon? Or will you be waiting indefinitely to take the reins?"

Prescott's jaw must tighten—I can almost hear it. "He's not stepping down yet, but he's entrusting me with what matters. I've been handling the cyber division for years. I'll be ready when the time comes."

"That time is now." Father's voice goes hard. Heavy. "This marriage isn't just important—it's necessary. We need a male heir to take over as the Fifth. I'm not getting any younger. I need time to train the boy, ensure he understands his place."

My chest constricts. A male heir. That's all I am. A vessel for their precious heir. A womb with a pedigree.

"I understand the gravity." Prescott sounds almost contrite. "I'll do my duty to ensure the continuation of both families within Sentinel."

Another pause. I picture Father nodding, satisfied. "Good. Malfor is counting on this alliance to strengthen Sentinel as a whole. We cannot disappoint him."

"I won't, sir." That confidence again, bordering on arrogance. "With our combined resources, we'll be unstoppable. Financial and technological dominance. I have ideas for integrating AI into operations that could give us a significant edge."

Father makes a sound—not quite approval, but close. "As much as I hate to admit it, her art expertise provides perfect cover for our operations. She's too well-respected for anyone to question her movements. Which is precisely why she must never know the full extent of our involvement."

The words slam into me. My art. My career. My one source of pride—it's just a cover for them. A convenient disguise.

"Understood." Prescott sighs, and there's something different in his voice now. Softer? "It's... not easy keeping her in the dark. It would be simpler if we could tell her everything."

My pulse stutters. What?

"I don't disagree."

That's Father's voice. But it can't be. Because that tone—gentle, almost tender—is one I've never heard directed at me. Not in twenty-five years.

"But it's for her protection. She hates me for keeping her here, but the less she knows, the safer she'll be. The safer we'll all be." A pause. The clink of ice in a glass. "Merlin isn't dead. Not like we thought. That exhibit was a shot across our bow. We have to assume Paul de Gaulle is either working for Merlin or carrying on his work. And I'm not convinced she's not sympathetic to his cause."

My lungs forget how to work.

"For now, we proceed as if she's compromised." Father's voice hardens again. "She remains in the dark."

I stumble back from the door, hand pressed over my mouth to stifle any sound. My shoulder hits the opposite wall, and I brace myself there, legs shaking.

Merlin. Paul. Sentinel. The words swirl in my head like debris in a hurricane, refusing to form a coherent picture.

My entire life has been a lie. Not just controlled—weaponized. Twisted into something I don't recognize.

And Prescott... his talk of caring, of wishing he could tell me. It doesn't match the man who threatened me over breakfast, who discussed my body like a commodity.

But Father. That gentle tone when he spoke about protecting me. Was that real? Can any of this be real?

I press my palms against my eyes, willing the spinning to stop.

Paul confided in me. Showed me his paintings. Told me about Merlin—or did he? Did he actually tell me anything, or did I fill in the blanks with what I wanted to believe?

Our relationship began with a lie. He knew who I was before we met. The chalet. The paintings. All of it was carefully orchestrated.

But the way he touched me. Looked at me. Painted me.
Was any of it real?
I don't know. Don't know who to trust. Father? Paul? Merlin?
Maybe none of them.

Maybe I'm just a pawn in a game where all the players are liars.

I make my way back to my room on autopilot, feet carrying me through familiar halls that suddenly feel foreign. Threatening. How many of these walls hide secrets? How many of these paintings are forgeries, stolen, covers for God knows what?

In my room, I try to work. Spread papers across my desk—authentication reports, provenance research, correspondence with galleries. The familiar documents should ground me, but the words blur together, meaningless.

I sketch. Attempt to lose myself in the familiar scratch of charcoal on paper, but my hand won't cooperate. The lines come out jagged, wrong.

Hours pass. The sunlight shifts across the floor, turns golden, then amber. My body feels disconnected from my mind, going through motions while my thoughts chase themselves in circles.

Sentinel. Fifth. Malfor. Merlin. Paul.

The pieces won't fit together.

A soft knock at the door makes me jump, charcoal skittering across the page, leaving a dark slash.

"Miss Faulks?" Marcus's gruff voice, muffled through wood. "Your father requests your presence in his study."

I close my eyes. Take a breath that doesn't quite fill my lungs. "I'll be right there."

The walk down the hallway feels endless. Marcus's bulk moves ahead of me—not quite escort, not quite guard. Something in between. The paintings on the walls seem to watch me pass, their subjects' eyes following my movement.

Accusing.

How long has this house been a prison? Since Mother died? Since I was born? Since generations before me made choices that locked us all into these roles?

Father's study smells like leather, old books, and the expensive scotch he drinks in the evenings. He stands by the window, hands clasped behind his back, staring out at the grounds. The sunset paints everything in shades of blood and gold.

He doesn't turn when I enter. Just gestures toward a chair.

"Sit."

I obey. Lower myself onto the edge of a leather armchair, spine straight, hands folded in my lap. The perfect picture of a dutiful daughter.

Inside, I'm screaming.

The leather creaks as I shift. The clock on the mantel ticks— too loud, each second a small eternity. Outside, birds call to each other, oblivious to the tension in this room.

Finally, he turns. Fixes me with that hard stare I've known my entire life. "I hope you understand the gravity of your actions this morning. Bringing up delicate family matters in front of Prescott was unacceptable."

"I'm sorry." The words taste like ash. Like surrender. "I was confused. Overwhelmed."

"Understandable." Something flickers across his face. He moves to his desk and pours himself a drink from the crystal decanter. Doesn't offer me one. "But you must realize there are things in this world better left undisturbed. Our family's history is... complicated. Knowing too much could put you in danger."

Danger. The word he used with Prescott, in that gentle tone I'd never heard before.

I lean forward, unable to help myself. Hope flickers—stupid, fragile thing. "Then help me understand. Please, Father. I can handle the truth."

He shakes his head. Swirls the amber liquid in his glass, watching it catch the dying light. "No. You can't. Not yet." He drinks. "Perhaps after the wedding. When you're settled into your new role."

The hope dies. Quick and brutal. "My new role. As Prescott's wife."

"As a true Faulks." He sets down the glass with a decisive click. "Carrying on our legacy. Our responsibilities."

"What if I don't want that responsibility?" The words slip out before I can stop them. Reckless. Dangerous.

His expression hardens. The brief softness—if it was ever really there—vanishes. "You don't have a choice. None of us does. The sooner you accept that, the easier this will be."

I match his stare, refusing to look away even as fear makes my palms slick. "The sooner you trust me enough to tell me the truth about our family and our responsibilities, the sooner I'll accept my role."

Cheap shot. Throwing his words back at him. But I can't resist.

Silence falls. Heavy. Oppressive. The clock ticks. The ice melts in his drink with tiny cracking sounds. Outside, the sky deepens from gold to purple to indigo.

I want to scream. To rage. To flip his desk, shatter that crystal decanter, and demand that he see me as something more than a pawn.

But I don't. Because I know it would do no good. His mind is made up. My fate is sealed.

"May I go?" My voice barely rises above a whisper.

He nods. Turns back to the window, dismissing me. "Yes."

I stand on shaky legs, willing them to carry me to the door. To not collapse. To maintain this facade of composure for just a few more seconds.

"And Viv?"

I stop. Don't turn around. Can't bear to see his face. "Yes?"

"I think it's best to limit your outside communications for a while. Focus on the wedding preparations." A pause. "Marcus will accompany you if you need to leave the house."

The last shred of freedom, snipped away. Clean. Surgical. Final.

"Yes, Father." The words come out woodenly. Mechanical. "Of course."

I reach for the door handle—brass, cool under my palm.

"I do love you, Viv." His voice is soft. Almost pained. "Everything I do is to protect you."

My hand freezes on the handle. There's something in his tone—raw, haunted. Like he's carrying a weight I can't see.

"There are worse prisons than the ones you know about." So quiet I almost miss it. "Worse sacrifices than the ones you've been asked to make. I've built walls to keep you safe, even knowing you'd hate me for them."

A chill runs down my spine. The way he says it—*walls*—like he's talking about something more than metaphor. More than the locked doors and surveillance cameras.

"Sometimes love looks like cruelty." His voice drops further. "Sometimes the only way to keep someone alive is to let them believe you're the monster."

I want to turn around. To ask what he means. But something stops me—some instinct that knows if I look at his face right now, I'll see something I'm not ready to understand. That he's protecting me instead of protecting his secrets.

Without a word, I slip into the hallway. Pull the door closed behind me.

Back in my room, I curl up on the window seat, forehead pressed against the cool glass. The gardens spread below, perfectly manicured. The roses are beginning to bloom, their petals unfurling in the warm spring air. They'll be at their peak in three months.

Just in time for my wedding.

Unless Paul gets my message.

Unless he comes.

Unless this isn't all a lie.

I close my eyes, but that makes the tears come faster. Hot. Silent. Useless.

The weight of secrets and lies presses down, threatening to crush me. But beneath it all—buried deep—a spark of defiance still burns.

I am Vivianne Faulks. And I will not go quietly into the cage they've built for me. I have to believe that. Have to cling to it. Because if I let go, there's nothing left.

I will find a way out.

I have to.

The alternative is unthinkable.

The rumble of engines pulls me from my thoughts. I lift my

head, peer down at the driveway where a convoy of black SUVs winds up toward the house. Three. Four. Five of them. Their tinted windows reflect the last rays of sunset, turning them into moving mirrors.

My stomach drops.

They stop in front of the main entrance. Doors open in synchronized precision. Men in dark suits emerge—tall, broad-shouldered, moving with the coordinated efficiency of soldiers.

Or guards.

My door swings open without warning. No knock. No courtesy.

Marcus fills the doorway. "Miss Faulks. Your father requests your presence in the main hall. Immediately."

Two summons in one day. My mouth goes dry. "What's happening?"

He doesn't answer. Just waits, immovable, until I stand and follow.

The stairs feel steeper than usual. Each step takes effort, like walking through water. Through the windows, more men circle the house, speaking into radios, pointing at corners, doors, and windows.

Father stands in the center of the foyer, surrounded by the men from the SUVs. Their faces are blank. Professional. But there's an undercurrent of tension in their postures, in the way they scan the space with trained eyes.

Assessing. Cataloging. Planning.

Father's gaze locks onto mine as I descend the last few stairs. "Ah, Viv. Good. Some changes are being implemented. For your safety."

Safety. The word tastes like a lie.

One of the men steps forward. He's older than the others, maybe fifty, with silver at his temples and eyes that miss nothing. "Miss Faulks. Donovan Price. We'll be upgrading the security measures around the estate. I'll need your cooperation to ensure everything runs smoothly."

"I don't understand." I look between him and Father. "What's going on?"

"Just a precaution, my dear. With the wedding approaching, we can't be too careful." Father's smile is tight. Doesn't reach his eyes.

"We'll be installing additional surveillance cameras." Donovan's voice is flat. Informative. Like he's discussing the weather. "Inside and outside the house. There will also be a rotating security detail on the grounds. Twenty-four seven."

The implications hit like a fist to the gut.

Cameras. Inside the house. In the hallways. Watching. Recording.

Twenty-four-seven security detail. Guards. Barriers. No way in or out without being seen.

They're not protecting me.

They're containing me.

I open my mouth to protest, but Father's eyes narrow. A warning. Clear and unmistakable.

My words die in my throat.

"Thank you, Donovan." Father's voice is smooth. Pleasant. "My daughter will provide any assistance you need. Won't you, dear?"

Not a question. Never a question.

I nod. The movement feels disconnected from my body, like I'm watching someone else surrender.

"Excellent." Donovan gestures to his men. They disperse throughout the house like water finding cracks—methodical, thorough, unstoppable.

The sounds start immediately. The whir of drills. The click of locks being changed. The mechanical hum of cameras being mounted and adjusted.

Each sound is another nail in my coffin.

Father dismisses me with a wave. I retreat to my room on legs that feel like they belong to someone else.

The men work through the night. From my window, they circle the grounds, installing motion sensors and cameras. Bright work lights flood the gardens, turning everything stark and shadowless.

I sink onto my bed, pulling a pillow to my chest. The tears want to come, but I blink them back. Crying won't help. Won't change anything.

I need a plan. A way to reach Paul before it's too late.

But as the camera's red light blinks its steady rhythm—watching, recording, reporting—I wonder if I haven't already lost.

The wedding looms. Three months away. Getting closer with each tick of the clock.

I'm running out of time.

SIXTEEN

Vivianne: Sixty-Seven Days

THE WALLS ARE CLOSING IN. EACH HOUR THAT PASSES, THE NOOSE tightens another notch. Cameras in every corner—their red lights blinking like demon eyes. Guards patrolling the halls with military precision. The constant weight of being watched, cataloged, and contained.

I can't breathe in this house anymore.

I have to get out.

Midnight. The house settles into its nighttime rhythm—creaking floorboards, the distant hum of the heating system, the whisper of wind against windowpanes. Most of the staff have retired. This is my chance.

I slip out of my room, backpack pressed against my spine. Inside: cash from my emergency stash, my passport, a change of clothes, Grandmother's letters. The essentials for disappearing. My hiking boots dangle from one hand, laces tied together. I'll put them on outside. For now, thick socks muffle my footsteps on the carpet.

The hallway stretches before me, dimly lit by wall sconces.

Each shadow could hide a guard. Each corner could reveal Marcus, Donovan, or one of the faceless men in dark suits.

My pulse pounds so hard I taste it—metallic, sharp, like fear has a flavor.

I make it to the grand staircase. The marble gleams below, polished to a mirror shine. I start down, keeping to the edge where the steps are less likely to creak.

Halfway down, a voice cuts through the darkness.

"Miss Faulks?"

I freeze. Every muscle locks. The backpack suddenly weighs a thousand pounds.

Marcus's silhouette materializes at the bottom of the stairs—broad shoulders, that slight limp from an old injury. "Is everything alright?"

Think. Think.

"I couldn't sleep." My voice comes out steadier than I feel. "Thought I'd get some water."

He moves closer, and the light catches his face. Concern etched into the lines around his eyes. The same concern he's worn since I was a child, since he pulled me out of the pool when I nearly drowned at seven.

This would be easier if he were cruel.

"Let me get that for you, miss." His gaze drops to the boots in my hand. Lingers there. "You shouldn't be wandering around at night."

My fingers tighten around the laces. "I can manage."

"I'm afraid I must insist." His tone shifts—still kind, but firm. Immovable. "Your father's orders. You're not to be unescorted anywhere. Even within the house."

The walls contract. The air thins.

"Of course." I force the words out. "How silly of me to forget."

He leads me back upstairs. His footsteps are heavy, deliberate.

Mine feel like a death march. At my door, he pauses.

"Miss Faulks." His voice drops low. "I know this is difficult. But please understand—we're just trying to keep you safe."

Safe. The word tastes like a lie.

I nod. Don't trust myself to speak. The door closes, and I sink to the floor, back pressed against cool wood. The backpack slides off my shoulders.

Attempt one: failed.

I crawl into bed and cry myself to sleep.

PRE-DAWN LIGHT BLEEDS GRAY THROUGH MY WINDOWS. I'VE always loved sunrises—used to sneak out to watch them from the east garden, the world quiet and new and full of possibility.

Surely they can't deny me that.

I dress quickly in yesterday's clothes. No backpack this time. Nothing suspicious. Just a girl wanting to greet the day.

The hallway outside my room is empty. Silent except for the ticking of the grandfather clock at the far end. Hope flutters in my chest—fragile, desperate.

I make it all the way to the back door. My hand closes around the handle, cool brass under my palm.

A hand falls on my shoulder.

"Going somewhere, Miss Faulks?"

Donovan. His cologne hits me—something sharp and woody, like pine needles and cold. I turn slowly. His face is impassive, professional, but his grip on my shoulder is iron.

"Just to the garden." I force a smile, feeling it stretch across my face, artificial. "I love watching the sunrise."

"I'm afraid that's not possible. The grounds are off-limits without a proper escort." He shakes his head.

Heat flares in my chest. "This is ridiculous. It's my home. I should be able to go where I please."

"Your safety is our primary concern." His voice is maddeningly calm. Like he's discussing the weather. "Perhaps we can arrange for you to view the sunrise from one of the upstairs windows?"

I want to scream. To claw at his face. To run.

Instead, I nod stiffly. Let him escort me back to my room like a prisoner being returned to her cell.

The door closes. I press my forehead against the window glass, cold against my skin. Outside, the sky shifts from gray to pink to gold. The roses in the garden open their faces to the light.

Beautiful. Untouchable. Just like my freedom.

Attempt two: thwarted.

THE DAY CRAWLS BY. I PACE MY ROOM UNTIL I'VE WORN A PATH IN the carpet. Eleven steps from the window to the door. Eleven steps back. The walls seem closer each time I turn.

Late afternoon, I try again.

The kitchen is chaos at this hour—staff preparing dinner, the clatter of pots and pans, voices calling orders. Mrs. Holloway runs a tight ship, but even she can't watch everyone at once.

If I can slip through unnoticed, the service entrance is right there. One door. Freedom.

I make my way downstairs, trying to look casual. Like I'm not planning anything. Like my pulse isn't hammering in my throat.

The smell hits me first—roasting meat, fresh herbs, something sweet baking. My stomach growls despite the anxiety churning inside.

I'm reaching for the kitchen door when—

"Miss Faulks?"

Mrs. Holloway. The housekeeper. Her gray hair pulled back in its severe bun, glasses perched on her nose, eyes sharp as ever.

"Is there something you need?" Her tone is gentle. Patient. Like she's talking to a child.

My mind scrambles. "I was feeling peckish. Thought I might grab a snack."

"Oh, you poor thing. All this wedding stress." Her expression softens. She pats my arm. "Why don't you return to your room? I'll have someone bring up a tray."

The kindness makes it worse. How can I explain that this place is suffocating me? That I'd rather starve on the streets than eat another meal in this house?

I can't. So I nod. Murmur thanks. Turn away.

Attempt three: foiled.

NIGHT FALLS. THE HOUSE DARKENS. AND WITH IT, MY desperation grows teeth.

I can't stay here. Won't. Not one more day. Not one more hour.

This time, I don't bother with doors or stairs. They're watching those. Expecting them.

But the old servant's passages—those haven't been used in decades. Father probably doesn't even remember they exist.

The wardrobe in my room is massive, ornate, and older than I am. I shove it aside, muscles straining, sweat beading on my forehead. It scrapes against the floor—too loud, much too loud— and I freeze, listening.

Nothing. No footsteps. No voices.

I keep pushing until the wardrobe reveals the small door behind it. The wood is old, the paint peeling. The handle sticks, then gives with a reluctant groan.

Stale air rushes out—thick with dust and age and secrets. The passage yawns before me, darker than dark.

I step inside. Pull the door closed behind me.

The darkness is absolute. Suffocating. I feel along the wall with trembling hands, finding the steep stairs by touch alone. They're narrow, twisting, carved directly into the stone. My fingers trace rough mortar and cold rock.

Down. Down. Each step careful, measured. One slip and I'll tumble, break my neck in the dark where no one will find me.

Cobwebs catch in my hair, across my face. I brush them away, skin crawling. Something skitters nearby—rats, probably. The sound echoes off the stone, making it impossible to tell how close.

The air grows colder. Damper. The smell changes from dust to earth, to the sharp tang of wine.

The cellar.

My foot hits flat ground, and I nearly sob with relief. Pale moonlight filters through high windows, just enough to see by. Rows of bottles glint like eyes. The floor is packed earth, cool under my feet.

I navigate between the racks, heading for the far corner. There—the old coal chute. Haven't used it since the house converted to gas heating, probably fifty years ago.

It's smaller than I remember. Much smaller.

But I'm desperate.

I grab the iron ring and pull. The door swings open with a metallic shriek that makes my teeth ache. I freeze, listening.

Silence.

The chute angles steeply. Stars glimmer through the opening at the top. Fresh air, cool and sweet, kisses my face.

Freedom.

I climb in feet-first. The metal is cold, rough with rust. It scrapes my sides as I wriggle upward, pushing with my feet, pulling with my hands. The space is so tight my ribs can barely expand to breathe.

For a terrifying moment, I'm stuck. Can't move forward or back. Panic claws at my throat.

Then something gives. I surge upward, tumbling out onto grass wet with dew.

I'm out. Actually out.

For a heartbeat, I just lie there, gasping. The sky above is vast and dark and full of stars. The air tastes like possibility.

Then—

A shout from inside the house. Muffled but distinct.

They know.

Adrenaline slams through me. I lurch to my feet and run.

The manicured lawn gives way to rougher ground. My socks are immediately soaked, cold seeping into my feet. But I don't stop. Can't stop.

The woods loom ahead—a dark wall of trees. I plunge in, branches whipping my face, catching in my hair. Thorns tear at my nightgown. I don't care.

Behind me, more shouts. Closer now.

"Miss Faulks! Stop!"

"She went toward the woods!"

"Get the lights!"

The underbrush grabs at my ankles. Roots snake across the path, invisible in the darkness. I stumble and catch myself on a tree trunk. The bark scrapes my palms raw.

Keep moving. Just keep moving.

Flashlight beams cut through the trees behind me—white, stark, searching. They sweep back and forth like prison spotlights.

I veer left. Then right. Trying to lose them in the maze of trees.

But the Faulks estate is vast, and I've never been this deep in the woods. The darkness is disorienting. Every tree looks the same. Every shadow could hide pursuit.

My breath comes in ragged gasps. My legs burn. A stitch forms in my side, sharp as a knife.

An owl shrieks somewhere close. The sound is primal, predatory. I nearly scream.

The voices behind me grow louder. They're gaining.

How? How are they so fast?

Then I realize—they know these woods. Patrol them nightly. While I'm running blind, they're following familiar paths.

I push harder, legs pumping, arms swinging. My foot catches on something—a root, a rock, doesn't matter. I'm falling.

The ground rushes up. I hit hard, the impact driving the air from my lungs. Leaves and dirt fill my mouth. The taste of earth and decay.

Get up. Get up NOW.

I scramble to my feet. Take two steps.

The ground disappears.

For a sickening moment, I'm airborne. Then I'm tumbling, rolling, the world spinning in a blur of dark and darker. Trees, sky, ground—impossible to tell which is which.

Branches claw at me. Rocks slam into my ribs, my shoulders, my head. Pain explodes in bright stars.

I land at the bottom of a ravine with a bone-jarring thud. For a long moment, I can't breathe. Can't move. Can only lie there, stunned and aching.

Blood fills my mouth. I've bitten my tongue. Or split my lip. Maybe both.

My head throbs. When I touch my temple, my fingers come away wet and dark.

Have to move. Have to—

A light finds me. Bright. Blinding.

"I've found her!" Male voice. Triumphant. "Over here!"

No. No no no.

I try to stand. My legs don't work right. Everything tilts.

Hands grab me—rough, efficient. Pulling me upright.

"Easy now, Miss Faulks." Donovan's voice. Close to my ear. "You're safe. We're taking you home."

Home. The word is a curse.

"No." It comes out as a whimper. "Please. No."

But he's already lifting me, carrying me like a child. My protests dissolve into incoherent sounds. The world swims, edges blurring.

I must have hit my head harder than I thought.

Other guards surround us as we emerge from the woods. Their flashlights create a bubble of harsh white light. Beyond it, the darkness presses in—hungry, mocking.

So close. I was so close.

The house rises before us, every window ablaze. It looks like a palace. Like a postcard of wealth and privilege.

It's a prison.

Father stands on the front steps. Even from a distance, the rigid set of his shoulders is visible, the tight line of his jaw.

As we approach, his expression shifts—anger morphing into shock. His eyes widen, taking in my appearance.

"My God." His hand reaches toward my face, stops just short of touching. "Look at you. Your face—" His voice cracks. "You're covered in scratches. Are those bruises forming?" His gaze sweeps over me, cataloging damage. The concern in his eyes looks almost real. "You could have been seriously hurt." Softer now. Almost gentle. "Do you understand how dangerous that was?"

I want to laugh. Want to scream. Want to tell him that staying here is more dangerous than any ravine.

But I'm so tired. So broken. The words won't come.

I slump in Donovan's arms, and Father steps back. The concern vanishes, replaced by cold efficiency.

"Take her inside. Call Dr. Morrison. And double the security detail."

They carry me through the door. The marble floor gleams, spotless and cold. My reflection stares back from the polished surface—wild-eyed, disheveled, streaked with blood and dirt.

I don't recognize myself.

Is this what I've become? A desperate animal, clawing at her cage?

The door to my room closes with a final click. Donovan sets me on the bed, surprisingly gentle. Then he's gone, and I'm alone.

Outside, Father's voice carries through the walls. Giving orders. Tightening security.

The walls press closer. The air grows thick.

I've failed.

I'm trapped.

And the wedding looms—sixty-seven days away. I counted this morning, marked it on the calendar like counting down to my execution.

I curl into myself as dawn breaks. The light creeps through the windows, gray and cold. My body aches. Every breath hurts.

The tears come. Harsh, wrenching sobs that shake my frame. Each one tears something loose inside.

But beneath the despair, beneath the pain and fear and exhaustion—

A spark.

Tiny. Stubborn. Refusing to die.

This isn't over.

I will find a way out.

I have to.

Because the alternative—marriage to Prescott, life as a broodmare for Sentinel, whatever that means—is worse than death.

As sleep finally claims me, dragging me under with heavy hands, my last thought is of Paul.

Where is he?

Does he know what's happening?

Will he come before it's too late?

I can only hope.

For now, it's all I have left.

SEVENTEEN

Paul: Guardian HRS

THE FIRE CRACKLES IN THE HEARTH, ITS WARM GLOW A STARK contrast to the turmoil in my chest. Outside, the first signs of spring are emerging in the Swiss Alps. Patches of green peek through the thinning snow, a world awakening from its long slumber. But my thoughts are far from this peaceful transition.

Two months. Two agonizing months since I last saw Vivianne, our stolen moment at her engagement party cut brutally short. The memory haunts me—her lips on mine, the spark of hope in her eyes, and then... gone. Whisked away by her father calling in the distance.

I slam my fist into my open palm, the sharp sting a welcome distraction from the regret gnawing at my gut. I should have taken her at that damn engagement party, consequences be damned. Now she's trapped, and I'm left pacing, helpless.

"You'll wear a hole in that rug if you keep that up." Merlin's gruff voice cuts through my brooding.

I turn to face him, frustration bubbling up. "We're running out of time."

"I know, son. But we can't rush in half-cocked. The Faulks

estate is a fortress now." He sighs, setting down the book he's been pretending to read.

I pace the length of the room, my footsteps echoing off the wood-paneled walls. "You think I don't know that? I've flown back and forth from here to the States more times than I can count. And each time, it's worse."

My mind flashes to my last reconnaissance mission. The sprawling grounds of the Faulks estate, once merely guarded, now bristle with activity.

"There are men everywhere. Armed patrols circling around the clock. They've installed motion sensors and infrared cameras. I wouldn't be surprised if they have satellite surveillance at this point."

I run a hand through my hair. "I've broken into museums, for Christ's sake. Swapped out priceless paintings under the noses of the world's best security. But this?" I shake my head. "I can't even get within a hundred yards of the main house without tripping a dozen alarms."

My fist connects with the mantle, pain shooting through my knuckles. "We should never have let her go back there. I had her in my arms, Merlin. Right there. And I let her slip away."

"And what would you have done?" His eyebrow arches. "Kidnapped her in front of half of New York's elite?"

"She was in my arms. I held her. I kissed her."

His weathered hand grips my shoulder, both comforting and restraining. "Paul, my boy, you can't lose sight of the bigger picture."

A muscle twitches in my jaw. "Vivianne is the bigger picture."

"Is she?" His eyes narrow, his voice taking on that lecturing tone I've heard countless times. "What about the Swan? What about everything we've worked for?"

The pendant. Of course. That damned piece of jewelry that's caused so much grief. "To hell with the pendant."

His grip tightens. "If you had taken Vivianne at the engagement party, we'd have lost any chance of locating the Swan. Not to mention, any hope of recovering it would be gone."

"If I had taken her, she wouldn't be trapped like she is now." The words burst from me, raw and angry.

"There are things more important than one woman." His voice softens, but the steel in his eyes remains. "Lives depend on retrieving the Swan."

I open my mouth to argue, but Merlin cuts me off with a sharp gesture.

"It's not about family legacy. The Swan is more than a pendant with a flaw." He leans in close, voice dropping to a whisper. "There are engravings on it. Microscopic. Invisible to the naked eye."

My brow furrows. "Engravings? You never mentioned—"

"Because I wasn't sure you were ready to know." His gaze darts around the room as if checking for unseen listeners. "Those engravings... they're coordinates. Locations of... well, let's just say they're locations that certain very powerful people would kill to know about."

The weight of his words sinks in. "What kind of locations?"

"The less you know right now, the better." He shakes his head. "But trust me when I say that pendant in the wrong hands could destabilize governments and start wars."

I lean back, processing this new information. The Swan was always important—a family heirloom, a reminder of Merlin's lost love.

But this?

This is something else entirely.

"Does Faulks know?" My voice is barely audible.

"I've never been certain, but I always suspected. Too many things don't add up, and the Swan... it's the only thing that explains it all." Merlin's expression darkens.

"So you think Vivianne's father knows what the pendant is?"

"Yes." Heavy with implications. "The Faulks family has always been too well-connected, too strategically positioned. If they know about the Swan's true significance, it explains their obsession with keeping it hidden from the world and guarding their secrets so fiercely. It's more than a bauble. Always has been."

My fists clench at my sides.

The room falls silent as the true weight of what we face settles over me. Suddenly, it's not just about reclaiming a family treasure or righting old wrongs. The stakes have risen exponentially, and Vivianne, unwittingly, is at the center of it all.

The silence stretches between us, thick with decades of shared history and conflicting priorities. Merlin is right, at least in part. But the thought of Vivianne, trapped and alone, overrides everything else.

"And the date of the wedding?" Merlin leans forward. "Has it been announced? Are you certain of the timing?"

"No official announcement yet." I shake my head.

"So how can you be sure?" His eyes sharpen.

I pull out my phone, bringing up the post I've read a thousand times. "Because of this."

I hand him the device, watching as his eyes scan the screen:

Feeling nostalgic today. Remembering that beautiful garden in Paris, with its hidden corners and secret pathways. How I long to walk those grounds again, to feel that sense of freedom and possibility. Perhaps in three months, when the roses are in full bloom? #ParisianDreams #GardenEscapes #CountdownToAdventure

"This could mean anything." Merlin looks up, brow furrowed.

"No." I take the phone back. "The garden in Paris—that's where we truly connected. And three months... it has to be the new wedding date."

"It's thin." A warning in his voice.

"Not so thin. After announcing her engagement to Prescott, the air was thick with whispers about the wedding date. Everyone had a theory, but nothing concrete."

I run a hand through my hair. "Some were saying it's a shotgun wedding, that Vivianne's pregnant. Others swore it would be a long engagement for appearances' sake. But no one knew for sure. The Faulks are keeping it all very hush-hush. But Vivianne made that post with intent. She's telling us when."

"You're putting a lot of faith in a social media post."

"It's all we have." I meet his gaze. "To anyone else, it looks innocent. But it's a cry for help. As clear as if she'd shouted it from the rooftops."

"Even if you're right, it could be later." Merlin sighs, rubbing his temples.

"Or it could be sooner." The urgency is clear in my voice. "We have to work with what we've got. We have a month to figure out what we're going to do. After that..." I don't finish the sentence. I don't need to. We both know what's at stake if we fail.

"We'll need to move fast. And Paul?" His eyes lock onto mine. "Remember, as important as Vivianne is, we can't lose sight of the bigger picture. The Swan must be our priority." Merlin nods slowly, his expression grave.

I nod, even as everything in me rebels against the idea. Because as much as I understand the importance of our mission, in my mind, there's nothing more important than saving Vivianne.

"We need to move faster." I turn back to Merlin. "Every day that passes is another day she's trapped."

His eyes soften, a rare show of emotion. "I understand. More than you know." His hand drifts to his pocket, where he keeps an old, faded photograph of Brigitte, the woman he loved and lost all those years ago.

"The Swan." Merlin's voice is urgent. "You're certain Vivianne saw it? You're absolutely sure it's there?"

I remember Vivianne's words. "She saw it. I painted it into the picture, and she recognized it. She told me she saw it. The Swan pendant is at the Faulks estate."

"After all this time... to be so close." His eyes blaze with a fire I haven't seen in years.

"We'll get it back. Along with Vivianne."

A shadow crosses Merlin's face. "What about Nicholas? If word gets out that the pendant has resurfaced..."

"Nicholas is dead." The memory of that night in the warehouse still fresh, still haunting. "He can't hurt us anymore."

Merlin nods, but doubt flickers in his eyes, the worry he can't shake. "You know as well as I do... Nicholas has a way of surviving. Even when we think he's down, he finds a way."

I clench my jaw. "Not this time. I watched him fall. I saw the blood. He's gone."

"You've seen him slip out of tighter situations. If Nicholas is alive... he'll come for it. And for Vivianne." But Merlin shakes his head.

I want to argue, to insist that Nicholas is dead, but the fear gnawing at Merlin's expression makes me hesitate. Nicholas was always unpredictable, always a step ahead, and Merlin has the right to be cautious.

"Even if Nicholas isn't a threat, with the Faulks' increased security at the estate, there's no way we can take the Swan." Merlin exhales, dragging a hand through his hair.

"The security is... intense. Armed guards, surveillance cameras, the works. It's like they're expecting an invasion." I turn to the window, watching snowflakes dance in the wind. "As much as I hate to say it, we need help." I run a hand over my face, feeling the weight of the situation pressing down.

My jaw clenches. The thought of Vivianne trapped behind those walls, a prisoner in her own home, makes my blood boil.

Merlin is silent for a long moment. When he speaks, his voice is carefully neutral. "I might have a solution."

I turn, eyebrow raised.

"There's an organization. They operate in... shall we say, gray areas of the law. Specializing in extracting people from impossible situations."

"Hostage rescue?" I run a hand through my hair. "Can they be trusted?"

"They're professionals, discreet. And they have resources we lack." Merlin shrugs.

The idea of involving outsiders sets my teeth on edge. More variables. More potential for things to go wrong. But we're out of options.

"Make the call."

Merlin nods, reaching for his phone. As he steps out, I turn back to the window, my reflection ghostly in the glass.

"Hold on, Vivianne," I whisper. "I'm coming for you."

The next few days pass in an agonizing blur. Every hour stretches into what feels like an eternity as we wait for a response from Guardian HRS.

I throw myself into preparation—poring over blueprints of the Faulks estate, satellite images, every scrap of intelligence we've gathered—but it's not enough to quiet the growing desperation in my chest.

Merlin and I exchange few words, both of us knowing that until we have confirmation, all we can do is wait.

And waiting has never been my strong suit.

EIGHTEEN

The Extraction Plan

THREE DAYS AFTER MERLIN'S INITIAL CALL, HIS PHONE RINGS. Tension spikes in the air as he answers. The conversation is brief, nothing more than a few gruff exchanges, but when he hangs up, there's a glimmer of hope in his eyes.

"They're coming. They'll be here tomorrow." The weight in his voice is slightly lifted.

Relief crashes into me, tempered by the anxiety still churning in my gut. "Good. That's... good." I can't shake the nerves coiling tighter. I'm a solo operator, not used to relying on others.

It's... difficult reaching out for help.

The next day dawns clear and cold. I'm up before the sun, restless energy thrumming through my veins. By the time a sleek black SUV pulls up the winding driveway, I'm pacing, practically crawling out of my skin.

Two men emerge from the vehicle. The first commands the space around him. He has a hulking build, muscles straining against his clothes, and a quiet authority that would make anyone think twice about crossing him. There's something about the way he moves—deliberate, precise—that tells me he's no stranger to dangerous situations.

But the second man draws the eye. A mountain of a man with a severe expression, shock-white-blonde hair, and piercing blue eyes, he's reminiscent of a Norse god—Thor incarnate. My fingers itch to paint him, immortalize him on canvas.

"Mr. de Gaulle." The first man extends a hand with a firm, steady grip. "I'm Sam, head of Guardian HRS. This is Forest Summers, the founder of our organization."

"Thank you for coming." I shake their hands, noting the quiet strength in their grips. "Please, come inside."

As we enter the study, they take in the room with those same keen, assessing gazes. These aren't just hired muscle; they're strategists, calculating every possible angle of the situation.

What do they see when they look at me? A desperate man? A lovesick fool? Or maybe, just maybe, they recognize something familiar—a man willing to move heaven and earth for what matters most.

We settle into the leather chairs around the fireplace. Sam leans forward slightly, clasping his hands as he speaks, his voice calm yet unmistakably authoritative.

"Before we begin, I need to be clear about one thing. Guardian HRS doesn't engage in kidnapping or any non-consensual extractions. Your colleague mentioned extenuating circumstances. If the subject doesn't want to leave—"

"She does." I cut him off, urgency clear in my voice. "Trust me, she wants out."

Sam's attention flicks to Forest, who watches me with an unnerving silence. It's as if he's measuring me, weighing the truth of my words without needing to speak.

A moment of quiet, then Sam claps his hands and moves the conversation forward. "Tell us the details."

I exhale, steadying myself. "Vivianne Faulks is being forced into a marriage she doesn't want. She's been under her father's control for years, but now it's getting worse. They've arranged for her to marry Prescott Harrington, but she's unwilling. She's tried to resist, but her father's a powerful man, and he has ways of making sure she complies. They've all but imprisoned her within the Faulks estate, cut off her ability to communicate."

Sam listens intently, his expression unreadable, but his mind is already working through the logistics.

"The estate is heavily fortified." Merlin interjects, tone cautious. "She's under constant surveillance, is never left alone, and has no freedom. Her father's not giving her a choice. She's being manipulated and controlled."

Forest's deep voice rumbles into the conversation, his first words since arriving. "You said she wants to leave. Are you certain of that? This isn't the kind of job we take lightly. If she has doubts, if she's not fully on board—"

"She's sure." My voice is firm. "Vivianne isn't some spoiled girl running away from a wedding. She's trapped. She's been trying to get out for months, and now she's running out of time. If we don't move soon, her father will have full control over her life, and she'll be stuck in that marriage for good."

"What's the estate like? What kind of security are we dealing with?" Sam sits back, his gaze never leaving mine.

I pull out the blueprints of the Faulks estate and lay them across the table. "The Faulks family is wealthy and well-connected. They've invested in top-of-the-line surveillance, armed guards, and a state-of-the-art security system. The estate is a fortress."

"With all the increased security, it's nearly impossible to get in unnoticed." Merlin leans forward. "They're expecting the wedding to go off without a hitch, and they've locked down the estate to keep any unwanted eyes out."

Forest studies the blueprints, arms crossed over his massive chest. "We'll need to disable the security systems and neutralize the guards. Getting in is one thing. Getting out with Vivianne is another."

"First, we need to contact Vivianne and ensure her needs align with yours." Sam leans back, giving me that same intense, calculated stare. "If she doesn't want to be extricated, we won't act."

Frustration bubbles up inside me. "You don't understand. There's no way to reach her. She's locked down. It's impossible."

Sam and Forest exchange a look that says they know something I don't, and I suddenly feel like I'm missing something crucial.

Sam's lips curl into a small, amused smile. "Our people are already in place and attempting contact."

"What?" I blink, caught off guard.

"We don't sit around twiddling our thumbs." Forest's voice is calm but with a hint of snark. "Our team is in the process of confirming whether Vivianne wants out."

"We should have confirmation at any time." Sam leans forward slightly, expression unchanging.

"Their tech is extreme. You're telling me you've bypassed all that without anyone noticing?" Merlin shakes his head, incredulous.

"We're not worried about their tech. We've handled worse. We mean it when we say we can slip in and out unnoticed." Forest shrugs with casual confidence that borders on arrogance.

I pause, stunned by the sudden shift, but relief creeps in around the edges. "And once you've confirmed she's ready to leave?"

"Then we work on the extraction plan." Sam's eyes lock on mine.

I clench my jaw, the need to move forward eating at me, but I can't argue with them. They're professionals, and they've clearly done this before.

"Fine. But don't waste time. She doesn't have much of it."

"We'll get her out." Sam's tone is steady but firm. "But make no mistake—this won't be easy. We'll need every detail you can give us, and you need to trust our methods. There may be things you disagree with."

"Such as?"

Sam leans back, kicking his ankle over his opposite knee with a relaxed confidence that only adds to my growing frustration. "The timing, for one thing."

"What about the timing?" Unease settles like a stone in my chest.

"If she truly wants to get away from her family—for good— then a public extraction is best." Sam's tone is matter-of-fact.

"I don't follow."

"We're looking at removing her during the ceremony." Forest shifts slightly, folding his arms across his chest.

"The wedding?" I leap to my feet, the idea sending a jolt of anger and panic through me. "That's too late. This needs to happen now."

"Think about it." Sam's expression doesn't change, calm as ever. "There will be hundreds of guests at the wedding—plenty of ways for our team to blend in with the crowd. You'll have service personnel, caterers, photographers... it's the perfect cover. No one will notice a few extra people slipping in and out."

"That's your plan? To take her in front of all those people?" Incredulity sharpens my voice.

"If she wants to sever ties with her family, it must be public. Doing it during the ceremony makes it clear to everyone that she's choosing to leave them. No questions, no rumors of coer- cion. If we pull her out in secret, there will always be whispers, always a threat looming over her. They won't stop coming after her." Forest nods, his gaze sharp, almost brutal.

I swallow hard, the weight of their logic pressing down on me, but I can't shake the urgency gnawing at my gut. "You don't understand... I need her out of there yesterday." I pull away, running a hand through my hair. "And what if something goes wrong? What if they realize what's happening?"

"That's why we're here. To make sure it doesn't go wrong." Sam's eyes are cold and calculating.

"But for this to work, we need every detail. There can't be any surprises once we're inside." Forest's voice is low and hard.

"Is there anything else we need to know?" Sam leans forward, fixing me with a look that leaves no room for ambiguity.

For a split second, I hesitate. The Swan. That damn pendant. But this... this is about getting Vivianne out safely. "No. Nothing that will affect the extraction."

Forest studies me for a moment longer, his piercing blue eyes sharp as ever, then nods. "Good. Because once we're in, we can't afford any surprises."

"We have to trust them. It's the only way." Merlin exhales slowly, his gaze flicking between me and Sam.

I clench my jaw, every instinct screaming at me to act now, but the rational part of me knows they're right. "Fine. We'll do it your way."

"Don't worry. We'll get her out, and when we do, they won't be able to touch her." Sam's lips twitch into the slightest smile.

I glance at Merlin, knowing we've already left out one crucial piece of information: the Swan. That's a complication we'll handle ourselves. While they're liberating Vivianne, Merlin and I will liberate the Swan from the Faulks family for good.

Two weeks. Fourteen days. It feels like an eternity when every second ticks down. No formal wedding date has been announced yet, but it doesn't matter.

The Faulks name carries so much weight within the elite that when the invitations go out, they're not requests—they're commands. People will drop everything to attend the social event of the century. It doesn't matter if they're halfway across the world or in the middle of a crisis.

When the Faulks call, people answer. And as much as it kills me to admit it, Sam and Forest are right.

This needs to be public.

As Sam and Forest dive into the details with Merlin, I slip out onto the balcony. The night air is crisp, biting at my exposed skin. I welcome the cold, let it ground me in the present.

I close my eyes, picturing Vivianne's face. Her brilliant smile, the sparkle in her eyes when she talks about art. The quiet strength that radiates from her very being.

Behind me, the murmur of voices as plans are made and strategies formed. But my mind is already racing ahead, to the moment I'll hold Vivianne in my arms again, to the future we'll build together, free from the shadows of the past.

NINETEEN

Vivianne: The Bees

THE CRYSTAL CHANDELIER BLEEDS COLD LIGHT ACROSS THE formal dining room, turning everything sharp-edged and clinical. Like an operating theater. Like a place where things get dissected.

Two and a half months since I posted that desperate plea on social media. Sixty-seven days of waiting. Of hoping. Of watching that hope curdle into something that tastes like despair.

Two weeks until the wedding.

No word from Paul.

I smooth my dress for the third time in as many minutes. The silk is cool under my fingers, already perfect, but my hands need something to do. Something to keep them from shaking. From reaching for the phone they took away.

From clawing at the walls.

Prescott sits to my left, radiating satisfaction like heat from a furnace. His cologne—too heavy, too sweet—coats the back of my throat. Makes me want to gag. He shifts, and his thigh presses against mine under the table. Deliberate. A reminder of ownership.

Father sits at the head of the table like a king holding court.

Every line of his body speaks of control—spine straight, shoulders back, hands folded precisely on the table. Even the way he breathes feels calculated.

Donovan stands by the door. Silent. Watchful. Always watching.

The clink of silverware against china seems obscenely loud. I push a piece of lamb around my plate, leaving tracks in the sauce. The meat smells rich, perfectly seasoned. My stomach churns with nausea.

When did I last eat? Really eat, not just move food around until someone stopped watching?

"The lamb is exquisite." Prescott's voice cuts through the silence. He lifts his wine glass, swirls the dark liquid. "Don't you agree, darling?"

The endearment scrapes against my nerves like nails on glass.

"It's lovely." I force my mouth into something resembling a smile.

Father's gaze flicks between us. Assessing. Measuring. Finding me wanting, as always. He sets down his knife, the blade aligned perfectly with his plate.

"I'm glad you're both enjoying it. Now, about the final preparations—"

Prescott straightens in his chair. The movement is eager, puppyish. The chair scrapes against hardwood—too loud, making me flinch.

"Of course, sir." He leans forward, elbows on the table. "I've been in touch with the event planner. Everything's on schedule."

A single, economical nod from Father. "And the guest list?"

"Nearly finalized. All key players from both families. Plus a curated selection of business associates." Prescott ticks items off on his fingers. "Social connections that matter."

They continue talking. Numbers. Seating charts. Strategic

positioning of guests. Their voices blend into a constant drone, white noise that makes my head ache.

I'm fading. Becoming invisible. Dissolving into the silk wallpaper and polished wood.

My fingers twitch under the table. Itching for my phone. For any connection to the world beyond these walls. But it's gone. Confiscated. Another freedom stripped away.

I clear my throat. The sound barely registers above the conversation.

"Perhaps we could—"

"The flowers will be white roses and lilies." Prescott barrels through my words like they don't exist. Like I don't exist. "Classic. Elegant. Befitting our status."

Our status. Not mine. Ours. As if I've already been absorbed.

"Good choice. What about the music?" Father nods again, and something that might be pride flickers across his face. Never directed at me. Never.

"String quartet for the ceremony. For the reception, that jazz ensemble you mentioned." Prescott preens, shoulders rolling back, chin lifting. "From the Harrington gala."

"Well done."

The praise washes over Prescott. He practically glows with it.

My stomach twists. Bile rises, sharp and acidic.

"I was thinking—" I try again. Push the words out harder this time.

"The menu." Prescott doesn't even glance my way. "Five courses. Seasonal delicacies. The chef comes highly recommended."

The conversation swirls around me. Past me. Through me. Decisions made about my wedding—my life—without a single question directed my way.

The walls inch closer. The chandelier's light sharpens, turns knife-edged. The air thickens until each breath feels like drowning.

Blood rushes in my ears, drowning out their voices.

"What about postponing?"

The words explode out of me. Too loud. Sharp enough to shatter the careful atmosphere they've constructed.

Silence crashes down.

Father's fork clatters against his plate. The sound echoes—china on china, metal on porcelain. His head swivels toward me, movements slow and deliberate. A predator noticing prey that dared to move.

Prescott goes very still. His hand, reaching for his wine, freezes mid-air. Then lowers. Slowly. His fingers curl into a loose fist on the table.

"Postpone?" The word drips from his mouth like venom. His eyes narrow to slits. "Why on earth would we do that?"

I swallow. My throat clicks, too dry. "It's just... everything is so rushed. Wouldn't it be nice to have more time? To make sure everything is—"

"We've discussed this." Father's voice is flat. Final. He doesn't raise it. Doesn't need to. The authority is bone-deep, bred into every syllable. "The date is set."

"But surely a few more months wouldn't—"

"Viv." Just my name. But the way he says it—a warning, a command, a threat all wrapped in two letters.

"It's all happening too fast." The words tumble out now, desperate and graceless. "Too close to the engagement. People will wonder. They'll think—" I force myself to say it. "They'll think it's a shotgun wedding. That I'm pregnant."

One eyebrow rises. The corner of his mouth lifts—not quite a smile, more like a sneer. "And what if they do?"

The casual dismissal hits like a slap. Physical. Stunning.

"It wouldn't be such a bad thing." He picks up his wine glass and swirls it. Studies the legs running down the crystal. "If it were true."

My stomach lurches. For a second, I think I might be sick right here at the table. All over the fine china and perfectly arranged roses.

Prescott's hand slides across the tablecloth. His fingers find mine. Close around them. Not gentle. Possessive. Claiming.

"The sooner we're married—" His thumb strokes across my knuckles. The touch makes my skin crawl. "—the sooner we can start our family."

We. He said *we.* As if pregnancy is something we do together. As if I'm not the one who'll carry it. Birth it. Bleed for it.

I blink, stunned into silence. The room tilts. Spins.

"But the invitations haven't even been sent." I grasp at straws. Anything. "No one will be able to come on two weeks' notice. They'll have other commitments—"

Father's fork hits his plate. Sharp. Deliberate. The sound cuts through my words like scissors through paper.

"You think anyone would dare miss this event?" His eyes narrow.

"If they're already booked—"

"If I snapped my fingers—" He demonstrates. The snap cracks through the room. "—and told them the wedding was tomorrow, they'd drop everything. Cancel vacations. Postpone surgeries. Reschedule their entire lives to be here."

He leans forward. The light catches his face, turning it harsh and angular. "The Faulks name commands attention. We don't need a long engagement. We certainly don't need your approval to move forward."

Each word lands like a blow. Calculated. Precise. Meant to hurt.

"But the caterers, the florists—"

"Silence."

One word. Absolute authority. No room for argument.

My throat closes. The air vanishes from the room.

"There's no need to delay." He picks up his knife and fork. Cuts into his lamb with meticulous precision. "Everything is in place. This wedding proceeds as planned."

The finality of it presses down. A physical weight crushing my chest.

I look between them. Father, cold and immovable. Prescott, smug and satisfied. The walls contract further. The noose tightens.

There's no escape.

The realization settles over me like a lead blanket. Heavy. Suffocating.

Prescott's hand closes over mine again. Tighter this time. His fingers dig in just enough to bruise. A reminder of who holds the leash.

"Now—" His voice smooths out, takes on that practiced charm. "—let's discuss the honeymoon arrangements."

Honeymoon. The word makes my skin crawl.

They launch back into planning. Details that have nothing to do with me. My gaze drifts to the floor-to-ceiling windows over-looking the gardens.

The sun hangs low. The sky bleeds orange and purple, like a bruise spreading across the horizon. Long shadows stretch across the manicured lawn.

Movement catches my eye. Subtle. Barely there. Something flickering at the edge of the tree line.

My pulse skips.

The pull is instant. Visceral. Like a fishhook lodged under my ribs, tugging me toward the window. Toward outside. Toward air that doesn't taste like Prescott's cologne and Father's disap-pointment.

"I think I'll take a walk." The words come out before I think them through. "In the gardens. Before the sun sets."

Father's attention snaps to me. Sharp as a blade. His eyes narrow, calculating. Assessing threat levels. Escape routes.

"A walk?" He exchanges a glance with Prescott. Silent communication passes between them.

"I just need air." I force a shrug. Keep my voice light. Casual. Like I'm not screaming inside.

The silence stretches. Taut as a wire ready to snap.

Father's gaze slides to Donovan. A single nod—barely perceptible.

"Donovan will accompany you." Not a suggestion. A command. "And don't wander too far."

I bite back the response clawing up my throat. Angry words only make things worse.

"Fine." I stand, smooth my dress. The silk whispers against my legs.

Donovan moves into position. Not beside me—that would be too obvious. Behind. Just far enough to seem respectful. Close enough to grab me if I run.

The garden doors open, and cool air hits my face. Sweet. Clean. Everything the dining room isn't.

I breathe deep, pulling it into my lungs, letting it wash away the suffocating atmosphere. The scent of roses and jasmine. Fresh-cut grass. Earth.

For a moment—just a moment—I can almost believe I'm free.

The gardens sprawl before me. Geometric precision. Every hedge trimmed to mathematical perfection. Every flower bed a calculated arrangement of color and height. French Renaissance style, Father always says with pride.

More like a maze designed to trap rather than delight.

I walk slowly. Heels clicking on stone paths. The sound echoes, then gets swallowed by the vast emptiness. Birds settle into trees, their evening songs fading. The breeze rustles through leaves.

Behind me, Donovan's heavier footfalls. Steady. Relentless. The shadow I can't shake.

The gardens may be beautiful, but they're still part of my prison. The perfectly trimmed hedges are just walls made of leaves. The fountains and statues—just decoration on my cage.

I glance back. Donovan trails at a respectful distance. His face impassive. Professional. But his eyes track every movement.

The flicker of movement catches my attention again. Deeper in the gardens. Near the far hedge line.

Something tugs at me. Draws me forward.

"Everything okay, Ms. Faulks?" Donovan's voice carries across the space between us.

"Fine." Too sharp. I force myself to soften it. "Just enjoying the fresh air."

But the pull intensifies. Like a current I can't resist.

I keep walking. Deeper into the gardens. Away from the house.

That's when I notice them.

Bees.

One buzzes past my ear. Fat. Fuzzy. The sound of its wings unnaturally loud in the quiet evening.

I swat at it absently. Early for bees. Especially bumblebees.

Another drifts by. Then another.

My brow furrows. This is strange. Wrong.

More appear. Their movements lazy at first. Aimless. But as I walk, they seem to multiply. Little black bodies suspended in the cooling air. Their collective hum grows louder. More insistent.

The sound fills my ears. Drowns out everything else.

I stop. Stare at the growing swarm.

This isn't normal. There are too many. Far too many for this time of evening. This time of year.

They circle. Hover. Their pattern seems deliberate.

A cluster lands on a nearby bush. I blink, certain my eyes are playing tricks. But no—they're arranging themselves. Forming a shape.

An arrow.

Pointing ahead.

I freeze. Pulse hammering against my ribs.

"I'm losing my mind."

The stress has finally broken me. I'm hallucinating. Has to be.

The bees lift off. Swirl in the air. Reform.

Another arrow. Hovering. Impossibly precise.

Blood pounds in my ears. Adrenaline spiking.

"Ms. Faulks?" Donovan's voice sounds distant despite his proximity. "Is something wrong?"

"No." The word comes out strangled. "Just... stretching my legs."

I can't look away from the bees. From the impossible thing happening right in front of me.

They move again. Leading me deeper into the gardens. Away from the house. Away from Donovan's sight line.

I follow. Can't help it. Drawn forward like a sleepwalker.

The gravel crunches under my feet. Each step feels both terrifying and inevitable. The hedges grow taller. The path narrows. Shadows deepen as we move into more secluded areas.

Donovan follows, but he's falling behind. The winding paths and tall hedges break his sight line.

The bees lead me to a hidden alcove. Tucked away. Private. The air here feels different—charged, electric. Like right before lightning strikes.

Donovan stops at the entrance. Far enough to give me space.

Close enough to intervene if needed. He pulls out his phone. Checks something. Distracted for precious seconds.

The bees hover near wildflowers. Their wings blur with movement.

Then—impossibly—they arrange themselves into letters.

U C us?

My breath catches. Stops entirely. The world narrows to those three letters formed by living insects.

"Yes." The whisper barely makes it past my lips.

I blink hard. Expecting the hallucination to dissolve. But the letters hold. Steady. Real.

The sweet scent of nectar. The earthy smell of soil. The cool air on my skin. All real. All grounding me in this impossible moment.

The bees scatter. Regroup. Form new words.

Paul.

Comes.

Soon.

My pulse stops. Then restarts, double-time. Hope—that dangerous, fragile thing—sparks to life in my chest.

The bees shift again. Their tiny bodies realigning with impossible precision.

R U held...

A pause. More bees join the formation.

...against UR will?

The question floats in the air. Undeniable. Inescapable.

My throat tightens. The answer is so simple. So obvious. But saying it out loud—even to a swarm of bees—feels like crossing a line I can't uncross.

I glance back. Donovan's still focused on his phone. The shadows stretch longer. Darker.

"Yes." The word scrapes out. Raw. Honest.

The bees swirl. Dance. Reform.

Escape?

"How?" My voice breaks. "I can't. They won't let me leave. I've tried. They watch everything. Every door. Every window. Every—"

The bees shift before I finish.

Rescue.

The word hits like electricity. Every nerve fires at once. Desperation I've been burying for months surges to the surface.

"Please." Stronger now. More certain. "I need help. I—"

The bees scatter briefly. Then reform one last time.

Help will come.

Then they disperse. Melting into the dusk like they were never there.

The garden goes still. Silent except for my ragged breathing. But the buzzing continues inside my chest. Inside my head. A promise humming through my veins.

Paul is coming.

He hasn't forgotten me.

"Ms. Faulks?" Donovan's voice cuts through my reverie. "We should head back inside."

I turn. Force my expression neutral. My pulse races. My hands shake. I clasp them together to hide it.

"Of course."

As I follow him back toward the house, I cast one last glance over my shoulder. The flower bed looks perfectly ordinary in the fading light.

But I know better.

The mansion looms ahead. Every window blazing with light. A gilded cage I've been trapped in for too long.

But now there's hope. A countdown that means something other than doom.

Paul is coming.

I step back into the oppressive atmosphere of the house. The cold air. The watching eyes. The suffocating control.

But this time, I carry a secret.

I'm not alone.

TWENTY

Paul: Reconnaissance

THE TENSION IN THE ROOM IS PALPABLE AS I STAND BEFORE THE detailed holographic projection of the Faulks estate. One week. Just seven days until Vivianne is supposed to walk down the aisle and into a life of misery. My jaw clenches at the thought.

"Let's go over this one more time." Sam's steady voice cuts through my brooding. He gestures to the 3D map, zooming in on the main house. "The ceremony will take place here, in the grand ballroom."

I nod, my eyes tracing the unfamiliar layout. "It's likely the largest space on the property. Floor-to-ceiling windows along the east wall, ornate double doors to the south. Security will be tight, but they'll have to let their guard down somewhat to accommodate the influx of guests."

"That's our in. We'll have Delta team posing as catering staff, security personnel, and guests." Forest, the mountain of a man with piercing blue eyes, leans forward.

As if on cue, Mitzy steps forward. Her psychedelic rainbow pixie hair glows under the room's lights, matching her enthusiastic personality. She manipulates the holographic display with a few deft movements.

"Our bumblebee drones—" She pulls up a schematic of the tiny machines. "—will provide real-time surveillance. I'll keep a few with Vivianne to track her movements; the others can be used if needed to interfere with the estate's security systems. Wish I could use the RUFI on this op, but that's a no-go."

"Is that how you made contact with Vivianne?" I raise an eyebrow, impressed despite myself.

"Yes."

"RUFI?" Merlin asks.

"Robotic dogs." Mitzy answers as if robotic dogs are commonplace. "We've integrated them into our teams, but they're not good for this."

I glance at Merlin, catching the determined set of his jaw. I know what he's thinking, and it sends a spike of anxiety through me.

"Delta team will be arriving shortly for final planning." CJ clears his throat. "They're experts at these kinds of ops."

"I need to be part of the extraction team. I can't sit on the sidelines while you're rescuing Vivianne." The words burst out before I can contain them.

Sam and Forest exchange a look that sets my teeth on edge.

"That's not a good idea." Sam's voice is careful. "You're too easily recognizable. We have to assume Vivianne's father will have security there, specifically looking for you."

"But—" Anger flares in my chest.

"We understand your connection to Vivianne." Forest cuts in, voice firm. "But emotions cloud judgment."

I want to argue further, but they have a point. Still, the thought of not being there for Vivianne when she needs me most is unbearable.

As the team dives deeper into the plan, my attention drifts to

Merlin. He studies the holographic display intently, his eyes darting from one point to another. I know exactly what he's thinking.

The Swan.

When there's a lull in the conversation, I pull Merlin aside, keeping my voice low. "You can't go after the Swan."

"This might be our only chance." Merlin's eyes flick to mine, a hint of defiance in their depths.

"No." I cut him off sharply. "I'm not jeopardizing Vivianne's safety for a piece of jewelry."

"It's more than a piece of jewelry, and you know it." Merlin counters. "It's about justice. About righting old wrongs."

"This isn't the time or place. Let it go. Please." I shake my head, frustration bubbling up.

But as I look at the determination in his eyes—the same determination that's driven him for decades—my resolve weakens.

"It's our best chance. Besides, they've all but cut you out of getting Vivianne, and the big guy is right. You're too identifiable. You're no use there, but I could use you to get the Swan."

"Fine." The word comes out as a mutter, and I barely believe it's leaving my mouth. "But we do this smart. We can't risk the extraction."

"We need to find out where it's kept." Merlin nods, a spark of excitement in his eyes. "Vivianne's seen it, hasn't she?"

"Yes." I nod slowly, the beginnings of a plan forming in my mind. "I'll need to get to her somehow. Either before or during the extraction."

As we rejoin the main group, Mitzy is going over the details of the security systems. Despite my earlier resistance, I pay close attention. Every bit of information could be crucial, not just for Vivianne's rescue, but for our own clandestine mission.

As the planning session continues, Mitzy frowns at the holographic display. "We still need to get final instructions to Vivianne about the extraction. The bumblebee drones are great for simple messages, but for something this complex..."

My opening. "I can do it. I can get a message to her without raising suspicion." I may not be able to free her alone, but I can do this.

"It's risky. If you're spotted—" Sam raises an eyebrow, skeptical.

"I won't be." I cut him off. "This is what I do."

Forest and Sam exchange a look.

"Too risky." Forest mutters.

"Look, if I can slip into the Louvre, the Met, and the Musée d'Orsay without a hitch, I can get in and out of the Faulks estate without anyone knowing." I shake my head, leaning in. "I'm trusting you to get Vivianne out. You need to trust me when I say I can pull this off."

Besides, if Merlin and I are going after the Swan, we need the recon.

I meet their eyes, daring them to challenge me. This is what Merlin and I need—there's no way I'm backing down now.

"It could work. If you can get in, give Vivianne the details, and get out without being seen..." Forest nods slowly.

"Fine. Get in, deliver the message, get out. No heroics, no early extraction attempts. Understood?" Sam sighs, tone firm.

"Understood." I nod, my mind already working through how I'll ask Vivianne about the Swan.

"The estate's security system is top-of-the-line, but my bees can interfere with their cameras and sensors." Mitzy leans over the hologram, excitement gleaming in her eyes. "We'll have a small window, though—Faulks is paranoid, but there are gaps in their coverage." She highlights several spots on the map with quick, confident gestures, then looks up. "So did we agree on sending Paul in ahead of time?"

"Yes." I don't wait for them to change their minds.

"When?" Mitzy looks not at me but at Forest.

Watching them work, I'm struck by how fast they've put this plan together. I've spent years slipping in and out of places like the Louvre and the Met, replacing priceless paintings without a trace. What they've done in hours would have taken me months —if not longer.

Not to mention, this isn't a heist. Replacing a masterpiece is one thing; rescuing a person from a fortress is a whole different game.

"We'll disrupt the cameras here, here, and here." Mitzy continues laying out the final details. "Once we do, we'll have a narrow window before they catch on."

This crew is something else—efficient, precise, and operating at a level I've never had to reach. But the weight of what's coming presses down.

This is no ordinary job.

The planning session continues late into the night. By the time we break, my head is spinning with details—guard rotations, security protocols, escape routes. It's a far cry from my usual solo operations, and I find myself both impressed by the Guardians' thoroughness and chafing at the constraints of working with a team.

As the others file out, I linger behind, staring at the holographic display of the Faulks estate. Somewhere in there, Vivianne is counting down the days until her freedom is taken away forever. And somewhere in there is the Swan pendant, a key to unlocking the mysteries of the past.

"We can do this." Merlin's presence beside me registers before he speaks.

"I hope you're right. Because if something goes wrong..." I don't finish the thought. I don't need to. We both know what's at stake.

I cast one last look at the hologram as we leave the room. In just a few days, that virtual representation will become a battlefield. And I'll be damned if I let Vivianne or the Swan slip through my fingers.

TWENTY-ONE

Vivianne: Silence

THE DAYS CRAWL BY, EACH ONE A TORTUROUS REMINDER OF MY impending fate. Two weeks. Fourteen days. Three hundred and thirty-six hours until I'm supposed to walk down the aisle and surrender my freedom.

The mansion buzzes with frantic activity. An army of caterers, florists, and decorators swarms through the halls, transforming the already opulent space into something fit for a royal wedding. The air is thick with the cloying scent of lilies—Prescott's choice, not mine. Their perfume makes my head spin, my stomach churn.

The room feels smaller by the second, the scent pressing in from every corner. My sinuses swell as their syrupy perfume clogs my nostrils, thick and oppressive. The flowers' poison clings to me like smoke. I have to get out—now—before I either pass out or puke all over Prescott's precious masterpiece.

I lurch toward the nearest exit, my heels skimming the edge of a Persian rug as I stagger into the hallway. The reek is thinner here, but still heavy with the lingering floral scent. I shove open the first door I find and stumble into the servants' area, into a different kind of chaos.

Silver gleams under harsh overhead lights as trays of cutlery line the long worktable. Servants polish each piece methodically. A worker runs a rag along a crystal glass, the squeak of it scraping down my spine like nails on a chalkboard. Plates clink against one another with every adjustment, the sound brittle and endless.

I escaped the lilies only to be assaulted by silver polish—sharp and chemical, cutting through the cloying sweetness of flowers and settling deep in my lungs. My head spins, the nauseating blend of floral musk and metal cleaner swirling in my gut. I gag, my throat convulsing, but there's nothing left to bring up.

I need air. Now.

Shoving through another door, I stumble down a narrow corridor, my dress catching on the edges of furniture as I half-run, half-stagger toward the garden doors.

The evening air wraps around me, sharp and crisp, washing away the lingering stench of lilies and silver polish. I bend over, hands braced on my knees, dragging in desperate gulps of fresh air. My pulse slows, just a little, and the dizziness eases. For a brief, blissful moment, I believe I've found sanctuary.

Then I lift my gaze, scanning the bushes and treetops. A quiet hum of insects weaves through the twilight, but it's nothing more than ordinary garden life.

No sign of the bumblebees. No erratic flight patterns, no subtle hums arranging themselves into words. No message telling me Paul is coming, no sign that help is on the way. Just rows of sculpted hedges, perfectly trimmed roses, and the soft rustling of leaves in the breeze.

I wrap my arms around myself, as if holding my body together will stop the unraveling inside me. Maybe I imagined the message. Maybe the bumblebee drones were nothing more than a hallucination—a desperate trick my mind conjured to give me hope.

Footsteps crunch on the gravel path behind me. I spin around, breath catching in my throat.

Donovan. The head of security strides toward me, his tailored suit straining across his broad shoulders, the gleam in his eyes more condescending than concerned.

"Miss Faulks." His voice is too smooth, too practiced. "You know you're not supposed to wander."

I take a step back, but his hand catches my arm—not rough, but firm, with a weight that makes it clear I have no choice.

"Let's get you back inside." The words are murmured, as if coaxing a child.

I yank my arm, but his grip tightens just enough to let me know resistance won't end well. He turns, steering me toward the mansion with all the ease of someone escorting a prisoner back to their cell.

The doors loom ahead, swallowing the last sliver of sky. I stumble along beside him, swallowing the lump rising in my throat. One last glance over my shoulder, searching for a glimmer of hope among the flowers, a sign that the bumblebee drones are still out there, still watching.

But there's nothing.

Just silence.

TWENTY-TWO

Vivianne: Five Hundred Names

ONE WEEK

"Viv." My father's voice pulls me back from the window. The garden blurs back into focus—empty flowerbeds, no bees, no messages. Nothing.

"Are you listening?"

"Yes." I turn, smoothing my features into a neutral expression. Compliant.

His eyes narrow. He's been watching me long enough to know better. "Five hundred guests."

The number lands in my stomach like a stone. Five hundred witnesses. Five hundred people who'll smile and congratulate and never once ask if this is what I want.

"That's quite a lot."

Prescott shifts in the armchair—the one that was Grandmother's, the carved mahogany with the needlepoint she stitched herself. His jacket drapes across the arm now. His tie hangs loose. He's stretched his legs out like he's been coming to this house for years instead of months.

"The Vanderbilts had four hundred. We can hardly do less."

Father nods, already moving on. "You'll need to address the invitations. All of them."

The words take a moment to penetrate. "Address by hand?"

"Is that a problem?" Something in my tone makes Father's jaw tighten.

Back down. I should back down. "It's just... there's only a week. Five hundred envelopes, that's over seventy a day, and with the fittings and—"

"You will do it." He doesn't raise his voice. He's never needed to. "Etiquette demands it. Unless you're suggesting we send printed invitations like we're hosting a garden luncheon?"

Heat climbs my neck. "No, of course not. I only meant—"

"Then we're settled." He glances at his watch—platinum, a gift from Prescott after they finalized the merger. The merger that required a marriage to seal it. "Prescott and I need to finalize the contracts. You'll start this afternoon."

The dismissal is clear. I should nod, should murmur agreement, disappear to my room where I can address invitations until my hand cramps and five hundred strangers know exactly when to arrive to watch me sign my life away.

"I can't."

The words escape before I can stop them. Quiet, but they land in the silence like breaking glass.

Prescott's posture changes. Nothing dramatic—just a subtle shift forward, weight redistributing. His expression doesn't harden. That would be simpler. Instead, something almost like pleasure flickers across his face. Like I've done something unexpectedly entertaining.

"Can't?" He rises from the chair. Not quickly. Not with any visible aggression. Just... purposefully. The way a cat rises when it's spotted movement. "That's an interesting word choice, darling."

My spine wants to curve, wants to step back. I lock my knees. Stepping back would be blood in the water.

"I meant I don't have time. To do it properly."

"Ah." He crosses the room. Each step deliberate. "See, that's better. Much more... reasonable."

He stops close enough that his cologne hits me—something expensive and cloying that's started to make me nauseous. His hand finds my elbow. To anyone glancing in, it might look affectionate. Possessive in the way engaged couples are possessive.

His thumb presses into the soft underside of my arm. Steady pressure. Not bruising. Not yet. Just enough to send a clear message: *I could.*

"The invitations are your responsibility, Viv." Father's voice comes from behind his phone now, already scrolling through messages. Not even watching. "You'll make time."

"And you'll be gracious about it." Prescott's thumb finds the spot where my pulse hammers against skin. "Won't you?"

The pressure increases. Just slightly. Just enough.

I meet his eyes. Mistake. There's something eager there, something waiting to see if I'll push back again. Hoping I will.

"Of course." My voice comes out steady. Small victory.

"Good girl." He releases my arm, but his hand trails down to capture my fingers. Brings them to his lips. The kiss is brief. Proprietary. His eyes never leave mine, and there's a promise there that makes ice flood my veins. "We want this to be perfect for you. Don't we?"

"Your mother would have wanted this." Father's voice cuts across whatever Prescott was about to say. "A proper ceremony. Your grandmother certainly did, before she passed."

The invocation of my grandmother hits exactly as he intended. She would've been relieved that I'd be taken care of, that the family legacy would continue. She would roll in her grave if she knew what her son was willing to do to secure a business alliance.

"Of course." I force the words through numb lips. "I'm sorry. I'm just... overwhelmed."

"Overwhelmed." Prescott's breath ghosts across my ear. His hand stays locked on my waist. "That's one word for it."

Father checks his watch again. "The two of you can discuss the details. I have a conference call in ten minutes. Viv, those invitations need to start today."

He's halfway to the door before pausing. "And Viv? The servants have been gossiping about your... mood. I won't have it. Whatever personal feelings you may have, you'll keep them private. This family's reputation depends on it."

The door closes behind him with a decisive click.

I count the beats of silence that follow. One. Two. Three. Four.

Prescott's hand slides from my waist to the small of my back. "Alone at last."

I try to step away. His hand becomes a bar.

"We should discuss the wedding night." His voice is conversational. Pleasant, even. "I want to make sure we understand each other."

"There's nothing to discuss." My voice barely works.

"Oh, I disagree." He turns me to face him. Both hands on my waist now. Heavy. Inescapable. "See, I've been very patient. Very... restrained. Your father insisted. No intimacy before the wedding. No... marks."

The way he says *marks* makes my skin crawl.

"But after?" He leans closer. "After, you're mine. Legally. Completely. I intend to make full use of my rights as your husband."

"Rights." The word tastes like ash.

"God-given rights." His smile doesn't reach his eyes. "A husband's authority over his wife. Her body. Her obedience."

Submission. Duty. Honor.

The words sound so different in Prescott's mouth. Twisted. Weaponized. He says them like they're chains he's owed, shackles he has every right to lock around my wrists.

Paul uses the same words, but they come wrapped in protection, in devotion, in the kind of reverence that makes me want to give it. He earns every ounce of my surrender with the way he looks at me—like I'm something precious he's been entrusted to guard. Like my willingness is a gift he'll spend his whole life being worthy of.

Prescott demands. Paul cherishes.

Prescott takes. Paul receives.

One wants to break me. The other would bleed himself dry before letting me crack.

"You're a monster." The words come out as a whisper.

"Perhaps." He doesn't look offended. If anything, he looks pleased. "In seven days, there won't be a single thing you can do about it."

His hand comes up to cup my face. Gentle. Tender, even. His thumb brushes my cheekbone.

"Our wedding night—" His voice drops lower. "—I'm going to strip you out of that white dress. Lay you down in our marriage bed. And I'm going to take what's mine. Every inch."

My breath catches. Can't help it.

"And here's what I want you to understand." His thumb traces my jaw now. "If you fight me—and God, I hope you do—it will only make me enjoy it more. Your father wants a grandson. An heir. And I'm going to spend our wedding night buried inside you until I've given him one."

Bile rises in my throat.

"In fact..." His eyes darken with something that makes me

want to shower for a week. "I'm hard right now, just thinking about it. Just imagining you struggling beneath me, that pretty mouth forming all those protests that won't matter anymore."

"Let go." I barely recognize my own voice.

"Not yet." But his hands drop. He steps back, adjusting his tie, his expression smoothing into something almost respectable. "You should get started on those invitations. Five hundred is quite a lot, after all."

He collects his jacket from Grandmother's chair and shrugs into it. Buttons it with careful precision.

At the door, he pauses. "Oh, and if you embarrass me in front of our guests—if you show anything other than devotion— I'll make sure our wedding night lasts for days. Do we understand each other?"

I don't answer. Can't.

His smile says I've given him exactly what he wanted. "I'll see you at dinner. Wear the blue dress. I prefer you in blue."

The door closes. His footsteps recede down the hall. The front door opens and closes.

Silence.

My legs give out. I sink onto the sofa—not Grandmother's chair, can't sit there now that he's touched it—and stare at my hands. They're shaking. My whole body is shaking.

Five hundred invitations.

Seven days.

I turn back to the window, searching the garden with desperate eyes. Empty flowerbeds. No bees. No messages.

Where are you, Paul?

The afternoon sun slants through the window, warm on my face, and I'm so cold I might never be warm again.

Seven days until I become Prescott's wife.

Seven days until I stop being Vivianne entirely.

Unless Paul comes. Unless the rescue he promised materializes from nothing. Unless—

"Miss Faulks?"

I jump. Mrs. Holloway stands in the doorway, her expression carefully neutral. She's been with the family since before I was born. She loved my grandmother. Adored my mother when she came and made this place her home. She knows exactly what's happening here.

"Your father asked me to bring you the guest list. For the invitations." She sets a leather portfolio on the side table. Doesn't quite meet my eyes. "And the calligraphy supplies."

"Thank you."

She hesitates. Opens her mouth. Closes it.

"Mrs. Holloway?"

"Nothing, miss." But her hand trembles slightly as she smooths her apron. "Will you be taking lunch in here?"

"I'm not hungry."

Another hesitation. "You should eat something. Keep your strength up."

For what? For addressing five hundred invitations to people who'll watch me marry a monster? For surviving a wedding night that Prescott's already promised will break me?

"I'll have tea. Thank you."

She nods and withdraws, closing the door softly behind her.

Five hundred names to write. Five hundred envelopes to address. Five hundred witnesses to summon to my execution.

I pick up the calligraphy pen. My hand still shakes.

The first name on the list: Mr. and Mrs. William Vanderbilt.

I dip the pen in ink. Press it to paper. Form the first letter.

And count down the hours until Paul comes to save me.

He will come.

He has to.

Because if he doesn't, in seven days, I'll cease to exist.

TWENTY-THREE

Paul: Six Days

The holographic display bathes the war room in cold blue light, turning everyone into ghosts. I lean forward, hands braced on the table's edge, staring at the three-dimensional rendering of the Faulks estate. Every window. Every door. Every potential exit.

Every barrier between me and Vivianne.

My fingers itch to reach into the hologram, to tear through the digital walls and pull her out. Five weeks since she posted that cryptic message about Paris gardens and three-month countdowns. Five weeks of planning, preparing, assembling this team.

Six days until the wedding.

Six days until I lose her forever.

"You listening, de Gaulle?"

Jenny's voice cuts through my thoughts like a switchblade. She stands across the table, arms crossed, one eyebrow raised. The woman radiates authority—shoulders back, spine straight, every inch the tactical commander. Her dark skin gleams in the holographic light, and those sharp eyes miss nothing.

"Every word." I straighten, meeting her gaze. Refusing to be cowed.

She doesn't look convinced. The silence stretches, taut as wire, until Merlin shifts beside me. His hand lands on my shoulder—a warning or support, maybe both.

"The estate's security is formidable." Jenny manipulates the display. The hologram zooms in, revealing guard positions, camera placements, and patrol routes marked in pulsing red. "Twenty-four-seven surveillance. Rotating guard shifts. Motion sensors on every accessible entry point."

"Which is why we're not breaking in." Mac's voice rumbles from the corner like distant thunder. The man is a mountain—six and a half feet of solid muscle packed into tactical black. His arms are crossed, biceps straining against fabric. "We're walking in."

"Elaborate." Merlin leans forward, his weathered hands folding on the table. Always calm. Always assessing. Seventy years of stealing priceless art has taught him patience I'll never master.

Jenny taps the display. Two figures materialize—generic male silhouettes with credential badges floating beside them. "Mac and Blaze infiltrate as last-minute security hires. We've already planted your backgrounds in their system. Ex-military. Impeccable references. Exactly what Faulks is looking for to beef up protection for his daughter's wedding."

"Because nothing says 'happy celebration' like a small army." Blaze speaks for the first time since we gathered. He's leaner than Mac, all coiled energy and restless movement. His eyes never stop tracking—cataloging exits, assessing threats, calculating angles. "What's our cover story for the sudden hiring?"

"Increased threat assessment due to the bride's high profile." Charlie's voice is honey and smoke. She's perched on the table's edge, one long leg crossed over the other, blonde hair pulled back in a severe ponytail. Beautiful enough to stop traffic. Dangerous enough to cause a pileup. "Rich families love being paranoid. Makes them feel important."

"Plus, the groom's family has their own security concerns." Forest adds from where he's slouched against the wall. The man is built like his name suggests—solid, immovable, radiating quiet strength. "Harringtons have made enemies. Easy to sell the extra muscle as preventative."

The hologram shifts again. The estate's floor plan spreads before us—a maze of corridors, ballrooms, and private quarters. Jenny's fingers dance through the projection, highlighting sections in different colors.

"Jon and Brett, you're on the catering team." She doesn't look at the two men, just points. "That gives you access to the main house. Kitchen. Dining areas. Anywhere food and drink need to go."

I glance at the pair. They stand close—not touching, but orbiting each other like binary stars. Jon is darker, broader, his presence solid and grounding. Brett lighter, leaner, moving with a fighter's grace. The way they communicate without words speaks of years together. Battle. Blood. Brotherhood.

"Catering." Brett's mouth quirks. "Haven't done food service since that job in Prague."

"That wasn't food service." Jon's response is dry. "That was a disaster with appetizers."

"You're the one who set off the—"

"Focus." Jenny's single word cuts through the banter. No raised voice. Just authority. The room snaps to attention. "Charlie and I will infiltrate as either florist assistants or waitstaff. Our primary objective is to make contact with Vivianne. We need to reach the bridal suite and assess her physical and mental state."

My chest tightens. *Physical and mental state.* Clinical terms for whether the woman I love has been broken by her captors.

"She's strong." The words come out rougher than intended. "Vivianne won't break."

Jenny's gaze locks onto mine. Assessing. Measuring.

"Everyone breaks eventually. It's just a matter of how much pressure gets applied and for how long."

The truth of it sits heavy in the room. I want to argue. To insist Vivianne is different, special, unbreakable.

But I remember Catherine. My sister, whom I thought was invincible. Who walked into that museum in Florence with absolute confidence.

Who never walked out.

"What about us?" Merlin's question pulls me back from the edge of that particular abyss. "Where do Paul and I fit in this operation?"

Jenny manipulates the display again. The estate's perimeter appears, surrounding properties marked in yellow. "You're our insurance policy. Off-site, monitoring communications, ready to provide intel or extraction support if things go sideways."

"Absolutely not."

The words are out before I can stop them. I push away from the table, the chair scraping harshly against concrete. "I'm not sitting in a van while Vivianne is in there. I'm going in."

"No." Jenny doesn't move. Doesn't raise her voice. Just states it as fact. "You're emotionally compromised. Emotional compromise gets people killed."

"I know the art world. Know these people. I can—"

"Get Vivianne killed along with yourself and anyone near you when you do something stupid." She steps around the table, closing the distance between us. Up close, the scars are visible—one along her jawline, another disappearing into her hairline. Combat wounds. Proof she's earned the right to make these calls. "This isn't negotiable, de Gaulle. You want our help? You follow our rules."

The air crackles with tension. Everyone's watching. Waiting to see if I'll push back. If I'll throw away this chance because my pride can't handle being benched.

Merlin's hand finds my shoulder again. "She's right, mon ami."

I want to shrug him off. Want to argue that it's my operation, my plan, my woman we're saving.

But it's not. Not really. The moment I called in the Guardians, I handed over control.

"Fine." The word tastes like ash. "We stay off-site."

"Good." Jenny turns back to the display, and the moment passes. "Now, let's talk about contingencies."

The briefing continues for another two hours. Escape routes. Communication protocols. What to do if Vivianne can't or won't leave. What to do if Faulks or the groom make an appearance. What to do if everything goes to hell.

That last section takes the longest.

Mitzy bounces forward when Jenny finally calls for tech review, her rainbow hair catching the holographic light like a prism. She's brilliant, her eyes holding the sharp focus of someone who sees the world in ones and zeros.

"Okay, okay, okay." She spreads an array of items across the table. Watches. Earrings. Tie clips. Pens. All looking completely ordinary. "These are not your grandfather's spy gadgets."

She picks up a watch—sleek, expensive-looking, the kind any security professional might wear. "Micro-camera. Comms unit. Emergency beacon. Plus—" She presses something on the side, and the air around it shimmers. "—a targeted EMP. Thirty-foot radius. Kills all electronics dead."

"How long?" Mac reaches for the watch, turning it over in his massive hands with surprising care.

"Sixty seconds. Ninety if you're lucky." Mitzy grins. "Plenty of time to get somewhere you shouldn't be."

She moves to the earrings—elegant drops that catch the light. "Fast-acting sedative. Aerosol delivery on contact. Touch these to someone's skin, they're down in three seconds, out for twenty minutes."

"And these?" Charlie holds up what looks like a simple hair clip.

"Tracker. Plant it on someone, we can follow them anywhere within a ten-mile radius." Mitzy's grin widens. "Also doubles as a lock pick if you're desperate."

The technology is remarkable. My work with Merlin has always relied on simpler tools—talent, timing, insider knowledge. This level of sophistication is military-grade. Maybe beyond.

"Where did you get this equipment?" The question slips out before I can stop it.

Mitzy's grin falters. She glances at Sam, who's been silent throughout the briefing. He steps forward, and the easy-going mask he usually wears drops away.

"We have resources." His voice is flat. Final. "That's all you need to know."

The message is clear—don't ask questions we won't answer.

Fair enough.

"One more thing." Jenny pulls up a new image. A man in his late forties, distinguished-looking, with salt-and-pepper hair and calculating eyes. "Donovan Price. Head of Faulks estate security. Former military. Delta Force. He's not just muscle—he's smart, experienced, and loyal to Henry Faulks above all else."

"Which means?" Forest asks.

"Which means if he suspects anything—anything at all—he won't hesitate to lock down the entire estate." Jenny's expression goes grim. "If that happens, we abort. Vivianne's safety is priority one. We don't take risks that might get her hurt."

The words hang in the air. An acknowledgment that, for all our planning, all our preparation, success isn't guaranteed.

Failure might mean leaving Vivianne behind.

"That won't happen." My voice is quiet but certain. "We're getting her out."

"Your confidence is touching." Jenny's tone is dry. "But confidence doesn't stop bullets."

"Neither does pessimism."

For a moment, we stare at each other. Then her mouth quirks —not quite a smile, but close. "Fair point. Alright, people. Final equipment check, then get some rest. Tomorrow we start surveillance runs. I want to know every car that comes and goes from that estate, every delivery truck, every pattern we can exploit."

The team disperses. Mac and Blaze huddle over the security details. Jon, Brett, and Charlie review the catering schedule. Forest and CJ confer quietly in the corner.

I stay at the table, staring at the holographic estate. Somewhere in that maze of wealth and privilege, Vivianne is trapped. Counting down to a wedding she doesn't want. To a life she never chose. Which brings up memories of Catherine and the job where everything went wrong. We lost Catherine that day. Buried her a week later. Six months after that, we lost Nicholas after his trial.

"You're thinking about Catherine."

I don't turn at Merlin's voice. He knows me too well. "How did you guess?"

"Because I'm thinking about her too." He moves beside me, his reflection ghostly in the holographic light. "About all the ways that job went wrong. All the signs we missed."

"We're not missing signs this time." I finally look at him. Really look. The lines around his eyes have deepened over the past month. The silver in his hair, catching the blue light, makes him look older. Tired. "We're going to save her, Merlin. And we're getting the Swan back."

Something flickers across his face. "Paul—"

"Don't." I shake my head. "We can do both."

"Can we?" His voice is soft. Sad. "Or is that what we told ourselves in Florence?"

The question sits between us. Heavy. Damning.

"This is different." But even as I say it, I'm not sure I believe it.

"Is it?"

Before I can answer, Jenny's voice cuts through the room. "De Gaulle. Merlin. Conference room. Now."

We follow her through a door I hadn't noticed—clever camouflage built into the farmhouse's rustic paneling. The space beyond is small, windowless, soundproofed. A room built for secrets.

Sam and Forest are already inside, standing with arms crossed. The easy camaraderie from earlier is gone, replaced by something harder. More dangerous.

"Sit." Jenny doesn't make it a request.

We sit.

She remains standing, looming over us in a clearly intentional way. Establishing dominance. Control. "Before we go any further, there's something we need to discuss. Your agenda."

My stomach tightens. "What agenda?"

"Don't insult our intelligence." Forest's voice is cold. "You're not here just to save Vivianne. You're after something else. Something you think is in that house."

"I find that comment insulting. Vivianne is my priority." Merlin and I exchange glances. How much do we tell them? How much do they already know?

"The Swan pendant." Sam leans against the wall, casual. But his eyes are sharp. Alert. "A ruby the size of a quail's egg. Stolen in World War II. Missing ever since."

"Until Paul painted it around Vivianne's neck." Jenny's gaze locks onto mine. "Painted her wearing something she'd never seen before. Something that just happens to match her grand-mother's earrings. Earrings that came from a matching set."

"We did our homework." CJ crosses his arms. "The question is—did you think we wouldn't?"

The silence stretches. Taut. Dangerous.

"Yes." Merlin's voice is calm. Steady. "We're after the pendant. It belonged to someone I loved. Someone who died because of it. I want it back."

"And that won't compromise the mission?" Jenny's tone makes it clear what she thinks of that idea.

"It won't—"

"Bullshit." Sam pushes off the wall. "You're telling me that if you have to choose between grabbing that pendant and getting Vivianne out safely, you'll pick Vivianne every time? No hesitation?"

The question hangs in the air.

I open my mouth. Close it. Because the truth is, I don't know. I'll choose Vivianne every time. Merlin, however, wants the Swan. That pendant represents everything he lost. Everything that was stolen from him.

But Vivianne—

"Yes." The word comes out stronger than I feel. "Vivianne comes first. Always."

"And you?" Jenny's attention shifts to Merlin. "Can you make that same promise?"

For a long moment, Merlin remains silent. When he speaks, his voice is rough. Raw. "I've already lost everyone I loved for that pendant. I won't lose anyone else."

It's not exactly a yes. But it's close enough.

Jenny studies us both. Measuring. Weighing. Finally, she nods. "Alright. But understand this—if you do anything that puts Vivianne or my team at risk, I will personally ensure you regret it. Are we clear?"

"Crystal."

"Good." She moves to the door. Pauses. "One more thing. Vivianne's father—Henry Faulks. What's your read on him?"

I think about the man who controlled every aspect of Vivianne's life. Who arranged her marriage like a business transaction. Who values legacy and power over his daughter's happiness.

"Dangerous." The word feels inadequate. "He'll do whatever it takes to maintain control."

"His purpose being?"

"Sentinel." Merlin speaks before I can. "An organization we know almost nothing about. Only that it's old, powerful, and the Faulks family has been part of it for generations."

Jenny's expression shifts. Something flickers there—recognition? Concern? It's gone before I can identify it.

"Sentinel." She repeats the word like a curse. "Well. That complicates things."

"You've heard of it?" I lean forward.

"If Henry Faulks is part of Sentinel, if that's what's driving this marriage..." She trails off. Thinks. "We need to adjust our approach. Be even more careful."

"How much more careful can we be?"

"You'd be surprised." Her smile is grim. "Now get some rest. Tomorrow, we start surveillance."

We file out. The war room has mostly emptied—just Mitzy still tinkering with equipment, her rainbow hair bent over circuit boards and micro-electronics.

I make my way to the room they've assigned me. Small. Spartan. A bed, a desk, a window overlooking dark fields.

Sleep won't come. I know it won't. So I sit by the window, staring out at nothing, thinking about Vivianne.

Six days.

In six days, I'll see her again. Touch her. Hold her.

Or I'll lose her forever.

The door opens quietly. I don't turn—I already know it's Merlin from the weight of his footsteps.

"Can't sleep either?"

"Not even close."

He settles into the room's only chair with a soft grunt. We sit in comfortable silence for a while, two men bound by blood and loss and stolen art.

"Paul." His voice breaks the quiet. "What Jenny said about choosing. About prioritizing Vivianne over the pendant."

"I meant it."

"I know you did. But I also know you." A pause. "You're thinking you can do both. Save her and retrieve what was stolen. That you're clever enough, fast enough, lucky enough to pull off both objectives."

I don't answer because he's right.

"Catherine thought that too." His voice goes rough. "Thought she could get the Caravaggio and get out clean. We all did."

"This isn't Florence."

"No. It's worse." He moves to the window beside me. "Florence was a heist. This is a rescue from people who won't hesitate to hurt Vivianne if they think it serves their purposes. And you want to add recovering the Swan on top of that?"

"The pendant is important—and this may be our only chance to retrieve it."

"Agreed. But the pendant is an object." He turns to face me. "Vivianne is a woman. The woman you love. Don't let me lose someone else I care about because I couldn't let go of the past."

The words hit like a blow. Physical. Stunning.

"I can do both." But even to my ears, it sounds hollow.

"Maybe." He moves to the door. Pauses with his hand on the handle. "Or maybe you'll have to choose. And when that moment comes—when you're standing in that house with seconds to decide—make sure you choose right."

He leaves. The door clicks shut. And I'm alone with my thoughts.

With the truth I don't want to face.

I stare out at the darkness, and for the first time since this all began, I wonder if I can do this. If I'm strong enough to make the right choice when it matters.

The hologram flickers to life on the desk—Mitzy must have left a portable unit. The Faulks estate rotates slowly, its walls glowing soft blue.

Somewhere in there, Vivianne is counting down the hours.

Waiting for rescue.

Trusting me to choose her.

I reach out, my fingers passing through the holographic walls. Grasping at nothing.

Please let me be strong enough.

But in the reflection on my window, I'm not sure I recognize the man staring back.

TWENTY-FOUR

Vivianne: The Rehearsal Dinner

THE NAPKIN DEBATE HAS BEEN GOING ON FOR TWENTY MINUTES.

Twenty. Minutes.

I stare at the fabric swatches spread across Father's desk—ivory, cream, pearl, eggshell—all variations of the same colorless nothing. Mrs. Holloway hovers nearby, wringing her hands, waiting for a decision I don't care to make.

"The ivory is too yellow." Prescott leans over my shoulder, his cologne coating the back of my throat. "Pearl is better. More elegant."

Elegant. Everything must be elegant. Perfect. Befitting the union of two powerful families.

I want to laugh. Or scream. Or both.

"Fine." The word comes out flat. Dead. "Pearl."

Mrs. Holloway scurries away, relieved to escape. I don't blame her.

The days blur together now. Tastings where I push food around plates. Fittings where seamstresses pin and tuck fabric I never chose. Endless conversations about flowers and fonts and whether the string quartet knows our first dance song.

Our. As if I had any say in it. As if this wedding is something we're building together instead of a cage being constructed around me, one pearl napkin at a time.

Through it all, I escape to the gardens whenever possible. Searching for bumblebees. For any sign that Paul's message was real. That help is coming.

But the flowers remain stubbornly still. Only regular honeybees going about their business, oblivious to my desperation.

Days before the wedding, I'm trapped in Father's study again. The air is thick with cigar smoke and expensive whiskey. The smell makes my stomach turn.

"The rehearsal dinner is in three days." Father doesn't look up from his papers. His pen scratches across documents—contracts, probably. Or prenuptials. Legal shackles to match the emotional ones. "I expect you to be on your best behavior. No more moping around like you're attending a funeral."

The bitter laugh claws up my throat. I swallow it back.

A funeral would be preferable.

"And for God's sake, eat something." Prescott eyes me from his perch against the desk. His gaze travels over me—assessing, cataloging, finding me wanting. "That dress cost a fortune. I won't have you looking like a skeleton walking down the aisle."

I wrap my arms around myself. The gesture is automatic. Defensive. I've lost weight—the stress and constant nausea have stripped flesh from bones I didn't know I could spare.

But hearing him say it. Reducing me to an ornament that's not polished enough for display.

Something hot and sharp lodges under my ribs.

"I'll try." I force the words out. Keep my eyes down.

"You'll do more than try." Father's voice cracks like a whip.

"This union is too important to be jeopardized by your childish behavior."

The word detonates something inside me.

"Childish?" My head snaps up. "Is it childish to want some say in my own life? To not want to be sold off like—"

The room goes silent. That terrible, suffocating silence that means I've crossed a line.

Father rises slowly from his chair. His face darkens—first red, then purple, like a storm gathering. "How dare you."

"You're embarrassing yourself." Prescott moves faster than I can react. His hand clamps around my upper arm, fingers digging into the soft flesh above my elbow. Pain blooms, sharp and immediate.

I try to pull away. "Let go—"

He shoves. Hard.

I stumble backward, catching myself on the bookshelf edge. Pain radiates from my arm where his fingers branded me. My elbow hits wood, sending another shock of pain up to my shoulder.

Prescott stands there, straightening his cuffs. Calm. Composed. Like he didn't just put his hands on me.

Father has already returned to his papers. Dismissing me. Dismissing what just happened.

I flee.

My feet carry me through corridors, past staff who won't meet my eyes, out into the gardens where the sunset bleeds orange and red across the sky like a wound.

I collapse onto a stone bench. The marble is cold through my thin dress, but I barely feel it. Everything is numb except my arm, which throbs with each heartbeat.

The tears come finally. Hot. Angry. Useless.

"Please." I whisper to the empty air. To Paul. To whoever might be listening. "If you can hear me... I can't do this anymore."

But only the wind answers. Rustling through leaves. Carrying away my words like they never existed.

No bumblebees appear. No magical messages.

Just silence.

The days crawl by. Each one heavier than the last.

Father makes it clear—crystal clear—that any further "outbursts" will not be tolerated. He doesn't specify what that means. Doesn't need to. The threat hangs in the air like smoke.

Prescott's touches linger longer now. His grip tighter. Fingers pressing into my waist, my shoulder, my wrist. Not quite hard enough to bruise where people can see. But the message is unmistakable.

You're mine. Or you will be soon enough.

The night before the rehearsal dinner, I lie in bed staring at the ceiling. Sleep is impossible. My mind races with thoughts of escape that go nowhere. Dead ends and locked doors and guards who watch my every move.

What if I tried again? How far could I get?

And what happens when they catch me?

Tap.

I freeze. Hold my breath. Wait.

Tap tap.

It's coming from the window.

My pulse slams against my ribs as I slip out of bed. The floor is cold under my bare feet. Each step feels loud enough to wake the house.

I ease aside the curtain.

Bumblebees hover outside the glass. Their bodies glow faintly in the moonlight—impossible, beautiful, real.

They move, forming letters against the dark.

Wedding. Be ready.

My hands shake as I unlatch the window. Cool night air rushes in, carrying the scent of roses, earth, and possibility.

"How?" The whisper barely makes it past my lips. "What do I need to—"

But they're already dispersing. Melting into the darkness like they were never there.

I close the window. Lean my forehead against the cool glass.

They're coming. Paul is coming.

For the first time in months, hope flickers in my chest. Small. Fragile. But alive.

I don't sleep. Can't. My mind spins with possibilities, fears, and desperate plans.

Dawn breaks slowly. The sky shifts from black to gray to pale gold. I watch it all from my window, memorizing the colors in case I never see them again.

Because this is it. Today is the rehearsal dinner.

Tomorrow is my wedding day.

The day Paul will come for me. Or the day I lose everything.

The house erupts into chaos before I've finished my first cup of coffee. Hair stylists. Makeup artists. The seamstress with last-minute adjustments to the dress I didn't choose.

They pull and pin and paint. Transform me into someone I don't recognize. A bride. A doll. A prize to be displayed.

Through it all, I'm hyperaware. Watching. Listening. Searching for any sign, any clue of what's to come.

As evening approaches, luxury cars begin arriving. The circular drive fills with Mercedes, Bentleys, and sleek black town cars. Guests emerge in designer clothes and too much jewelry, laughing, air-kissing, pretending we're all here for something joyful.

I stand at the top of the grand staircase. Prescott's arm wraps around my waist—possessive, proprietary. His fingers dig into my hip through the silk of my dress.

"You look beautiful, darling." His breath is hot against my ear. Too close. Always too close. "Keep this up, and we might just make it through without incident."

I suppress a shudder. Force my mouth into a smile as the first guests reach us.

"Mrs. Whitmore, how lovely to see you." I shake hands. Smile. Lie. "Yes, we're so excited. Thank you for coming."

"Mr. Castellano, what a pleasure." Another handshake. Another empty pleasantry. "Of course. We're thrilled you could make it."

The faces blur together. Names I'll never remember attached to people I'll never see again. They all say the same things. Offer the same congratulations. Ask the same questions about flowers, venues, and honeymoon destinations.

And I smile. And nod. And die a little more with each guest.

The last guest finally passes through. My cheeks ache from smiling. My feet throb in heels too high for standing this long.

Then I hear it. Faint but unmistakable.

Buzzing.

My pulse leaps. I scan the room, trying not to be obvious. There—near a vase of white roses on the hall table. A single bumblebee hovers, impossibly still.

The estate has transformed. The marble floors gleam under chandeliers that cast diamond patterns across every surface. Guests drift through the space like colorful birds—silk rustling, jewelry glinting, champagne glasses catching light.

Servers weave through the crowd. Crisp white shirts. Black

waistcoats. Invisible until someone needs them. They carry silver trays laden with champagne flutes and tiny, perfect appetizers.

The air is thick with competing scents—truffle oil, caviar, the cloying sweetness of the lilies lining every surface. My stomach churns.

A server approaches. Male. Nondescript. His face partially hidden by the brim of his cap, pulled low.

Nothing remarkable. Just another piece of background staff.

He raises his tray toward us. Champagne flutes arranged in precise rows.

Then his hand jerks.

The movement is so small I almost miss it. But the result is spectacular.

A flute tips. Champagne arcs through the air in a glittering cascade. The cold liquid hits my dress, soaking through silk in an instant.

I gasp. Step back. The champagne is frigid against my skin, spreading across my stomach and thighs.

"Oh, I do apologize, Miss." The server's voice is low. Cultured. Familiar in a way that makes my pulse stutter.

He straightens, adjusting his thick-rimmed glasses with one hand. Wild gray hair frames his face—too long, slightly unkempt. The kind of dishevelment that looks accidental but probably isn't.

Our eyes meet.

Kind eyes. Warm. Unmistakable despite the disguise.

Anthony.

Paul's butler. Here. In my father's house. Dressed as a server and spilling champagne on me like he's just another clumsy employee.

Recognition floods through me so fast I feel dizzy. I start to open my mouth—

"You clumsy old fool." Prescott's voice cuts through the

moment like a blade. His face flushes red, veins standing out in his neck. "Do you have any idea how much that dress costs?"

Anthony bows his head, the picture of contrition. He pulls a napkin from his pocket and starts dabbing at the champagne spreading across my dress.

His hand brushes mine.

"Go to your room." The words are barely a breath. So quiet I almost think I imagined them.

Then he's stepping back, apologizing profusely in a voice that carries across the room—making a scene and drawing attention.

"Let's not make this worse." I place my hand on Prescott's arm before he can escalate further. Force a laugh that sounds almost genuine. "It's fine, darling. Accidents happen."

His jaw works. The calculation is visible—make a scene or let it go. Finally, he nods. Stiff. Angry. But controlled.

"I should change." I turn to him, widening my eyes in what I hope passes for apologetic. "I won't be long."

He frowns. Studies my face for signs of deception. I keep my expression neutral. Slightly embarrassed. Nothing more.

"Be quick about it." A command, not a request.

I nod. Start toward the stairs. Each step measured. Careful. Not too fast or he'll get suspicious.

But my pulse pounds so hard I can feel it in my throat. In my fingertips. In the champagne-soaked silk clinging to my skin.

The staircase stretches endlessly. I climb deliberately slowly, aware of eyes tracking my movement. Of Prescott watching from below. Of guests pretending not to stare while absolutely staring.

Finally, I reach the landing. Turn down the corridor toward my room.

The sounds of the party fade. Laughter and conversation give way to the muffled quiet of the private quarters.

I reach my door. My hand trembles as I turn the handle. Push it open.

Close it softly behind me.

For a moment, everything is still. The room is dark except for moonlight spilling through the windows. Shadows pool in corners. The air smells like the jasmine perfume I wore earlier. Like the champagne drying on my dress.

Then a shadow moves.

I freeze. Every muscle locks. My pulse roars in my ears.

From the darkest corner near my wardrobe, a figure emerges. Silent. Controlled. Like he's part of the darkness itself.

Paul.

He steps into the moonlight, and the breath leaves my lungs in a rush.

Months. It's been months since I've seen him. Since the engagement announcement, when everything changed.

His hair is different—dyed a mousy brown that washes out his features. Makes him forgettable. Colored contacts dim his eyes to a muddy hazel instead of the striking charcoal gray I remember.

But I know him. Would know him anywhere.

He's leaner. The athletic frame I remember has been honed to something harder. More dangerous. His suit—perfectly tailored, expensive—does nothing to hide the power coiled in his shoulders, his thighs.

My gaze drops to his hands. Those beautiful, capable hands that paint masterpieces. That touched me like I was art. They flex at his sides, fingers moving restlessly.

He's grown stubble. Just a shadow along his jaw, but it changes his face. Makes him look older. Rougher.

And his mouth. God, his mouth. Full lips pressed into a thin line of concentration. Lips that whispered poetry and filth against my skin. That made me come undone with words alone.

Every cell in my body recognizes him. Reaches for him. Like my soul knows his and is trying to bridge the distance.

"Paul." His name falls from my lips. Barely a breath. A prayer.

For a heartbeat, we just stare at each other. The space between us crackles with tension. With months of separation and desperate hope.

Then we're moving.

I don't remember deciding to go to him. Don't remember crossing the room. But suddenly we're colliding—a tangle of arms and desperate hands and mouths seeking mouths.

Paul wraps his arms around me, crushing me against his chest. I cling to him, fingers fisting in his jacket, pulling him closer, closer, never close enough.

He smells like paint and coffee and something uniquely him. The scent floods my senses, makes my eyes sting with tears.

"Vivianne." My name on his lips sounds like a benediction. Like salvation. His voice is thick, rough with emotion. "God, I've missed you."

I pull back just enough to see his face. To drink in every detail like I'm dying of thirst and he's water.

My hands come up, cupping his cheeks. The stubble is rough against my palms. Real. Solid. Here.

"You're here." The words shake. "You're really here."

His eyes—even dulled by contacts—burn with an intensity that steals my breath. One hand tangles in my hair, cradling my head. The other wraps around my waist, pulling me flush against him.

His pulse pounds against my chest. Racing. Matching my own frantic rhythm.

"I'm here, ma chérie." The endearment breaks something inside me. "I'm here."

Our lips meet.

The kiss is fire. Desperation. Months of need concentrated into this single point of contact.

His mouth moves against mine—urgent, hungry, claiming. I open for him, and he deepens the kiss immediately. His tongue sweeps into my mouth, tasting, exploring, reclaiming territory that's always been his.

I pour everything into the kiss. All my fear. All my hope. All the love I've carried like a torch through these endless months.

Paul matches me. His hands are everywhere—in my hair, on my waist, sliding up my ribs. Not sexual. Just desperate to touch. To confirm I'm real.

A low moan escapes my throat. Paul answers with a growl that vibrates through his chest into mine. His grip tightens. The hand in my hair tilts my head back, changing the angle, somehow making the kiss even deeper.

I can't breathe. Don't want to breathe. Just want this. Him. Us.

When we finally break apart, we're both gasping. Panting. Paul rests his forehead against mine, and for a long moment, we just breathe each other's air.

"I'm getting you out of here." His voice is low. Fierce. Each word a vow. "Tomorrow. I promise. I won't let you stay in this godforsaken place any longer."

Tears prick the corners of my eyes. Relief. Joy. Love. All of it overwhelming.

"I love you." The words spill out. "I love you so much."

His thumb brushes across my cheek, wiping away a tear I didn't realize had fallen. "I love you more, ma chérie. And I always will."

"How?" The question comes out shaky. Uncertain. "How will you save me? My father—he's... and Prescott—they watch every-thing. Every door. Every window. Every—"

"I have help." His hands frame my face, forcing me to meet his eyes. "You'll know when it's happening. But not tonight."

My pulse stutters. "Then why—" I pull back slightly. Confusion cutting through the relief. "Why are you here now? Why risk—"

"I need to know something."

The shift in his tone sends a chill down my spine. The fierce lover becomes something else. Something focused. Determined.

Mission-driven.

"What?" My frown deepens.

"I need to know where your father keeps the Swan."

The words land like a slap. Physical. Stunning.

My pulse stutters. Stops. Restarts at double time.

"Why?" The word barely makes it past my lips. "Why would you—"

"The Swan is more than a family heirloom." He's still holding my face, but his grip has changed. Less tender. More intense. "It was entrusted to your grandmother for safekeeping during the war. But it was never meant to be kept."

"I don't understand."

"It holds something. A secret. Information." His eyes search mine. "People are willing to kill for it. That's why it needs to be returned to its rightful owner."

"Returned?" The word tastes bitter. "You mean stolen."

He doesn't flinch. Doesn't look away. "I mean recovered."

I pull free from his grasp. Step back. The distance between us suddenly feels vast.

"You want to steal it." Not a question. A realization. "That's why you're here."

"No." He reaches for me, but I dodge his hand. "I'm here for you. Always for you. But Vivianne, that pendant—"

"Is my family's." The words come out sharp. Defensive. "It's been in our family for generations."

"It was never theirs to keep." His voice hardens. "Your grandfather—Henry Faulks—took it. Stole it from the woman it was entrusted to. Brigitte kept it hidden during the war, but it was supposed to be returned—"

"My grandmother." The pieces click together. Slowly. Painfully. "The letters. Anthony. The pendant in your painting—it matched her earrings because it was part of a set."

"Yes." He steps closer. I hold my ground. Barely. "Anthony entrusted the Swan to her before he went to war. She was supposed to keep it safe until he returned."

"But she married my grandfather instead."

"Yes."

The betrayal cuts deep. Not just Grandmother choosing the wrong man, but keeping something that wasn't hers. Building a legacy on stolen property.

Just like Father said—our family's wealth comes from making hard choices.

How many of those choices were theft?

"Paul." I press my hands to my face. "You can't—"

"I must." He closes the distance between us. His hands close over mine, pulling them away from my face. "Please understand. If the wrong people get their hands on it, they'll use it to destroy more than you can imagine."

"What's inside it?" I search his face. "What secret?"

"I don't know." The admission costs him. "But Anthony spent his entire life searching for it. And people have died trying to keep it hidden."

"And you think stealing it from my father will somehow make things right?" Anger flares hot in my chest. "That taking it will—"

"I think leaving it here will get you killed." His voice drops. Goes cold. "Your father knows someone's coming for it. He's preparing. And when they come, Vivianne, you'll be caught in the crossfire."

The words hit like ice water. "What?"

"Sentinel." He practically spits the word. "Your father is a part of their organization. Whatever they're doing, whatever power the Swan represents—they'll kill to keep it. And they won't care who gets hurt in the process."

My mind races. The conversations I've overheard. Father's paranoia. The increased security.

We're preparing for war.

"He said that." The words come out whisper-soft. "My father. He said we're preparing for war."

Paul's expression darkens. "Then we're running out of time. Vivianne, please. I'll get you out tomorrow. I swear it. But tonight, I need to know where the pendant is."

The choice crystallizes before me. Sharp. Impossible.

Trust Paul and betray my family.

Or protect my family's secrets and lose the only chance at freedom I have.

"And if I don't tell you?" My voice shakes.

His expression softens. Just a fraction. "Then I'll still save you, ma chérie. No matter what. But this may be our only chance to recover the Swan."

"I know where it is." The words come out slowly. "From when Father took me to the vault."

Paul goes very still. "He showed you?"

"Not intentionally." I sink onto the edge of my bed. My legs won't hold me anymore. "He was panicked. After your exhibit. After he saw the paintings, I followed him when he checked to see if the pendant was still safe."

"Where is it?"

I close my eyes. The journey unfolds in my mind. The hidden door. The secret corridors. The vault filled with stolen art and impossible treasures.

"It's here. In the house. Hidden behind the wine cellar." The words feel like betrayal leaving my lips. "Multiple locks. Retinal scans. Hidden doors. It's not just a vault—it's a fortress."

Paul kneels before me. Takes my hands in his. "Vivianne. I know this is difficult. But that necklace—"

"Is my family's legacy. I know." I look up, meet his eyes. "My father said those exact words. It's our legacy. And now you're asking me to help you steal it."

"I'm asking you to help me return what was stolen." He squeezes my hands. "Your family built their legacy on theft, ma chérie. On keeping something that was never theirs."

The truth of it sits heavy in my chest. All those conversations with Father about hard choices. About doing what's necessary. About family coming first.

How much of our wealth—our entire lives—is built on lies?

"My father—" I start, but Paul interrupts.

"Your father is playing a dangerous game. Sentinel, the Swan, whatever secrets it holds—it's bigger than family pride. Bigger than legacy." His voice drops. "The Swan isn't what you've been told. It's a key. One that could bring destruction."

My pulse quickens. "What do you mean?"

"His grip on my hands tightens. "Power like that, in the wrong hands, could tip the balance of nations."

"You're saying my father—"

"I'm saying he's willing to sacrifice everything. Your family. Your future. You." The words land like blows. "I know you don't want to believe that. But look at what's happening. He's not protecting you. He's using you."

Tears sting my eyes. Because he's right. I know he's right.

Father's obsession with the wedding. With Prescott. With producing an heir.

The increased security. The paranoia. The constant surveillance.

None of it is about protecting me. It's about protecting his secrets.

Paul cups my face. His thumb brushes away a tear. "I need you to trust me."

"You're asking me to betray my family." My voice breaks.

"I'm asking you to save them. Even if they don't see it that way."

The silence stretches. Heavy with the weight of impossible choices.

Father's voice echoes in my memory. *Sometimes love looks like cruelty. Sometimes the only way to keep someone alive is to let them believe you're the monster.*

What if he's been protecting something he doesn't understand? What if the legacy he's built is a poison that's been slowly killing us all?

"Okay." The word comes out small. Broken. But certain. "I believe you. What do you need me to do?"

"Tell me everything you remember from when you saw the Swan."

And I do. I tell him everything, down to the smallest detail.

Relief washes over his face. He pulls me close and presses a kiss to my forehead. "Just be ready. Tomorrow, everything changes."

I melt into his embrace. Let him hold me. Let myself believe—just for a moment—that everything will be okay.

But as his arms tighten around me, as his pulse beats against mine, I can't shake one terrible thought.

What if I'm choosing wrong?

What if trusting Paul means destroying everything?

And what if Father was right all along?

The questions spiral in my mind. Unanswerable. Terrifying.

Paul pulls back just enough to look at me. "I need to go. They'll be looking for you soon."

"Wait." I grab his hand. Hold tight. "Tomorrow. When you come for me. Will it be dangerous?"

He doesn't lie. Doesn't try to reassure me with false promises. "Yes."

"Will people get hurt?"

"I'll do everything in my power to prevent that." His eyes hold mine. Steady. Honest. "But I can't promise chaos won't happen."

I nod. Swallow hard. "Okay."

He leans in. Kisses me one more time. Soft. Tender. Goodbye and hello and promise all wrapped into one.

Then he's moving toward the window. Silent as shadow.

"Paul."

He pauses. Looks back.

"Don't die." The words come out fierce. Desperate. "Whatever happens tomorrow. Whatever it takes. Don't die."

His smile is sad. "Same to you, ma chérie."

Then he's gone. Out the window into darkness. Like he was never there.

I stand alone in my room. Champagne on my dress. The taste of him still on my lips.

Tomorrow, I either escape this cage or lose everything trying.

I move to the mirror. The woman staring back looks haunted. Desperate. Scared.

But beneath the fear, something else burns.

Hope.

Dangerous, fragile, impossible hope.

I change. Fix my hair. Arrange my face into the mask I've perfected over these endless months.

Then I go back downstairs.

Back to the party.

Back to playing the role of the perfect bride.

For one more night.

TWENTY-FIVE

Vivianne: The Wedding Day

FIVE IN THE MORNING, AND I HAVEN'T CLOSED MY EYES ONCE.

The taste of Paul's kiss still lingers on my lips, a phantom warmth that makes everything else feel cold by comparison. My fingers drift to my mouth, tracing where his were just hours ago.

Was he really here? Did he really promise to come for me, or have I finally cracked under the pressure, my mind conjuring rescue where none exists?

No. The champagne stain on my discarded dress proves it was real. He was here. He's coming.

Today.

I sit at my window, knees drawn to my chest, watching the estate wake beneath a sky bleeding from black to bruised purple. The gardens spread below like a battlefield preparing for war—which isn't far from the truth. White chairs arranged in perfect rows, hundreds of them, each one a witness to my upcoming execution. The altar stands at the far end, draped in white silk and roses, looking more like a guillotine than a place where love should bloom.

A security guard passes beneath my window, his flashlight

cutting through the pre-dawn gloom. Then another. And another. Donovan Price has them doing rounds every fifteen minutes now instead of every hour. Father's paranoia has infected everyone, turning our home into a fortress.

Or a prison.

I pull my hidden notebook from behind the radiator, its pages worn soft from my desperate sketching. The pencil trembles in my hand as I flip to a fresh page. I need to capture it before the memory fades—the Swan, as I saw it that night Father dragged me to the vault.

My pencil moves, recreating the massive ruby from memory. The size of a quail's egg, Paul had said, but that doesn't capture its presence. It had seemed alive in that glass case, pulsing with secrets and old pain. The gold setting, intricate as lace, delicate as spider silk, but somehow strong enough to bear the weight of all that blood-colored stone.

But it's what lies within the ruby that haunts me.

The swan itself, frozen inside the jewel's heart. Not carved, not painted—a flaw in the stone that nature shaped into something impossible. Wings spread wide, neck extended, forever suspended in that moment between earth and sky. Between bondage and freedom.

Like me.

I add shadows, depth, trying to capture how the light had bent through the stone, how the swan had seemed to move when Father lifted the pendant. My grandmother wore this once. Young Brigitte, in love with Anthony, who became Merlin, before my grandfather stole both her and the necklace. Building our family's empire on theft and betrayal.

The pencil stills.

Is that what I'm doing now? Betraying my family? Or am I finally breaking the chain of women in this family who surrendered to men who saw them as possessions?

The first delivery truck rumbles up the drive, its headlights sweeping across my window. Four forty-five. Earlier than expected. I lean forward, studying it in the growing light. "Celestial Catering" painted on the side in elegant script. Then another van—"Paradise Florals." Then another. And another.

Too many.

We're having five hundred guests, yes, but this is excessive even by Father's standards. Seven vans. Three trucks. More arriving.

My pulse begins to race.

I flip back through my notebook, past sketches of Paul's hands, his eyes, the way he looked at me in that garden in Paris before everything went wrong. Past drawings of escape routes I'll never use, floor plans of the house with all its secret passages. I find the page I'm looking for—my grandmother's face, drawn from memory and old photographs.

She was beautiful once. Really beautiful, not just the faded prettiness of old age. In the photos from before her marriage, she glowed. There was a wildness in her eyes, a freedom that got slowly extinguished year by year until only shadows remained.

I've read more of Anthony's letters hidden throughout her room. Tucked behind picture frames, sewn into the lining of old purses, pressed between pages of books she knew my grandfather would never read. Love letters that burn with passion and promise, each one a small rebellion she managed to keep.

"My dearest Brigitte," one had read. "Every sunrise I think of you. Every sunset, I mourn another day apart. But this war will end, my darling. All wars do. And when it does, I'll come for you. I'll cross oceans, I'll move mountains. Nothing will keep me from you. Not time, not distance, not the devils that walk this earth in uniform. You are my Paris, my freedom, my home. Wait for me. Just wait for me."

But she hadn't waited. Or maybe she had, and he never

came. Or maybe my grandfather made sure he couldn't come, the way Father is making sure Paul can't come for me now.

Except Paul is different.

The door to my room opens without warning. I barely manage to shove the notebook under my pillow before Mrs. Holloway enters with an army of stylists behind her.

"Time to begin, miss." The sorrow she tries to hide bleeds through anyway. She's been with this family long enough to know what this day really means.

The stylists descend like vultures—cheerful, chattering vultures who seem genuinely excited about transforming me into the perfect bride. They arrange their tools of torture across my vanity: curling irons that will burn my rebellion into submission, makeup brushes that will paint over my despair, hairpins that will pierce through any remaining hope.

"Such beautiful skin." One coos, running fingers along my cheek. "Like porcelain."

Yes, I think. *Porcelain. Beautiful, delicate, empty. Easy to shatter.*

"And this hair!" Another lifts the heavy mass of it. "We'll do an elegant updo, very classical. Mr. Harrington will love it."

Mr. Harrington—Prescott—will love it. Not a single person asks what I might love. But then, dolls don't get preferences.

They sit me in the chair, and the mirror shows them beginning to erase me. Foundation to cover the shadows under my eyes from sleepless nights. Concealer to hide the place where I've been biting my lip bloody with anxiety. Blush to approximate the glow of a happy bride.

Outside, more vehicles arrive. A van with no logo—suspicious. Two men in catering uniforms who move with too much precision, too much awareness. Not caterers at all.

Hope blooms in my chest, dangerous as a flame near gasoline.

"Hold still, dear." The makeup artist chides as I crane to see out the window. "We need these lashes to be perfect."

Perfect. Everything must be perfect for my sale—no, my wedding. Must remember to use the right words, even in my own mind. Father has ears everywhere, and sometimes I wonder if he can hear my thoughts, too.

Mrs. Holloway hovers near the door, ostensibly supervising but really standing guard. Her eyes meet mine in the mirror, and it's there—she knows something. Maybe not the specifics, but she knows today is different. A tension in her shoulders, a watchfulness that wasn't there during yesterday's preparations.

"Your grandmother—" She speaks suddenly, causing the stylists to pause. "—would want you to have this."

She pulls something from her pocket—a small silver hair comb, art deco style, with tiny sapphires that match my earrings. My grandmother's earrings.

"She wore it at her wedding." Mrs. Holloway ignores the stylists' protests as she slides it into my half-finished updo. "Said it was her 'something blue.' Though between you and me, miss, I think she'd understand if you decided you needed something else. Something... different."

Our eyes meet again. She knows. Somehow, she knows.

"Thank you." The whisper is all I can manage.

The stylists resume their work, chattering about the weather (perfect), the flowers (exquisite), the reception menu (divine). Their words wash over me like white noise as the estate transforms through my window. The sun is properly rising now, painting everything gold and pink, making it all look like a fairytale.

But I know better. Fairytales have happy endings. This is something else entirely.

Unless Paul keeps his promise.

Unless I'm brave enough to run when the moment comes.

The stylists step back, admiring their work. In the mirror, a perfect bride stares back—beautiful and empty as a museum piece. But underneath the makeup and the carefully arranged hair, my pulse beats wild as a caged bird's.

Today, one way or another, this cage opens.

Today, I either fly free or die trying.

Because I've decided: I won't say "I do." No matter what Father threatens, no matter what Prescott promises, no matter if Paul doesn't come. I won't speak those words that will seal my fate.

The swan in the ruby knew what I'm only now learning—sometimes being frozen between two states is better than surrendering to the wrong one. Sometimes the flight itself, even if it never ends, is better than the cage.

More vehicles arrive below. More strangers in uniforms, more boxes being unloaded, more preparation for this grand performance where I'm both the star and the sacrifice.

But they don't know the script has changed.

They don't know the cavalry is already here, hidden among the caterers and florists and photographers.

They don't know that Paul de Gaulle keeps his promises.

The stylists pack up their tools, pronouncing me ready for the next phase—the dress. But I'm not ready. I'll never be ready for the dress that will be my shroud, for the veil that will be my blindfold, for the rings that will be my shackles.

Yet I smile at them, thank them, play the part of the grateful bride.

Because in a few hours, when Prescott waits at that altar and Father walks me down that aisle, when five hundred of society's finest gather to watch me be sold—

That's when the real show begins.

TWENTY-SIX

Paul: Operation Swan Song

Four-thirty AM. The farmhouse kitchen smells of gun oil and bitter coffee.

I've been awake all night, memorizing every detail of the estate's layout until the blueprints are burned into my retinas. Every door, every window, every possible entry and exit point. But it's the path to the vault that I've traced a hundred times with my finger—wine cellar, 1947 Château d'Yquem section, hidden door, corridor, biometric lock. Vivianne's whispered instructions replay in my mind on an endless loop.

The Guardian team moves around me, transforming the rustic space into a tactical command center. Jenny checks her camera equipment one final time—the Nikon that conceals a Glock 19, two spare magazines, and a ceramic knife that won't trigger metal detectors. Mac and Blaze inspect their security uniforms, ensuring every detail is perfect down to the company logos and ID badges that Mitzy forged yesterday. John and Brett do the same with their catering company attire. Charlie adjusts her florist's apron, tucking communication equipment into the pockets.

"Stop pacing." Merlin doesn't look up from the EMP watch he's examining. "You're making everyone nervous."

"I'm not pacing." But I am. Back and forth across the worn wooden floors, unable to stay still when every cell in my body screams to move, to act, to get to Vivianne now.

"You're going to wear a groove in the floor." He looks up from the watch. "And that's coming from someone who once watched you stand perfectly still for six hours while casing the Louvre."

"That was different."

"How?"

"It just was." I can't explain that stealing paintings never made my hands shake like this. Never made my chest feel like it might explode from the pressure building inside. This isn't a heist —it's everything.

Jenny claps her hands once, sharp as a gunshot. "Circle up. Final briefing."

We gather around the table where she's spread out aerial photos of the estate. Red circles mark entry points. Blue lines show patrol routes. Green dots indicate camera positions. It looks like a battle plan because that's what it is.

"Team One." She points to John and Brett. "You're in with the catering company at 0500. Kitchen access, staff areas. Your job is to map internal movement patterns and identify any additional security we missed."

They nod. Both ex-military, they've done this type of reconnaissance before.

"Team Two." She indicates Charlie. "Florist delivery at 0515. You'll have access to the main house, specifically the bridal suite. Make contact with the target, assess her condition, and signal if there are any complications."

Charlie grins, checking the small camera hidden in her

bouquet holder. Despite her warm demeanor, she has a gift for reading situations quickly. "What counts as complications?"

"If she's drugged, restrained, or injured. If there's a guard posted inside her room. If she shows any hesitation about the extraction."

My jaw clenches at the word *drugged*. The thought of Prescott or her father—

"Team Three." Jenny continues, and I force myself to focus. "Mac and Blaze with the security company at 0530. Blend in with the existing detail, redirect actual security when the extraction begins, and make sure our exit routes stay clear."

"What about Donovan Price?" The question comes out sharp. "He's ex-Delta. He'll spot operators immediately if they don't fit."

"Which is why they're going in as legitimate last-minute additions from a regional security firm." Jenny's tone is patient but firm. "Price will read them as hired muscle for crowd control. As long as they stay professional and don't give him reason to look closer, we're good."

"We've worked events like this before." Mac nods. "Big society weddings love to over-staff security to impress guests."

"And me?" Sam asks from where he's been standing quietly by the window.

"You're our eyes." Jenny turns to him. "Mobile surveillance in vehicle two with Forest. You'll be monitoring all camera feeds, coordinating timing, and running interference if anything goes sideways. Forest stays in the van—you're too..."

"What?" Forest asks.

"Big." The word sparks a round of laughter. "Quiet down." She gives her team a look, but the corners of her mouth twitch with amusement. "You know what I mean. If Donovan Price or any of the other ex-military security see you, they'll make you instantly."

Forest doesn't argue. He knows his size and distinctive features make him memorable—exactly what we don't need on a covert operation.

Jenny turns to Mitzy, who's been quietly working on something that looks like a jewelry box filled with mechanical bees. "Technical support?"

Mitzy holds up one of the drones—no bigger than an actual bumblebee but gleaming with tiny sensors and cameras. "I'll deploy these in waves. First set at 0545 to map current security positions. Second wave at ceremony start to create blind spots in their camera coverage. Each bee can block a camera for approximately ninety seconds before needing to relocate."

"How many do we have?"

"Forty-seven operational units." She demonstrates on her tablet, showing how the bees will swarm specific cameras in sequence. "I can create a rolling blackout effect—cameras going down and coming back up in a pattern that looks like technical glitches rather than sabotage."

"Brilliant." Merlin murmurs, genuinely impressed. "The vault security?"

"The bees can handle the motion sensors in the corridor." Mitzy confirms. "But the biometric lock is isolated from the main system. That's where the EMP comes in."

Merlin holds up the watch—innocuous-looking, expensive but not ostentatious. "Thirty-second window once activated. The electromagnetic pulse will disrupt all electronics within a ten-foot radius, but it only works once. You need to be in position before you trigger it."

"Which brings us to extraction logistics." Jenny's gaze moves between me and Merlin. "Paul and Merlin, you two are going for the Swan. The vault is your priority. The rest of us handle Vivianne's extraction."

I nod. This was always the plan—the only plan that made sense. We can't leave the Swan behind, and I'm the only one besides Vivianne who knows where the vault is and how to access it. Merlin has the tools and experience to back me up. Together, we'll crack whatever security we encounter.

"Timing is critical." Jenny continues. "The ceremony starts at 1100. Charlie signals us when Vivianne is moved from her suite to the staging area. That's our window—everyone will be focused on the bride, the processional, the ceremony itself."

"How long do we have?" Merlin asks.

"From ceremony start to extraction point, I'm estimating twenty to thirty minutes before anyone realizes she's gone. Maybe less if Prescott or her father check on her early."

"The vault is in the wine cellar, correct?" Mac studies the blueprints.

"Yes." I trace the route again. "Accessible through the service corridors. Merlin and I will enter through the kitchen with Team One, then split off while everyone's attention is on the ceremony."

"And the Swan itself?" Blaze leans forward. "How big, how heavy, how are you transporting it?"

Merlin pulls out a specially designed case—foam-lined, temperature controlled, with built-in shock absorption. "The ruby is approximately four inches in diameter, maybe a pound in weight. This case will protect it and mask any electronic signature it might have."

"Once you have it, exfil is through the south service entrance." Jenny points to the map. "CJ will have vehicle three waiting there. Straight to the airport, private charter already arranged."

"What about Vivianne?" The question comes out before I can stop it, even though I know the answer.

"She goes out the north side with Charlie and me. We'll have her in a photographer's van—I've got credentials to be on-site shooting detail for a society magazine. Once we've got her, we head straight for the second airport. Different location, different flight plan."

It makes sense. Split the targets, split the risk. If one team gets caught, the other still has a chance.

"Questions?" Jenny asks.

"Yeah." Blaze crosses his arms. "What happens if Prescott or Donovan figure out what's happening before we're clear?"

"Then Mac and I become very loud distractions." Her voice is cool. Steady. "We can cause chaos, buy you time to get gone."

"And if that doesn't work?" John asks.

"Then we adapt." Jenny's tone goes flat. "This is a snatch-and-grab with high-value assets. Everyone in this room knows things can go sideways fast. That's why we have contingencies, escape routes, and more firepower than we should need." She looks around the table. "We're professionals. We extract the targets, we get out clean. Understood?"

A chorus of affirmatives.

"Good. Teams One and Two roll in thirty minutes. Everyone else, final equipment check."

The kitchen erupts into controlled chaos. Weapons concealed, uniforms adjusted one final time, comm checks performed. I pull Merlin aside.

"The path to the vault." I keep my voice low, pulling out the tablet with all my notes. "One more time."

He takes it, scrolling through my obsessively detailed annotations. "Wine cellar, northeast corner. The 1947 Château d'Yquem section—"

"Third rack from the door. The bottle second from the left triggers the mechanism."

"Hidden door opens to a corridor approximately forty feet

long. Motion sensors that Mitzy's bees will handle. Biometric lock at the end."

"Which you'll bypass with the EMP."

"Thirty-second window." He confirms. "I'll need you to work the manual override while the system's down. Can you do it?"

Can I pick a lock while my pulse is trying to beat out of my chest and every instinct screams at me to find Vivianne instead? "Yes."

He studies me for a long moment. "She matters to you."

"She's everything."

"They will get her out." He squeezes my shoulder. "And we'll get the Swan. Both. No choosing, no compromise."

On Jenny's signal, John and Brett head out first, their catering van disappearing down the pre-dawn road. Fifteen minutes later, Charlie follows in her florist truck, humming along to the radio like she's just making a delivery.

The rest of us load into our respective vehicles. I'm with Merlin in CJ's "plumbing van," which is actually a mobile surveillance center with monitors lining one wall and communication equipment taking up another. Jenny and Mac take the photographer's van. Blaze and Sam head out in the security company vehicle with Forest hidden in the back with all the monitoring equipment.

As we pull onto the road, the sun breaks over the hills, bathing everything in golden light.

"Team One in position." John's voice crackles through comms fifteen minutes later.

"Team Two arriving now." Charlie reports. "Flowers are gorgeous if I do say so myself."

On the monitors, her van pulls up to the service entrance. Guards check her credentials, wave her through. She disappears inside.

"Team Three approaching." Mac's voice. Our security van

pulls up to the main gate. More credential checks. Professional nods exchanged. They're in.

"Technical support deploying first wave." Mitzy announces from her remote location. The monitors fill with tiny dots as her bee drones spread across the estate like a mechanical swarm.

Jenny's voice cuts through the chatter: "All teams, this is Lead. Confirm ready status."

"Team One ready."

"Team Two in position, visual on target's suite."

"Team Three posted and monitoring."

"Surveillance ready." Sam confirms. "Forest has eyes on all feeds."

"Vault team?" Jenny asks.

Merlin looks at me. I nod.

"Ready."

"Copy all. We are go for Operation Swan Song." Jenny's voice is steady, professional. "Execute on my mark at ceremony start. Stay sharp, stay safe, and let's bring them home."

My hand goes to the tactical vest under my jacket. The weight of the Glock is reassuring. The lock picks in my sleeve, the smoke grenades in my pockets, the knife in my boot—all tools I hope I won't need but won't hesitate to use.

Merlin checks his own equipment one final time, then reaches into his jacket and pulls out something unexpected—a small pistol, vintage but well-maintained.

"Just in case."

"You hate guns."

"I hate losing family more." His faded blue eyes meet mine. "We're getting her out, and we're getting the Swan. Trust the team to do their part. We do ours."

On the monitors, guests begin arriving. Expensive cars, designer clothes, false smiles. Somewhere in that house, Vivianne is trapped in a wedding dress, preparing for a ceremony that will never happen.

Because we're about to steal both the bride and the treasure.

My pulse pounds as I check my watch. Two hours until the ceremony starts.

Two hours until we burn this whole charade to the ground.

TWENTY-SEVEN

Vivianne: The Gilded Cage

THE STYLIST, A SEVERE WOMAN NAMED CLAUDETTE, SMELLS OF hairspray and speaks only in commands. "Sit. Don't move. Tilt your head." She works in silence, transforming my long curls into an elaborate updo that requires forty-seven pins. I count each one as it scrapes against my scalp, a small rebellion that no one can take from me.

The makeup artist follows. Genevieve is gentler, but her tools are just as ruthless. Foundation that covers the circles under my eyes—evidence of three sleepless nights. Concealer for the bruise on my jaw from where Father grabbed me during our last argument. Powder to set it all in place, creating a mask of porcelain perfection.

"You have lovely bone structure." Genevieve tilts my chin to catch the light. "Like a painting."

I am a painting. Static, silent, decorative. Something to hang on Prescott's wall and show off to his colleagues.

She brushes shadow across my eyelids—champagne and gold to match the wedding colors. Liner that makes my eyes look larger, more innocent. Mascara that weighs down my lashes until blinking feels like an effort. Rouge on my cheeks. Gloss on my lips that tastes like chemicals and lies.

"There." She steps back to admire her work. "Beautiful."

The woman in the mirror is unrecognizable. She's perfect. Flawless. Empty.

Mrs. Holloway arrives as Genevieve is packing her brushes. The housekeeper who's known me since childhood looks at my transformed face, and her eyes go bright with unshed tears.

"Oh, Miss Vivianne." The whisper catches.

"Don't." I keep my voice soft. "If she cries, I'll break, and I can't break. Not yet."

She sets down the breakfast tray—croissants, fruit, coffee—but my stomach revolts at the sight. How am I supposed to eat when I can barely breathe?

"You should try." Mrs. Holloway slides the tray closer. "It's going to be a long day."

The longest. The last day I'll be myself before becoming Mrs. Prescott Harrington.

I force down half a croissant and immediately regret it. My stomach churns, threatening to expel even that small amount. I grip the edge of the vanity, breathing slowly through my nose until the nausea passes.

The knock on the door makes me flinch.

"Miss Faulks?" Donovan Price's voice carries through the wood—professional, emotionless. "Security briefing."

Mrs. Holloway opens the door. Donovan steps inside, his military bearing evident in every movement. He's efficient, thorough, and completely loyal to my father.

"The ceremony will begin at eleven hundred hours." He consults his tablet. "Security perimeter is established. Guests will pass through metal detectors at the gate. Your processional will start from the second-floor landing, proceed down the main staircase, through the gallery, and out to the garden pavilion."

He continues listing protocols—where I'll stand, when I'll move, how many steps from the house to the altar. Seventy-three, apparently. I'll be counting every one.

"Additional security personnel arrived this morning. Contract staff to supplement our team for crowd control. All properly vetted."

I nod mechanically. Like I care. What does it matter? Prison guards by any other name.

"Any questions?"

"No."

He leaves. Mrs. Holloway squeezes my shoulder once before following him out. The door clicks shut, and I'm alone again with my reflection and my racing pulse.

I don't know how long I sit there—minutes? hours?—before Father arrives.

He doesn't knock. Never has. This is his house, his domain, and I am simply another possession within it.

"Stand up."

I obey, my legs unsteady beneath the silk robe I'm wearing over my undergarments.

Father circles me like a buyer inspecting livestock. His cold blue eyes catalog every detail, searching for flaws. "Remember what's at stake today. This marriage secures everything—the company, our position, our future. Your duty is to smile, say your vows, and produce an heir within the year."

My hands clench at my sides, hidden in the folds of my robe. An heir. I'm nothing more than a broodmare.

"The Harringtons expect certain... standards." He continues his slow circuit. "You will be a perfect wife. Gracious, elegant, obedient. You will reflect well on this family. Any deviation from that—any embarrassment, any scandal—will have conse-quences."

I know what those consequences are. He's made them abundantly clear. Complete financial ruin. Social destruction. Criminal charges fabricated from thin air. My father has enough money and influence to bury me so deep I'd never see daylight again.

"Do you understand?"

"Yes, Father."

"Good." He moves toward the door, then pauses. "Your mother would have been proud."

The lie is so audacious it steals my breath. My mother would have burned this house down before allowing this.

The door closes behind him with a finality that echoes in my bones.

I'm shaking now, a fine tremor that starts in my hands and spreads through my entire body. I sink onto the chaise, pressing my palms against my thighs to make it stop, but it only gets worse.

Another knock. More measured, almost apologetic.

Marcus enters with a bottle of champagne on a silver tray. "From Mr. Harrington." His voice is quiet, his expression carefully neutral.

There's a card tucked beside the bottle. I open it with trembling fingers.

Can't wait to unwrap my gift tonight. Your innocence will look beautiful surrendered on silk sheets. —P

The vulgarity of it, the entitled cruelty, makes bile rise in my throat. I lunge for the bathroom, barely making it to the toilet before I'm sick. The half-croissant, the coffee, everything comes back up until I'm dry-heaving over the porcelain.

When I finally emerge, mouth rinsed, Marcus is still there. He pours the champagne down the sink.

"I took the liberty." His voice is soft. Our gazes meet for just a moment—a flash of sympathy quickly hidden. Even the staff knows what kind of man I'm being sold to.

"Thank you." The whisper is all I can manage.

He nods and leaves me alone again.

***

The wedding dress arrives at nine-thirty.

It's a masterpiece of couture—French lace, Italian silk, Austrian crystals. The bodice is structured like armor, with boning that will hold me rigid and upright even if I wanted to collapse. The skirt is layers upon layers of tulle and organza, so voluminous that I'll need help walking. The train is twelve feet long, heavy with beadwork that catches the light like captured stars.

It's suffocating perfection.

The seamstress and her assistant help me into it, their hands quick and efficient as they button the forty-seven closures running up my spine. Another number to count. Another way to be trapped—I'll never get out of this dress without help.

The corset cinches tight, forcing my posture straight, my breathing shallow. The weight of the skirt pulls at my hips. The sleeves—delicate lace—restrict the movement of my arms. Every inch of this gown is designed to constrain, to transform me into an ornamental object.

"Stunning." The seamstress steps back, declaring her work complete.

The woman in the full-length mirror is a stranger—a beautiful, expensive stranger being prepared for sacrifice.

My grandmother's earrings are the final touch. Ruby drops that match the necklace I should be wearing—the one currently locked in the vault below my feet. The Swan. The secret I whispered to Paul in the dark.

I fasten the earrings with shaking hands, the weight of them pulling at my lobes. These, at least, are mine. A piece of my grandmother, a connection to something real in this pageant of lies.

I move to the window, the dress rustling like dead leaves with each step.

The garden has been transformed. White chairs arranged in perfect rows, hundreds of them, creating an aisle down the center. The pavilion at the end is draped in silk and flowers. A string quartet tuning their instruments in the corner. Waiters setting up champagne stations. Security personnel positioned at every exit.

It's beautiful. Grotesque. A gilded cage dressed up as a fairy tale.

The guests are starting to arrive. Luxury cars pull up the drive, disgorging women in designer gowns and men in bespoke suits. Society's elite, here to witness my destruction and call it a celebration.

Another knock. Different this time—lighter, more cheerful.

"Florist delivery!" A woman's voice calls.

I turn from the window as a woman enters carrying an enormous arrangement of white peonies and roses. She's perhaps thirty, with bouncing blonde hair, vivacious blue eyes, and an easy smile that seems out of place in this house of cold perfection.

"Vivianne Faulks?" She clearly knows who I am.

"Yes."

"I'm Charlie. Margaux sent me to do the final floral setup for the bridal suite and to make sure your bouquet is perfect." She sets down the arrangement and pulls out a smaller bouquet— white roses, lily of the valley, sprigs of rosemary. "Something old, something new, something borrowed, something blue. The blue is subtle—tiny forget-me-nots hidden in the center."

Forget-me-not. An odd choice for a wedding bouquet. Almost like a message.

Charlie moves around the room, adjusting flower arrangements, checking that everything is perfect. But her eyes—her eyes are taking in everything. The locked door to the hallway. The window overlooking the garden. The layout of the suite.

She returns to where I stand, making a show of adjusting my bouquet. Her voice drops to barely a whisper. "Your friend sent me. The one who appreciates art." Her eyes meet mine meaningfully. "He asked me to make sure you still want what he's offering."

Paul. She means Paul.

My breath catches. My hands tremble around the bouquet stems.

"I need to hear you say it." Charlie's fingers stay busy with the flowers, her face angled away from the door. "Do you want out? Because once this starts, there's no going back."

Everything in me screams yes. Every cell, every breath, every desperate hope I've been trying to bury.

"Yes." The word escapes as a whisper. "God, yes. Please."

Charlie's smile doesn't change, but something shifts in her eyes—determination, satisfaction. "Good. When the ceremony starts, stay alert. No matter what happens, trust the chaos. Can you do that?"

I nod, not trusting my voice.

"You're braver than you know." She squeezes my hand once —brief, reassuring. Then, in a normal voice, "Everything looks beautiful. You make a stunning bride."

"Thank you." The words come from somewhere far away.

She hands me a business card—"Margaux's Floral Designs"—though we both know I'll never need it. Then she's gone, leaving only the scent of flowers and that dangerous, brilliant spark of hope burning in my chest.

THE FOLLOWING HOURS BLUR TOGETHER. THE WEDDING coordinator arrives, fussing over my dress, my hair, my posture. Photographers taking pre-ceremony shots. The house fills with noise—voices, laughter, the clink of champagne glasses.

Through it all, I'm numb. Floating outside my body, watching this happen to someone else.

At ten-forty-five, Marcus appears at my door. "It's time."

Something lurches in my chest. Too soon. Not ready. Will never be ready.

He escorts me downstairs to where Father waits at the base of the grand staircase. Behind him, the gallery stretches—guests assembled, waiting for the show to begin.

Prescott's mother stands near the door in ice-blue silk, her sharp eyes assessing me like I'm a piece of furniture she's not sure will match her décor. She nods once—approval or dismissal, I can't tell.

The wedding coordinator fusses with my train, arranging it just so. She checks her watch, her clipboard, her earpiece. Everything must be perfect. Everything must go according to plan.

Father offers his arm. His grip is iron as my hand settles in the crook of his elbow.

"Don't disappoint me." Quiet. Final.

I want to scream. To run. To set this entire house ablaze and dance in the ashes.

Instead, I nod.

We walk through the gallery—past the Monet I used to dream in front of as a child, past the sculpture of Diana the Huntress that Mother always loved, past the window seat where I'd read on rainy afternoons. Every step takes me further from the girl I was, closer to the woman I'll be forced to become.

The processional doors open. Sunlight streams in, bright and merciless.

Hundreds of faces turned toward me. Prescott at the altar in his custom tuxedo, that predatory smile fixed in place. The officiant with his book of vows. The string quartet with their bows poised.

Someone signals. The musicians lift their instruments.

The first notes of the wedding march begin.

Father pulls me forward.

And I step toward my own execution.

TWENTY-EIGHT

Paul: The Vault

THE MONITOR FILLS WITH WHITE SILK AND IMPRISONED BEAUTY.

Vivianne descends the grand staircase, and even through Jenny's button camera feed, she takes my breath away. The wedding dress is a masterpiece of perfection—countless pearls, French lace, a train that trails behind her like chains made of cloud. But it's her face that stops me cold.

Blank. Empty.

Like she's already gone somewhere deep inside where they can't reach her.

"Target is mobile." Jenny's voice crackles through comms, professional and detached. "Moving toward the garden ceremony site."

Target. Not Vivianne. Not the woman I love. *Target.*

"That's our cue." Merlin is already moving toward the van's rear doors.

On the monitor, Vivianne's father takes her arm. His grip is possessive, fingers digging into the silk at her elbow hard enough that she winces.

"Paul." CJ doesn't look away from his screens. "Remember the plan."

The plan. Right. The plan where I crawl through dirt and wine cellars while the woman I love is being sold off fifty meters away.

"Security is shifting to ceremony positions." Sam's voice cuts through. "Donovan's moving his primary team to the garden perimeter. You've got your window."

Merlin cracks the van doors and peers out. We're parked behind a maintenance shed, technically on the neighboring property but with a clear line of sight to the estate's service areas. The morning sun casts long shadows that we'll use for cover.

"Mitzy, we need those blind spots."

"Already on it." Her voice is calm, focused. "Bumbles deploying to cameras three, seven, and twelve. You'll have a rolling blackout—ninety seconds per camera, sequenced to give you continuous coverage."

On another monitor, the garden fills with guests. Five hundred of the elite, here to witness what they think is a fairy tale but is actually a public execution. Prescott stands at the altar, adjusting his cufflinks with the satisfied air of a man about to receive a long-awaited package.

I'm going to kill him. Not today, not during the mission, but someday when he least expects it, I'm going to—

"Move." Merlin's command cuts through my dark thoughts, and we're out of the van, running low across the manicured lawn.

The grass is still wet with dew, soaking through my shoes, making each step treacherous. We reach the first checkpoint—a decorative wall that separates the service area from the main grounds. I boost Merlin up and over, then follow, landing silently on the other side.

"Camera twelve going dark in three... two... one..." Mitzy counts down.

We sprint across the exposed ground, reaching the shelter of a delivery truck just as she announces, "Camera twelve back online. Camera seven going dark now."

It's like playing the world's most dangerous game of red light, green light. Move, freeze, move again. My pulse pounds so loud I'm sure the guards will hear it.

Through my earpiece, the wedding march begins. Strings and organ, traditional and suffocating.

"Bride entering garden area." Charlie's voice. "She looks... fuck, she looks like she's walking to her execution."

I force myself not to think about it. Can't think about it. One mission at a time.

We reach the wine cellar's service entrance—a simple wooden door that looks like it hasn't been updated since the house was built. But I know better. The wood is just a façade. Underneath is reinforced steel, and the lock...

I kneel, pulling out my picks. It's a Fichet Primlock, French-made, seven pins, false gates on three of them. Not impossible, but not simple either.

"You've got ninety seconds before the patrol comes around." Merlin keeps watch, voice low.

My hands steady as I work. This is what I know, what I'm good at. The picks slide in, feeling for each pin's position. First one sets. Second. The third is sticky—false gate trying to catch my pick.

"Sixty seconds."

Third pin sets. Fourth. Fifth is another false gate.

"Processional beginning." Jenny's report. "All eyes on the bride."

Vivianne walking down that aisle, every step taking her

further from freedom. My hand trembles, nearly dropping the tension wrench.

Sixth pin. Seventh. The lock turns with a satisfying click.

We slip inside, closing the door just as footsteps round the corner outside. The wine cellar is exactly what you'd expect from old money—stone walls that breathe history, perfect temperature control, thousands upon thousands of bottles that represent more wealth than most people see in a lifetime.

But we're not here for the wine.

"1947 Château d'Yquem." I orient myself, voice barely a whisper. According to Vivianne, it's in the third row, halfway down.

We move through the cellar like ghosts, our footsteps silent on the ancient stones. The bottles seem to watch us pass—silent witnesses to another crime in a house built on them. First row: Burgundies. Second row: Bordeaux. Third row...

There. A section dedicated to dessert wines, and among them, the distinctive gold labels of Château d'Yquem. The 1947 vintage sits in its own subsection, twelve bottles that would sell for more than a small fortune if they ever reached auction.

"Which one?" Merlin asks.

I close my eyes, replaying Vivianne's whispered instructions. "Third from the left, second shelf from the bottom."

But as I reach for it, the bottle isn't quite aligned with the others. It's tilted, just slightly, like someone has been here recently.

"Groom saying his vows." The report crackles through comms. The ceremony is moving fast. Too fast.

I grasp the bottle and pull. Nothing happens.

"Turn it." Merlin suggests.

I rotate the bottle clockwise. A soft click, then grinding as mechanisms struggle to engage. The entire wine rack shudders, then swings inward on hidden hinges, revealing darkness beyond.

The smell hits immediately—stale air, dust, and something else. Secrets left too long in the dark.

Merlin produces a small flashlight, its beam cutting through the gloom to reveal a wooden door, exactly as Vivianne described. But she was wrong about one thing—it's not just old, it's ancient.

"Bride's turn for vows coming up." Jenny again. "Security is completely focused on the ceremony."

Merlin kneels at the lock—a masterpiece of 19th-century craftsmanship that would be in a museum if anyone knew it existed. Seven levers, each one requiring precise pressure and timing.

"This is going to take time." He mutters, pulling out a set of picks that look as old as the lock itself.

"We don't have time." Through the comm, the priest's voice comes through, faint but clear: "Do you, Vivianne Amelie Faulks..."

"Then stop talking and let me work."

I pace the small space, three steps one way, three steps back. Every second that passes is another second closer to Vivianne being legally bound to that monster. My hands clench and unclench. I should be up there. Should be stopping this.

"First lever." Merlin announces quietly. Then, "Second."

"...take this man to be your lawfully wedded husband..."

"Third lever. Fourth."

"...to have and to hold from this day forward..."

"Fifth. Sixth is being stubborn."

My fist connects with the stone wall, pain shooting up my arm. "Hurry."

"Violence won't make this go faster." But his hands move more quickly now. "Sixth. And... seventh."

The lock disengages with a sound like a sigh, and the door swings open.

The corridor beyond is exactly as Vivianne described—narrow, maybe three feet wide, with modern additions that look obscene against the ancient stone. Motion sensors line the walls at regular intervals, their red lights blinking like eyes in the darkness.

"Mitzy." I speak into the comm. "We need those bees now."

"Already ahead of you. First wave incoming."

Through the doorway comes a sound like summer—dozens of mechanical bees, each no bigger than my thumbnail, their tiny rotors humming. They swarm past us and take positions directly in front of each sensor, their bodies blocking the infrared beams.

"You've got approximately three minutes." Mitzy warns. "Move fast."

We don't need to be told twice. Merlin and I rush through the corridor, our shoulders brushing the walls. The stone is cold, damp in places where groundwater has seeped through. Our footsteps echo despite our attempts at silence.

Halfway through, Charlie's voice crackles through my earpiece: "Something's wrong. The bride hasn't answered."

I stumble, catch myself against the wall.

"She's just standing there." Jenny reports. "Not speaking."

Good girl. Fight them, Vivianne. Give us time.

"The groom looks angry." Sam adds. "Father's moving toward her."

We reach the end of the corridor—the biometric door. State of the art, installed maybe five years ago. Fingerprint scanner, retinal scan, and a keypad for a twelve-digit code. Unbeatable under normal circumstances.

But we have Mitzy's special gift.

Merlin raises his wrist, where the EMP watch sits innocuously. "Once I trigger this, we have thirty seconds before the systems reboot. The door will be on manual locks only—we'll have to force it."

"Do it."

"Wait." He grabs my arm. "Listen."

Through the comms, chaos. Shouting. A crash.

"Flowers everywhere." Brett reports. "Someone knocked over the entire altar arrangement."

"Was it Charlie?"

"Negative, he's by the gift table. It just... fell."

A distraction. Someone's buying us time.

"Now." I tell Merlin.

He presses the watch face three times in sequence. No dramatic flash, no sound effect like in films. Just a subtle vibration, and every LED on the door goes dark.

Together, we grab the emergency manual handle—required by fire codes even in secret vaults—and pull. The door weighs at least 300 pounds and is designed to be opened by hydraulics, not human muscle. It fights us every inch.

"Ten seconds." Merlin gasps.

We pull harder. My shoulders scream. My hands slip on the metal.

"Five seconds."

With a grinding protest, the door swings open just as the lights flicker back on, systems rebooting. An alarm begins to shriek—piercing, overwhelming, designed to disorient as much as alert.

But we're in.

The vault spreads before us like a dragon's hoard. Paintings stack against the walls—a Monet, a Picasso, what might be a real Vermeer. Display cases hold jewelry that hasn't seen the light in decades. Ancient artifacts that belong in museums sit carelessly on shelves.

All stolen. All hidden. The Faulks family's real wealth, built on the bones of war and theft.

But we're here for only one thing.

"There." Merlin points.

A glass case, and within it, lying on black velvet like a drop of blood...

The Swan.

"Alarms are going off everywhere." CJ reports. "Security is scrambling. You need to move NOW."

I run to the pedestal. The glass case has its own lock—another antique, probably installed when the pendant was first hidden here. No time for picks. No time for finesse.

I wrap my jacket around my elbow and smash the glass.

The Swan is heavier than I expected, the ruby catching the emergency lights, seeming to pulse like something alive. Inside the stone, that impossible swan frozen in flight. Even in this moment of chaos, its beauty stops me cold.

"PAUL!" Merlin shouts.

I pocket the pendant, and we run. Back through the corridor where the bumblebees are already falling, their power exhausted. Back past the ancient door that we don't bother to close. Through the wine cellar where bottles rattle from our passing.

"Security converging on the house." Sam reports. "They know about the vault breach."

"Ceremony is in chaos." Jenny adds. "Complete pandemonium."

We burst from the wine cellar into blinding sunlight. The estate is in uproar—guards running toward the house, guests scattering, and somewhere in that chaos, Vivianne is either free or more trapped than ever.

"Van!" Merlin shouts, pointing.

CJ has brought it around, tires screeching as he slides to a stop beside us. We dive into the back, and he's moving before the doors close.

"Did you get it?"

"Yeah." I'm still gasping. "We got it."

"Our team is extracting the bride." CJ takes a hard turn that sends us sliding. "Complete chaos at the ceremony site."

On the monitors, fragments—white dress disappearing into smoke, guards with guns drawn, an elderly woman fainting into her chair. But no Vivianne. Can't tell if she's safe.

"Where is she?" The demand comes out raw.

"Charlie has her." Jenny's voice, steady despite the chaos. "Moving to extraction point two."

"Negative." Sam cuts in. "Father's blocking the route with security."

My hand goes to my gun. "Turn around."

"No." CJ's voice is firm. "This was the plan. You get the Swan, they get Vivianne."

"Turn the fucking van around!"

"Paul." Merlin's hand on my shoulder. "Trust them."

Trust. The hardest thing in the world when everything you love is on the line.

On the monitors, smoke grenades bloom like flowers. White dress flashing through the chaos. Guards converging. And somewhere in that beautiful catastrophe, Vivianne is fighting for her freedom while I sit here with a stolen ruby and a breaking pulse.

"Charlie's clear!" Brett shouts through comms. "They're at the van!"

"Moving to rendezvous." Another voice confirms.

I close my eyes, the Swan warm in my palm, and pray to every god I don't believe in that we haven't just traded one treasure for another.

That we've saved them both.

TWENTY-NINE

Vivianne: Vows and Violations

THE AISLE STRETCHES BEFORE ME LIKE A GUILLOTINE'S SCAFFOLD, every step taking me closer to my execution.

Five hundred faces turn to watch my descent into hell, their expressions ranging from envious to pitying to coldly calculating. Mrs. Astoria Vanderbilt dabs at her eyes with a lace handkerchief —not from emotion but from the pollen of the ten thousand white roses Father insisted on. Senator Blackwood whispers something to his mistress, both of them eyeing my dress with the appreciation of people who know exactly how much misery costs.

Fifty thousand dollars of Belgian lace. Seventy thousand dollars of hand-sewn pearls. A four-hundred-thousand-dollar dress for a marriage worth thirty million in merged assets.

They've turned me into a walking spreadsheet.

Father's grip on my arm is a vise wrapped in paternal affection. His fingers dig into the flesh above my elbow, finding the exact pressure point that sends shoots of pain up to my shoulder without leaving marks that would show in the wedding photos. He's perfected this hold over years—the loving father guiding his daughter while simultaneously dragging her to her doom.

"Smile." He whispers through his own practiced expression of joy. "Every camera in France is watching."

He's not wrong. Hundreds of phones rise, their black eyes recording every second of my humiliation for posterity and social media. The official photographer—a woman with sharp eyes—circles us like a predator, her camera clicking in rapid succession.

Each step is carefully measured to match the processional music—Pachelbel's Canon—because Father lacks the imagination to choose something original for selling his daughter. My train trails behind me, six feet of silk and suffering that my cousin's daughters carry with sticky fingers that will undoubtedly leave chocolate stains before this farce is over.

I catalog faces as we pass each row, my mind desperate for anything to focus on besides the altar ahead.

Row five: The Bernardis, who made their fortune in weapons manufacturing and now pretend they've always been old money.

Row twelve: Senator Dubois with his third wife, who's younger than his eldest daughter and already eyeing the groomsmen.

Row eighteen: My finishing school classmates, their faces carefully neutral because they know exactly what this is but would never dare say it aloud.

Row twenty-three: Mrs. Holloway, standing at the edge in her best dress, her eyes meeting mine with something that might be sorrow or might be resignation.

And then, scattered throughout like hidden promises, faces I don't recognize. The photographer whose movements are too precise, too aware. A caterer near the gift table whose shoulders suggest military training. A security guard scanning the crowd rather than watching the ceremony.

Hope flickers in my chest, dangerous and desperate.

But then the altar comes into view, and hope turns to ash.

Prescott stands there like he's posing for a portrait of

conquest. His coat fits perfectly, every hair in place, his eyes bright with anticipation that makes my stomach revolt. He watches me approach the way a spider watches a fly entering its web—patient, certain, already savoring the meal to come.

His best man, Thomas Ashford, leans in to whisper something that makes Prescott's smile widen. Probably discussing their plans for the bachelor party they held last week, the one where Prescott assured his friends that after tonight, I'd be "properly broken in."

The altar itself is a monument to excess. Roses, lilies, and gardenias create an archway with a scent that is overwhelming, cloying, like being buried alive in a florist shop. White silk drapes every surface, turning God's altar into a display of wealth that has nothing to do with love or sanctity.

The priest stands in the center of it all. His face serene, willfully blind to what he's really doing here. The Church has been well-compensated for his selective vision.

Three more steps.

Two.

One.

My father stops at the base of the altar, finally releasing my arm. The blood rushes back into the bruised flesh, pins and needles of returning circulation that I hide behind my bouquet— white roses for purity I lost long ago, not to Prescott but to the truth about what my family really is.

"Who gives this woman to be married?" The priest's voice carries across the silent garden.

"I do." Father announces, loud enough for the back rows to hear. Proud. Possessive. Final.

He lifts my veil, his lips brushing my cheek in a kiss that looks tender but feels like a brand. "Don't disappoint me." Quiet enough that only I can hear.

Then he places my hand in Prescott's.

The touch is an immediate violation. Prescott's palm is damp with anticipation, his fingers closing around mine with the grip of ownership. He pulls me up the two steps to stand beside him, and I'm close enough now to smell his cologne—too much, as always, trying to cover the scent of his excitement that borders on arousal.

"You look exquisite." His thumb strokes the inside of my wrist in a way that makes my skin crawl. "Worth the wait."

The priest opens his ceremonial book, its pages edged in gold that catches the morning sun. "Dearly beloved, we are gathered here today in the sight of God and these witnesses to join this man and this woman in holy matrimony..."

The words wash over me like water over stone, meaningless sounds that herald my imprisonment. My mind drifts, desperate for escape even if my body can't achieve it.

Where is Paul?

"Marriage is a sacred covenant." Father Francis continues. "Ordained by God, witnessed by the Church, and blessed by the community..."

Prescott's grip tightens, pulling me imperceptibly closer. To the crowd, it must look romantic. To me, it feels like drowning in slow motion.

"Prescott James Harrington—" The priest addresses him. "—will you take Vivianne Amelie Faulks as your lawfully wedded wife? Will you love her, comfort her, honor and protect her, forsaking all others, keeping only unto her for as long as you both shall live?"

"I have prepared my own vows." Prescott produces a card from his pocket with a flourish that draws approving murmurs from the crowd.

Of course, he has. Another performance in this theatrical production.

He turns to face me fully, taking both my hands, his grip ensuring I can't pull away without making a scene.

"Vivianne." His voice is pitched to carry to the back rows. "From the moment I first saw you at the Autumn Gala three years ago, I knew you would be mine."

Would be mine. Not that he would love me. Not that we would be together. That I would be *his.*

"Your beauty, your grace, your impeccable breeding—everything about you spoke to what I wanted in a wife. Someone to stand beside me as I build my empire. Someone who understands that marriage is about legacy, about power, about creating something permanent in an impermanent world."

The crowd seems to think this is romantic. Actual sighs from some of the women.

"I promise to provide for you, to protect what is mine, to ensure our children want for nothing. I promise to shape you into the perfect wife, the perfect mother, the perfect partner for the life I've planned for us. You will never have to worry about anything except pleasing me and raising our family."

My stomach turns. Every word is a bar in the cage he's building.

"I will possess you, body and soul." His eyes burn with something that isn't love but hunger. "I will guard you jealously, completely, ensuring no other man ever questions who you belong to. You are my greatest acquisition, and I will treasure you accordingly."

He lifts my hand to his lips, kissing my knuckles while maintaining eye contact. The possession in his gaze makes me want to run, but Father's presence behind me is a wall I can't cross.

"These are my vows to you," Prescott concludes. "To keep you, and make you mine in every way that matters."

The applause is immediate and enthusiastic. They think

they've witnessed a declaration of love instead of a declaration of ownership.

Father Francis clears his throat, looking slightly uncomfortable—perhaps even his willful blindness has limits. "Yes, well. Beautiful. Vivianne, would you like to share your vows?"

I haven't prepared anything. What would I say? *I promise to die a little more each day. I vow to dream of freedom every night. I swear to hate you with every breath I take.*

"She's overwhelmed." Prescott answers for me, his hand moving to the small of my back in what looks like support but feels like a shackle. "We discussed keeping her vows traditional."

We discussed nothing. He decided. Father approved. I was informed.

"Very well." Father Francis returns to his script. "If anyone here knows of any reason why these two should not be joined in holy matrimony, speak now or forever hold your peace."

The silence stretches.

One heartbeat.

Two.

Three.

I scan the crowd, desperate. *Someone. Anyone. Please.*

The photographer shifts slightly. The security guard's hand moves to his earpiece. The caterer takes a step forward.

But no one speaks.

The moment passes.

"Then let us continue." Father Francis says, and I taste copper where I've bitten my tongue hard enough to draw blood. "Vivianne Amelie Faulks, will you take this man to be your lawfully wedded husband? Will you love him, comfort him, honor and obey him, forsaking all others, keeping only unto him for as long as you both shall live?"

The words stick in my throat like broken glass.

Everyone is watching. Waiting. The silence stretches again, but this time it's wrong, uncomfortable.

"Vivianne." Prescott's fingers dig into my back. A warning.

I open my mouth. Close it. Can't make the words come.

"She's nervous." He tells the crowd with a laugh that doesn't reach his eyes. "Stage fright."

Sympathetic chuckles ripple through the assembly.

"Vivianne." Father Francis prompts gently. "You need to answer."

I look at him—this priest who has known me since birth, who should be protecting me instead of facilitating my sale—and still can't speak.

Father stands in the front row, his face darkening from pink to red. A warning.

Prescott's grip becomes painful. Another warning.

"I—"

The sound that splits the air isn't my voice.

It's an alarm. Piercing. Overwhelming. The kind that means something has gone catastrophically wrong.

For a moment, everyone freezes. Then chaos.

"Is that the fire alarm?" someone shouts.

"The security system—" Donovan Price has his radio out, barking orders. "Code Black. I repeat, Code Black. All units to the main house."

Father is on his feet, his face transforming from ceremonial father to the cold businessman I really know. "The vault." He snarls, and I know immediately—Paul did it. He actually did it.

"We finish this now." Prescott grabs my wrist hard enough to leave marks. "Say the words."

"The ceremony must pause." Father Francis protests. "If there's danger—"

"There's no danger." Father snaps, striding toward the altar. "Just a security breach. Continue."

But the guests are already moving, some running toward the house, others backing away from it. Phones are out everywhere, recording the chaos. The perfect society wedding has become a scandal in real-time.

"Vivianne, say the words." Prescott commands, shaking me slightly.

"No."

It comes out quiet, but in the spaces between alarm wails, it's perfectly clear.

"What did you say?"

"I said no."

His face contorts, the handsome mask slipping to reveal the monster underneath. "You don't get to say no."

"Actually, she does."

The photographer is suddenly beside us, her camera replaced with something that might be a taser. "Let her go."

"Who the hell are you?" Prescott demands.

"The cavalry." Someone else says, and the caterer from the gift table—massive, imposing—is there too.

Smoke grenades explode across the garden. White, thick smoke that turns the morning into fog. Guests scream, running in every direction. Father shouting orders, Donovan responding, guards converging.

"Time to go." The woman's command cuts through the chaos, and then we're moving.

Prescott tries to maintain his grip, but the large man picks him up and sets him aside like a child's toy.

"Run." The woman commands, and I do.

The wedding dress is impossible. It catches on everything—chairs, flowers, my own feet. The train tangles, tears, tries to pull me backward like the house itself won't let me leave.

My heels sink into the grass with every step. Without think-ing, I kick them off, running barefoot across the lawn as chaos erupts around us. More smoke grenades. Someone firing warning shots into the air. Guests screaming, scattering like startled birds.

Through the smoke, other figures moving—the security guards who aren't really guards, the caterers who were never here to serve food. All of them, here for me.

"The van." Another woman joins us, pointing through the smoke.

There—black, anonymous, engine running. Freedom in the form of a vehicle that would never be allowed in Father's pristine driveway.

But between us and escape stands my father himself, flanked by Donovan and six guards, all with weapons drawn.

"Stop right there." Father commands, and even now, even in this chaos, his voice makes me freeze.

The conditioning is so deep, obedience carved into my bones by twenty-five years of his absolute control.

"You're not leaving." He steps forward. The guards fan out, creating a human wall between me and the van. "You're my daughter."

Something breaks inside me. Maybe it's the adrenaline. Maybe it's seeing Paul's promise made manifest in the chaos around us. Maybe it's just twenty-five years of silence finally ending.

"I was never your daughter." My voice carries across the garden. "I was your asset. Your bargaining chip. Your merchandise."

The guests who haven't fled are filming everything. Good. Let them see.

"You ungrateful—"

"You sold me." My voice rises, fueled by years of suppressed rage. "You literally sold me to Prescott for a business merger. That's not a father. That's a pimp."

Gasps from the crowd. Someone's definitely livestreaming this.

"You know nothing about what I've done for you." Father spits. "The protection I've provided. The life you've lived."

"The cage you built." I take a step forward, and surprisingly, he takes one back. "The marriage you arranged. The education designed to make me a perfect wife instead of a complete person. All the stolen art in that vault, built on the bones of families destroyed by war."

His face is purple now, rage making him ugly. "You'll have nothing without me. No money. No name. No protection."

"I'll have everything that matters." The words come from someplace deep, someplace I didn't know existed. "I'll have freedom. I'll have choice. I'll have love that isn't contingent on obedience."

"Love?" Prescott stumbles through the smoke, his perfect hair mussed, his morning coat torn. "You're mine. We have contracts. Your father promised—"

The photographer drops him with a single punch. Prescott crumples like wet paper, all his posturing meaningless against someone who actually knows violence instead of just threatening it.

The crowd reacts with fresh screams, but also... applause? Some of them are actually applauding.

"Enough of this." Donovan raises his weapon. "Stand down or we will use force."

More smoke grenades. Flashbangs that turn the world white and ringing. The photographer, who's not a photographer, pulls me sideways.

"Stop them." Father's voice, desperate now. "Twenty million to whoever stops them."

But his guards are confused, blinded by smoke, unsure who's

a real guest and who's trying to take me away. The chaos is perfect, orchestrated, beautiful.

I'm thrown into the van, landing hard on my knees, wedding dress pooling around me like spilled milk. The others pile in after me. The doors slam.

"Go, go, go!" someone shouts.

Tires scream against gravel. The van lurches forward, throwing me against the wall. Through the back windows, my father stands in the smoke, his empire crumbling around him, his face a mask of rage and disbelief.

He's shouting something, but I can't hear it over the engine, the alarms still wailing, my own pulse pounding so hard I think it might escape my chest.

We tear through the estate's gates, past more arriving security, onto the main road, where we blend into traffic like we were never there at all.

I'm in a van with strangers, wearing a destroyed wedding dress, barefoot, with nothing but the earrings my grandmother left me.

And I'm free.

I start laughing. Or crying. Maybe both. The sounds tear out of me, years of suppression breaking like a dam. The woman pulls me into an embrace, and I sob into this stranger's shoulder, my body shaking with the force of everything I've held back.

"You're safe." Her voice is steady, grounding. "You're safe now."

Through my tears, I manage one question: "Paul?"

"On his way to the rendezvous." She confirms. "With the Swan."

The Swan. That cursed ruby that destroyed my grandmother's life and nearly destroyed mine.

But also the key to my freedom.

I close my eyes, feeling the van carry me away from everything I've ever known, toward something terrifying and uncertain and absolutely perfect:

A life that's actually mine.

THIRTY

Paul: Convergence

THE VAN TEARS THROUGH BACK ROADS AT SPEEDS THAT SHOULD terrify me, but all I can focus on is Jenny's voice crackling through the comm: "Package secured. Moving to rendezvous."

Package. Vivianne. Safe.

"How long?" The demand comes out rough.

"Three minutes." CJ never takes his eyes off the road. "Maybe two if I ignore physics."

"Ignore it."

Merlin sits beside me, the Swan heavy in his cupped hands like he's cradling something sacred. He hasn't spoken since we left the estate, just stares at the ruby with an expression I've never seen on his face—raw, vulnerable, a lifetime of loss etched in the lines around his eyes.

Through the windshield—an abandoned textile warehouse on the outskirts of the city, its broken windows like dead eyes. But the Guardian HRS van is already there, parked at an angle that suggests they came in hot.

CJ hasn't even stopped before I'm yanking the door handle.

"Paul, wait—"

I don't. Can't. I hit the ground running, my shoes slipping on gravel, nearly going down, but not caring. The van's back doors are opening and—

Vivianne.

She's trying to climb out, the wedding dress a destroyed cloud around her, one sleeve torn completely off, the train black with dirt and grass stains. Her elaborate updo has collapsed, and her hair hangs in golden tendrils around her face. Mascara streaks her cheeks like war paint.

She's the most beautiful thing I've ever seen.

Our bodies collide with enough force to drive the air from my lungs. Her arms wrap around my neck, mine around her waist, lifting her clear off the ground. She's sobbing and laughing simultaneously, her face buried in my shoulder, and I'm probably crushing her, but I can't let go.

I won't let go.

I'm never letting her go again.

"You came for me." She gasps against my neck.

"Always." I breathe into her hair. "Always, ma chérie. Always."

Her legs wrap around my waist, the dress making it awkward, but neither of us cares. Her pulse hammers against mine, proof that she's real, she's here, she's safe.

"I didn't say it." She pulls back just enough to look at me, eyes fierce despite the tears. "When he asked if I'd take Prescott, I didn't say yes. I couldn't."

"I know." I cup her face, thumbs wiping at the mascara stains. "Jenny told us. You were magnificent."

"I was terrified."

"You were everything."

She kisses me then, desperate and deep, tasting of tears and freedom. I kiss her back, pouring every moment of fear, every second of separation, every promise I couldn't keep until now into the connection between us.

"Hate to interrupt." Jenny's voice cuts through, dry as bone. "But we need to move. This location won't stay secure for long."

Reluctantly, I set Vivianne down but keep my arm around her, unable to break contact completely. The Guardian team is forming a protective circle, weapons still drawn, eyes scanning the perimeter.

"Anthony?" Vivianne spots him climbing out of our van.

He looks up at her voice, and something passes between them —recognition, understanding, shared loss. He holds up the Swan, its ruby catching the afternoon sun streaming through the broken windows.

"Mademoiselle Faulks." Formal, but his voice shakes.

"You're Anthony. From the letters."

Merlin goes completely still. "You found them?"

"Hidden all over her room. She kept them, every one." Vivianne steps toward him, the dress dragging behind her. "She loved you. Even after everything, she loved you until the day she died."

The sound Merlin makes is barely human—seventy years of grief condensed into a single moment. His legs give out, and I lunge forward to catch him, lowering him gently to sit on the van's bumper.

"She kept them." He stares at the Swan, voice barely a whisper. "Brigitte kept them?"

"Every one." Vivianne kneels beside him despite the dress. "Hidden where my grandfather would never find them. You were her great love. Her only love."

Merlin's hands shake as he pulls out his jeweler's loupe, holding the Swan up to catch the light. "I haven't seen it since the night I gave it to her. 1943. We were so young, so stupid, thinking love could survive war."

"What is it?" CJ moves closer, and everyone gathers around. "Beyond a ruby, I mean."

"It's a map." Merlin's voice is stronger now, shifting into teacher mode even through his tears. "Or rather, it contains coordinates."

He angles the stone so we can see inside, where that impossible swan seems to float in crystallized blood. "The flaw in the ruby—nature's accident that created the swan—that was what made it perfect for the purpose. But it's the surface that holds the secret."

"What do you mean?"

"Microscopic. Invisible to the naked eye. I need proper equipment to read them all, but I helped create them, so I know what's there." He looks up, meeting each of our eyes in turn. "GPS coordinates. Dozens of them. Maybe more."

"Coordinates to what?" Sam asks.

"Gold. Art. Currency. Everything the Nazis stole from Jewish families, from conquered nations, from anyone they deemed unworthy of wealth." Merlin's voice hardens, his fingers tracing the Swan's surface with reverence and revulsion. "Hidden in caves, bunkers, Swiss bank vaults that have been waiting seventy years to be opened."

He pauses, scanning our assembled group. "Have any of you heard of Der Goldzug? The Gold Train?"

Blank stares all around, except from Jenny, whose eyes narrow with recognition.

"Spring of 1945." Merlin continues, his voice taking on the cadence of a history professor. "The Reich was collapsing. The Russians were closing in from the east, while the Americans and British were closing in from the west. The Nazi high command knew it was over, but they weren't about to let their plunder fall into Allied hands."

He holds up the Swan, its facets catching the light. "They

loaded a train in Breslau—what's now Wrocław in Poland. Not just any train. Armored cars, reinforced steel, and the most advanced locomotive they had. Inside? The wealth of nations. Gold bars from the Czech National Bank. Art from the Budapest Museum. Jewish family fortunes from across Eastern Europe. Conservative estimates put the value at four billion Reichsmarks then. In today's money?" He shakes his head. "Twenty-seven billion dollars. Minimum."

"The train left Breslau on May 14th, 1945." He continues. "It was supposed to reach a bunker complex in the Owl Mountains. Seventy-three cars of stolen wealth, guarded by SS units who knew they were transporting the Fourth Reich's seed money— funds to rebuild when the world forgot."

"But it never arrived." Jenny's voice is quiet.

"No. It vanished somewhere between Wałbrzych and Wrocław. Seventy-three train cars don't just disappear, but this one did. The Soviets searched. The Polish searched. For seventy years, treasure hunters have combed every tunnel, every abandoned mine shaft." Merlin's eyes gleam. "They never found it because they didn't have this."

He taps the Swan. "The coordinates on here correspond to railway tunnels that were sealed in May 1945. Tunnels that don't appear on any official map because the Nazis used slave labor to dig them, then killed everyone who knew about them."

"You're saying the train is real?" Forest leans forward. "And it's still there?"

"Not just the train. The Nazis created an entire network. Some of the gold went to Switzerland—we know about those accounts, though the Swiss have been reluctant to release them. Some went to Argentina, funding the escape routes for war criminals. But the bulk of it? Hidden. Waiting."

His voice drops. "There's a coordinate here for Lake Toplitz in Austria. The Nazis dumped crates into that lake in the final days—supposedly just documents, but divers have died trying to reach the bottom. Another coordinate points to the Merkers Salt Mine, where Patton's Third Army found part of the Nazi gold reserves in 1945—but they only found what the SS wanted them to find. The real treasure was moved days before."

"How do you know all this?" Sam asks.

Merlin's face ages a decade in an instant. "Because I was there. Not for the loading—I was with the Resistance then. But after the war, when we were hunting war criminals, I interrogated an SS officer named Richter. He was dying, gut-shot, delirious with fever. He talked about the train, about the network of hiding places. He said there was a map, but it had been split up—pieces given to different officers to prevent any one person from claiming it all."

He looks down at the Swan. "What he didn't know was that the complete map, the coordinates of the caches, had been micro-engraved on a ruby by a Jewish jeweler in Prague—a man named Goldmann. Goldmann was clever. He smuggled the Swan to the Resistance."

Merlin's voice becomes distant, lost in memory. "It came to me through our network in early 1944. This impossible ruby with a swan trapped inside—Goldmann's final masterpiece and his greatest act of defiance. I knew what it contained, knew what it meant. But France was falling. The Nazis were closing in on our cell."

He looks at Vivianne. "So I gave it to the only person I trusted completely. Brigitte. Your grandmother. I told her it was a symbol of our love, and it was. But it was also the key to recovering billions in stolen wealth. I made her promise to keep it safe until I returned."

His voice cracks. "But I was captured two weeks later. Spent the rest of the war in a labor camp. By the time I escaped and made it back to Paris, Brigitte was gone. Her friend—my friend

—Henry Faulks had kept her safe during the occupation. Kept her too safe. They fell in love, or what she thought was love. Maybe it was just survival. When the Americans came, Henry had connections, papers, promises of a new life in America."

"She took the Swan with her." Vivianne's voice is soft.

"She took the Swan with her." Merlin confirms. "And for seventy years, I thought she'd betrayed me. Sold the secret to build the Faulks' fortune." He looks at Vivianne with wonder.

"That's what my grandfather discovered." Vivianne speaks slowly, piecing it together. "Somehow, he found out. The Faulks fortune was built on the Swan. On my grandfather tracking down just enough of the secondary caches to seem legitimate. A cave here, a Swiss account there, always with perfect paperwork to explain the windfall."

"The families." Merlin's grip on the Swan tightens, urgent. "The descendants of those who were robbed—they deserve this wealth. Museums that lost their collections. Synagogues that were burned with their treasures inside. Every coordinate on this stone represents thousands of destroyed lives. It has to go back to them."

"It will." Jenny's assurance is firm. "But Merlin, if even half of what you're saying is true, this is the largest recovery of stolen wealth in history. Governments will want to claim it. Switzerland will fight to keep its accounts secret. And Sentinel—if they know what the Swan contains—"

"They'll kill everyone in this room to get it." Forest finishes.

The weight of that statement settles over us. We're holding the key to tens of billions in stolen wealth—enough to fund a criminal empire for generations.

Vivianne stands, approaching Merlin slowly. "May I?"

He hands her the Swan without hesitation. She holds it, studying the bird within, and I see her grandmother in her face— not the broken woman from the photos, but the young Brigitte who loved a boy named Anthony before the world tore them apart.

She hands the Swan back to Merlin, then does something unexpected—she hugs him. He stiffens, then melts into it, and I see him as he might have been—young Anthony, full of hope and passion, before loss carved him into Merlin.

"She would be proud of you." He whispers. "You have her courage."

"And you have your justice." Her reply is quiet but certain. "Finally."

"Speaking of which—" Jenny cuts in, all business. "Faulks will mobilize everything he has to get the Swan back."

We load into new vehicles—clean ones, with false plates and no connection to the morning's chaos. Merlin clutches the Swan like a lifeline. Seventy years of searching ended. A love story that became a tragedy, finally finding something like a resolution.

But as I help Vivianne into the van, her wedding dress train catching on everything, I realize we've written a different ending. Where Anthony and Brigitte were torn apart by war and circumstance, we've fought through to the other side.

The Swan brought us together—a ruby born from pressure and time, holding secrets and sorrow. But we're not going to let it define us the way it defined them.

THIRTY-ONE

Paul: Prague

THE LIGHT IN PRAGUE IS DIFFERENT FROM PARIS. SOFTER somehow, filtered through centuries of coal smoke and history that clings to the buildings like memory. It's perfect for painting.

I've been at the canvas since dawn, trying to capture the way Vivianne looked last night—wrapped in my shirt, standing on our tiny balcony, the city lights turning her skin to gold. She doesn't know I'm painting this moment. She was lost in thought, probably processing the latest batch of testimony she'd given, unaware of how the weight she's carried for months is finally starting to lift from her shoulders.

Three weeks of freedom, and she's still learning how to breathe without asking permission.

"Paul?" Her voice drifts from the bedroom, husky with sleep. "Are you painting again?"

"Always." I call back, adding another stroke of gold to her hair in the painting.

She appears in the doorway wearing the same shirt from last night—my shirt—and nothing else. Her legs are bare, her hair a beautiful mess, and she's holding two cups of coffee like a peace offering.

"You were supposed to stay in bed." She hands me a cup. "It's Sunday."

"You were supposed to sleep past noon." I set down my brush, pull her between my legs where I'm sitting on the stool. "Bad dreams again?"

She nods, not lying but not elaborating either. The nightmares come less frequently now, but they still come. Prescott's hands. Her father's voice. The feeling of drowning in white silk.

"Want to talk about it?"

"No." She sets down her coffee and frames my face with her hands. "I want to forget about it."

She kisses me, slow and deep, tasting of coffee and promises. When she pulls back, there's paint on her fingers from where she touched my cheek.

I smile against her lips, my hands settling on her waist, drawing her closer. She's all soft curves and quiet need, and I want nothing more than to chase away those shadows for her. My thumbs trace lazy circles on her hips, under the hem of the shirt that dwarfs her frame.

"Then let's forget." I pull her in for another kiss—this one lingering, unhurried, like we're savoring the morning light filtering through the window.

Her fingers thread into my hair, tugging gently as she deepens the kiss, her body melting against mine. I wrap my arms around her fully now, hugging her tight between my legs, feeling the steady rise and fall of her breath sync with mine. The stool creaks under us as she shifts, climbing onto my lap to straddle me, her thighs bracketing my hips. The shirt rides up, exposing the smooth expanse of her skin, and I can't help but run my hands along her legs, savoring the sensation.

We kiss like that for what feels like hours—slow, exploratory, my lips trailing to her jaw, her neck, nipping softly at the pulse that flutters there. She sighs, arching into me, her hands working at the buttons of my shirt with deliberate slowness. One by one, they give way, and she pushes the fabric aside, her palms gliding over my chest, igniting sparks wherever she touches. I shrug out of it, letting it pool on the floor, and pull her closer, the heat of her core pressing against me through my jeans.

The laziness starts to fray at the edges as desire builds, her hips rocking subtly against me, drawing a low groan from my throat. I capture her mouth again, hungrier now, my hands slipping under the shirt to cup her breasts, thumbs teasing her nipples until they're peaked and she's gasping into the kiss.

"Paul." She whispers, her voice breaking on my name, and it's all the encouragement I need.

My fingers find the button of my jeans, freeing myself with quick, earnest movements, and she lifts just enough to help, guiding me to her entrance.

We move together like that, still on the stool—slow thrusts that build into something deeper, more insistent, her arms around my neck, my hands gripping her ass to hold her steady. The intimacy of it steals my breath; it's not just heat, it's us, reclaiming the space between nightmares and daylight. But as the rhythm quickens, her nails digging into my shoulders, the stool feels too precarious, too small for the fire we're stoking.

I stand, keeping her wrapped around me, her legs locking at my waist. She yelps a soft laugh that turns into a moan as I carry her the few steps to the wall, pressing her back against the cool plaster. The contrast makes her gasp, her body clenching around me, and I thrust deeper, earnest now, the steam of our bodies filling the air with the scent of paint and sweat and her.

Our kisses are frantic, tongues tangling, breaths mingling as I drive into her, each movement a promise to erase the past, to fill her with only this—us, hot and alive and unbreakable. She comes undone first, crying out against my shoulder, her body shuddering, and it pulls me over the edge with her, spilling into her with a guttural sound I can't hold back.

We stay like that for a long moment, foreheads pressed together, pulses pounding in unison, the world reduced to the press of our bodies and the quiet intimacy of after.

"You've got cerulean blue in your hair again." Her smile is lazy, satisfied.

"You've got cadmium yellow on your nose."

We're both laughing when the encrypted phone rings. The laughter dies immediately. That phone only rings for important things.

Vivianne answers, putting it on speaker. "Yes?"

"Ms. Faulks." The voice is crisp, professional. "Agent Harrison, FBI Financial Crimes Division. Are you ready for your deposition?"

She moves to the laptop, already set up with an encrypted video connection. I stay out of frame but close enough to hold her hand if she needs it.

The next hour is grueling. They walk her through every detail of her father's operations—the Swiss accounts, the art in the vault, the connections to Sentinel. She's steady, clear, devastating in her precision. This is the fifteenth deposition she's given to various agencies. Each one peels back another layer of the criminal empire her father built.

"Can you confirm the defendant's connection to the organization known as Sentinel?"

"Yes. I heard him identify himself as 'the Fifth' during a phone conversation. He mentioned someone called Malfor, who I now understand was the head of the organization."

"And Malfor's current status?"

"Dead, as I understand it. Found in his Swiss compound two weeks ago."

The agent's expression doesn't change. "The investigation into his death is ongoing. Professional execution, no organization has claimed responsibility."

Vivianne's gaze meets mine. We have our suspicions about who might have ordered that hit. Jenny and her team were very clear that Sentinel needed to be completely dismantled. Sometimes that requires more than legal measures.

"Moving on to the recovered assets." The agent continues. "The coordinates from the Swan pendant have led to the recovery of approximately eighteen billion dollars in gold, art, and currency so far. Is that your understanding?"

"Yes." Vivianne confirms. "Though I believe there's still more to be found."

What she doesn't mention is the five billion that will never be officially recovered. Merlin and I made that decision together. Guardian HRS has saved too many lives to operate on hope and good intentions. They need funding, resources, and the ability to move without asking permission. Five billion ensures they can keep saving people like Vivianne for decades to come.

Forest and Sam didn't even pretend to be surprised when we made the offer. Just nodded, said "It'll be put to good use," and that was that.

The deposition ends with the usual warnings about ongoing testimony, maintaining security, and the importance of her continued cooperation. Vivianne closes the laptop and slumps in her chair.

"How many more times?"

"As many as it takes." I pull her up into my arms. "Your testimony is destroying them. Your father, Prescott, and the entire network. You're giving those families justice after seventy years."

"I know. It's just—" She presses her face into my chest. "I want it to be over. I want to stop being Vivianne Faulks, star witness. I want to just be... us."

"Soon." I press a kiss to her hair. "The trials are moving fast. Your father's assets are frozen. Prescott's family is abandoning him to save themselves. Six months, maybe less, and we can disappear completely."

She pulls back, looks up at me with those extraordinary eyes. "Where would we go?"

"Anywhere you want. New Zealand. Japan. Argentina. Somewhere no one knows our names."

"What about your chalet? I liked it there."

"Then we stay there."

She kisses me again, different this time. Hungrier. Her hands slide under my paint-stained t-shirt, nails dragging lightly across my skin.

"Vivianne—"

"Shh." She pushes me backward toward the bedroom. "Less talking. More forgetting."

The morning light streams through our bedroom window, turning everything golden and sacred. I lay her down carefully, like she might disappear if I'm not gentle enough. But she's having none of that. She pulls me down, demanding, taking what she wants with a freedom that still makes my chest tight with emotion.

After, we lie tangled in sheets and each other, her head on my chest, my fingers tracing patterns on her bare shoulder.

"I love you." Quiet, certain. "I don't think I've said that enough. I love you."

"I love you too."

"No, you don't understand." She props herself up on an elbow, looks down at me with fierce intensity. "I love *you*. Not because you saved me. Not because you're my escape. I love YOU. The way you hum when you paint. How you can't make coffee without making a mess. The fact that you alphabetize everything except your paint brushes, which you organize by some system I still can't figure out."

"Color temperature." I start explaining. "I organize them by—"

She kisses me quiet. "I love that you're explaining your bizarre brush system while we're naked in bed. I love that you watch me sleep and think I don't know. I love that you've been painting me from memory for months, but you still look at me like you're seeing me for the first time."

"Vivianne—"

"I'm not finished." Her voice cracks slightly. "I love that you see me. Not the Faulks heiress. Not the asset. Not the victim. Me. Just me."

I pull her down, roll us so she's beneath me, cage her face between my hands. "You're everything. You know that, right? Everything."

We make love again, slower this time, memorizing each other with touch and taste and whispered promises. The sun climbs higher, warming our small, perfect world, and for a few hours, we forget about testimonies and trials and the weight of history we're helping to correct.

The doorbell breaks the spell.

We both freeze. No one knows this address except—

"It's me." Merlin's voice calls through the door. "And I brought lunch."

We dress quickly, laughing at ourselves for the moment of panic. When I open the door, Merlin stands there with bags from the Czech bakery down the street and a smile I rarely saw before the Swan was recovered.

"I'm interrupting." He takes in our mussed hair and the general air of afternoon debauchery.

"You're welcome." Vivianne counters, kissing his cheek and taking the bags. "Always."

We eat at our tiny table—bread and cheese, and those little Czech pastries Vivianne has become addicted to. Merlin provides an update on the latest recovery efforts. A cave in Austria yielded three tons of gold bars. The Swiss finally opened a set of accounts that had been dormant since 1945. Seventeen families have been reunited with artwork they thought was lost forever.

"There's a ceremony next month." Merlin sets down his coffee. "In Warsaw. They want to honor everyone involved in the recovery efforts."

"We won't be there." The refusal is immediate.

"I know. But they wanted you to know you're invited. Both of you."

"Maybe someday." Vivianne's voice is soft. "When it's safer."

Merlin studies us over the rim of his coffee, eyes amused, then lands on her bare left hand. "Speaking of ceremonies... when are you proposing?" He tips his head toward Vivianne. "I'd like to raise a glass to Paul and Vivianne Mercier while I'm still young enough to stand for the toast."

Vivianne laughs, color rising to her cheeks. "Subtle as ever."

"It's a rare gift,"I say.

The room narrows to the curve of her mouth, the way her thumb makes slow circles on the table between us. Not *do I want to marry her*—that's been true from the first impossible moment— but *can I ask her to carry the word again.* Wife. Ceremony. Promise. After everything.

Her eyes meet mine, steady, searching. She nods, almost imperceptibly, like she's giving me permission to ask and herself permission to want.

I reach for the string handle on the pastry box and work it loose, hands suddenly clumsy. "I should have a ring." My voice comes out rougher than I intend. "But I have this ridiculous bit of bakery twine and the only thing that matters."

I push back my chair and go to one knee on the chipped tile. The world goes very quiet.

"Vivianne Faulks." The name feels like a chapter closing. "Will you marry me? Will you be my partner in all of it—the quiet, the storms, the ordinary days—and become Vivianne Mercier?"

Her breath catches. For a heartbeat, all I see is the long shadow of her first wedding, the bruise of it. Then she exhales, eyes wet and bright, and holds out her hand. "Yes." Like a secret she's finally allowed to tell. "Yes!"

I tie the makeshift ring around her finger. It looks absurd and perfect. Merlin swears softly and wipes at his eyes, then pretends he didn't.

"Small ceremony." I stand and pull her into my arms. "Just us. Merlin as witness. Nothing like—"

"Nothing like before." She leans on my shoulder. She pulls back, smiling in that way that feels like sunlight. "Something real. Something ours."

Merlin clears his throat, back to brisk. "I know a magistrate here in Prague. Very discreet. Could be done tomorrow if you wanted."

"Tomorrow's too soon." Vivianne's voice is soft, then softer, to me, "But maybe in a year?"

"As you wish, ma chérie." The words settle in my bones like relief.

Later, when Merlin leaves with a hug that cracks my ribs, we stand in the doorway and look at the piece of string on her finger, and then at each other.

"Happy?" I ask.

"Yes." Her smile is real, and for the first time, I believe it.

The news plays on the café's small TV. Images of her father being led away in handcuffs. Prescott screaming about his rights.

The Swiss treasury announcing the largest repatriation of stolen assets in history.

Vivianne doesn't even look at the screen.

THIRTY-TWO

Epilogue: Vivianne

One Year Later

THE DRESS COST EIGHTY-NINE EUROS.

I found it in a tiny boutique in Prague, hanging between a vintage coat and a leather jacket that had seen better days. Simple cream silk, tea-length, with delicate cap sleeves and buttons down the back that I can actually undo myself. The shop-keeper tried to show me something fancier, with beads, lace, and a train. I just smiled and bought the simple one.

Now, standing in the garden of Paul's chalet above Lac Léman, wearing this dress I chose myself with wildflowers in my hair instead of a veil, I finally understand what a wedding should feel like.

Joy. Not performance or transaction or fear. Joy.

"You look beautiful, my dear." Dr. Phillips offers me his arm. He flew in from Boston yesterday, grumbling about airlines and his old bones, but his eyes were bright with happiness.

The garden is perfect—apple blossoms and early roses, the lake glittering below, mountains rising like witnesses all around. We strung lights between the trees and borrowed chairs from the local café. The altar is just an arch of branches Paul and Merlin built yesterday, threaded with spring flowers I picked this morning.

Everyone who matters is here.

Merlin waits at the altar beside Paul, both of them in simple suits, though Merlin has added a pocket square of brilliant blue that matches the spring sky. He's holding the rings—not the massive diamond set Prescott tried to chain me with, but simple gold bands Paul and I designed together, inscribed with the coordinates of the café in Paris where we first truly saw each other.

But it's Paul who stops me cold.

He's watching me walk toward him with an expression I've only seen in his paintings—wonder and desire and something sacred all mixed together. His hands are steady (mine are shaking), his eyes never leaving my face as Dr. Phillips and I make our way down the improvised aisle.

No Wagner's wedding march. Instead, a recording of Nina Simone singing "Feeling Good" drifts from speakers hidden in the trees. *Because it is a new dawn, a new day, a new life.*

And I'm feeling good.

"Who gives this woman to be married?" The officiant asks— not a priest but a local magistrate who speaks beautiful French- accented English and didn't ask questions about our somewhat complicated legal status.

"She gives herself freely." Dr. Phillips speaks the words we rehearsed, replacing the traditional patriarchal transfer. "But I'm honored to walk beside her."

He kisses my cheek, whispers "Be happy," and places my hand in Paul's.

The touch is electric, grounding, everything. Paul's thumb

brushes over my knuckles, and I can feel him trembling too, just a little. This matters. After everything we've survived, this moment of choosing each other freely matters.

"We're gathered here—" The magistrate begins, but I barely hear him. I'm lost in Paul's eyes, in the smile playing at the corners of his mouth, in the knowledge that we made it here despite everything and everyone who tried to stop us.

"I understand you've written your own vows?"

Paul nods, pulls out a piece of paper, then stops. Folds it up. Puts it back in his pocket.

"I had this whole speech prepared." He takes both my hands. "About art and beauty and how you're my masterpiece. But standing here..." His voice catches. "You're not my masterpiece. You're not anyone's creation but your own. You're the woman who refused to say 'I do' to save yourself. Who stood up to your father in front of five hundred witnesses. Who's spent the last year making sure every single stolen treasure gets returned to its rightful owners. You're the bravest person I know, and I'm so damn grateful you choose to be brave with me."

I'm crying now, not caring about ruining my makeup.

"I promise to love you without caging you. To stand beside you, not in front of you. To paint you a thousand times and never quite capture how magnificent you are. To make you coffee every morning, badly, until we're old and gray. To choose you, every day, in freedom and in love."

"Vivianne?" The magistrate prompts gently.

I don't need notes. The words have been living in my chest for months.

"You gave me my first choice." My voice is stronger than I expected. "In that museum, when you could have exposed my family's theft, you chose to protect me instead. Every choice since then has led us here. I choose you. Not because you saved me, but because you showed me I was worth saving."

I squeeze his hands, feeling the calluses from his brushes, the strength that's held me through nightmares and hearings and the slow work of rebuilding.

"I promise to love you wildly, freely, and completely. To be your partner in crime—literal and metaphorical. To pose for your paintings even when I'm feeling fat and cranky." A breath. "Which might be often in about seven months."

It takes him a second. Then his eyes go wide, dropping to my stomach (still flat, nothing showing yet) and back to my face.

"Really?"

"Really."

He kisses me before the magistrate can pronounce us married, lifting me off my feet, spinning me as our tiny audience erupts in surprised celebration. Merlin laughs—actually laughs.

"I now pronounce you man and wife." The magistrate's voice is dry when Paul finally sets me down.

The reception is at the tiny restaurant in the village where we've become regulars. The owner, Madame Dubois, closed the place just for us, stringing lights on the terrace and hiring a jazz quartet from Montreux. We eat simple, perfect food—nothing with foam or reduction or any of the nonsense from my engagement party. Just Swiss comfort food and good wine (sparkling apple juice for me) and laughter that comes easy and often.

Merlin gives a surprisingly emotional toast, talking about courage and second chances. "To Paul and Vivianne, who proved love wins. To the next generation—" He nods at my still-flat stomach. "—who will know only freedom."

Dr. Phillips pulls me aside during the dancing, pressing an envelope into my hands. "This came to the museum. I thought you should have it."

Inside is Mrs. Holloway's careful handwriting:

My dear girl, they're calling you a hero, you know. The woman who brought down an empire of thieves. Your father rages about it from his cell, but the staff smile. We always knew you were stronger than he understood. I wanted you to know—your grandmother would be so proud. She told me once that she'd made all the wrong choices for all the wrong reasons. You've made all the right choices for the right reasons. Be happy, dear one. Be free. With love, Mrs. H

P.S. - I've ensured your mother's jewelry box finds its way to you. Every girl should have something from her mother on her wedding day.

I'm crying again, but it's the good kind. The healing kind.

Paul finds me on the terrace and pulls me into a dance, even though I'm hiccupping with tears. "Happy?" The same question he's been asking all year, tracking my recovery like a chart.

"Yes." I mean it completely. "Scared about the baby. Worried I'll be a terrible mother. Terrified I'll turn into my father somehow. But happy. So happy it feels like flying."

"You'll be an amazing mother." He says it with such certainty that I almost believe him. "You know what not to do. That's half the battle."

"What if—"

"No what-ifs tonight. Tonight, we're married. Tomorrow, your position at the Sorbonne becomes official. Next month, my exhibition opens. The month after that, another Nazi bunker gets emptied, and the gold is returned. Life is good, Vivianne. We made it good."

He's right. The trials are over—Father got forty years, Prescott fifteen. The Sentinel organization has been dismantled, its assets seized and redistributed. Sixty-three families have been reunited with fortunes they thought were lost forever. Museums worldwide are rebuilding collections.

And us? We're here. Married. Free. Building a life that's completely ours.

The party winds down as midnight approaches. We say goodbye to our guests—Dr. Phillips to his museum. Merlin is staying in the village for a few days, finally taking a vacation after seventy years of fighting.

Paul and I drive back to the chalet under stars that seem impossibly bright. I can't stop touching my husband—*husband!*—as we climb the path.

At the threshold, Paul scoops me up, my dress tangling around his arms, both of us laughing as he fumbles with the door. We stumble inside, and he sets me down gently, hands framing my face.

"My wife." Testing the words.

"My husband." And then we're kissing, deep and consuming, the kind of kiss that leads to clothes scattered down hallways and promises whispered against skin.

Later—much later—we stand on the balcony wrapped in the sheet from our bed, looking out over Lac Léman. The moon is full, turning the water to liquid silver.

"No regrets?" Paul pulls me closer against his chest.

I think about it. Really think about it. About the woman who ran through gardens in a destroyed wedding dress, who stood up to her father, and who helped recover billions in stolen gold.

About the baby growing inside me, who will never know cages or contracts or the weight of a legacy built on theft.

"None." I mean it. "This is what freedom looks like."

Paul's hand drifts to my stomach, spreading across where our child grows. "It looks good on you."

"Everything looks good on me." I tease. "I'm an heiress, remember?"

"Former heiress. Current art historian. Future mother. Always mine."

"Always yours." I turn in his arms to kiss him.

The word hangs between us, powerful and perfect. *Choice.* The thing I never had and now have in abundance. In the quiet of our mountain home with the lake spread below and my husband's arms around me, I finally understand what my grandmother's letters meant.

True love leaves its mark on you forever.

Not a scar. Not a cage.

It gives you wings to fly.

YOU'VE MET Guardian HRS.
NOW DISCOVER WHERE IT ALL BEGAN.

THE ELITE OPERATIVES WHO RESCUED VIVIANNE DIDN'T JUST appear out of nowhere. They're **Delta Team**—the heart of Guardian Hostage Rescue Specialists—and they have their own stories. Each one packed with impossible missions, heart-stopping danger, and love that ignites in the most unexpected places.

But every team has an origin story.

RESCUING MELISSA is where Guardian HRS begins— the mission that forged Delta Team into the family you just watched save a bride from her own wedding.

And it's **FREE.**

If you loved watching Guardian HRS in action, you'll devour this series.

Claim your free copy of Rescuing Melissa here:

Four teams. Unlimited adrenaline.

Welcome to Guardian HRS.

—Ellie Masters

Keep current with Ellie Masters.
CLICK HERE

Receive news of her writing and new releases.

**Shop Ellie Masters Romantic Suspense and Steamy
Contemporary Romance by series.
Angel Fire Rock Romance
Guardian HRS: Alpha Team
Guardian HRS: Bravo Team
Guardian HRS: Charlie Team
Guardian HRS: Delta Team
Cerberus Personal Security
The LaRouge Triplets
The One I Want Series
Angel's Peak Series
Billionaire Boy's Club
The Lovers
Changing Roles**

ELLZ BELLZ

ELLIE'S FACEBOOK READER GROUP

If you are interested in joining the ELLZ BELLZ, Ellie's Facebook reader group, we'd love to have you.

Join Ellie's ELLZ BELLZ.
The ELLZ BELLZ Facebook Reader Group

Sign up for Ellie's Newsletter.
Elliemasters.com/newslettersignup

Also by Ellie Masters

The LIGHTER SIDE

Ellie Masters is the lighter side of the Jet & Ellie Masters writing duo! You will find Contemporary Romance, Military Romance, Romantic Suspense, Billionaire Romance, and Rock Star Romance in Ellie's Works.

YOU CAN FIND ELLIE'S BOOKS HERE:

ELLIEMASTERS.COM/BOOKS

Shop Ellie Masters Romantic Suspense and Steamy Contemporary Romance by series.

Angel Fire Rock Romance

Guardian HRS: Alpha Team

Guardian HRS: Bravo Team

Guardian HRS: Charlie Team

Guardian HRS: Delta Team

Cerberus Personal Security

The LaRouge Triplets

The One I Want Series

Angel's Peak Series

Billionaire Boy's Club

The Lovers

Changing Roles

Rescuing Eve

Rescuing Lily

Rescuing Jinx

Rescuing Maria

Bravo Team

Rescuing Angie

Rescuing Isabelle

Rescuing Carmen

Rescuing Rosalie

Rescuing Kaye

Cara's Protector

Rescuing Barbi

Charlie Team

Rescuing Rebel

Rescuing Stitch

Rescuing Mia

Jenna's Protector

Rescuing Sophia

Rescuing Malia

Rescuing Ally (Part 1)

Rescuing Ally (Part 2)

Delta Team

Rescuing Ember

Rescuing Aria

STANDALONES IN THE GUARDIAN HOSTAGE RESCUE

SERIES YOU CAN READ ANYTIME

Military Romance

Guardian Personal Protection Specialists

Sybil's Protector

Lyra's Protector

Angel's Peak Series

Steamy Instalove Small Town

EACH BOOK IN THIS SERIES CAN BE READ AS A STANDALONE AND IS ABOUT A DIFFERENT COUPLE WITH AN HEA.

SNOWED IN WITH THE MOUNTAIN DOCTOR

Rescued by the Mountain Guide

Stranded with the Resort Owner

Matched with the Small-Town Chef

Trapped with the Forest Ranger

Snowbound with the Vineyard Owner

Reunited with the Hometown Hero

Colliding with the Coffee Shop Owner

Falling for the Firefighter

Wrecked with the Reclusive Author

Tangled with the Single Dad

Whirlwinded by the Helicopter Pilot

Sheltered by the Veterinarian

Bound by the Sheriff

The One I Want Series

(Small Town, Military Heroes)

By Jet & Ellie Masters

~AND~

Science Fiction

Ellie Masters writing as L.A. Warren

Vendel Rising: a Science Fiction Serialized Novel

If you enjoyed this book by Ellie Masters, the LIGHTER SIDE of the Jet & Ellie writing duo, and aren't afraid of edgier writing, you might enjoy reading BDSM themed books written by Jet, the DARKER SIDE of the Masters' Writing Team.

The DARKER SIDE

Jet Masters is the darker side of the Jet & Ellie writing duo!

Romantic Suspense

Changing Roles Series:

THIS SERIES MUST BE READ IN ORDER.

Command Me

Control Me

Collar Me

Embracing FATE

Seizing FATE

Accepting FATE

HOT READS

A STANDALONE NOVEL.

Down the Rabbit Hole

Light BDSM Romance

About the Author

Ellie Masters is a USA Today Bestselling author and Amazon Top 15 Author who writes Angsty, Steamy, Heart-Stopping, Pulse-Pounding, Can't-Stop-Reading Romantic Suspense. In addition, she's a wife, military mom, doctor, and retired Colonel. She writes romantic suspense filled with all your sexy, swoon-worthy alpha men. Her writing will tug at your heartstrings and leave your heart racing.

Born in the South, raised under the Hawaiian sun, Ellie has traveled the globe while in service to her country. The love of her life, her amazing husband, is her number one fan and biggest supporter. And yes! He's read every word she's written.

She has lived all over the United States—east, west, north, south and central—but grew up under the Hawaiian sun. She's also been privileged to have lived overseas, experiencing other cultures and making lifelong friends. Now, Ellie is proud to call herself a Southern transplant, learning to say y'all and "bless her heart" with the best of them.

Ellie's favorite way to spend an evening is curled up on a couch, laptop in place, watching a fire, drinking a good wine, and bringing forth all the characters from her mind to the page and hopefully into the hearts of her readers.

FOR MORE INFORMATION
elliemasters.com

facebook.com/elliemastersromance
x.com/Ellie__Masters
instagram.com/ellie_masters
bookbub.com/authors/ellie-masters
goodreads.com/Ellie_Masters

Connect with Ellie Masters

Website:
elliemasters.com
Purchase Direct:
elliemasters.com/shopify
Amazon Author Page:
elliemasters.com/amazon
Facebook:
elliemasters.com/Facebook
Goodreads:
elliemasters.com/Goodreads
Bookbub:
elliemasters.com/Bookbub
Instagram:
elliemasters.com/Instagram

Final Thoughts

I hope you enjoyed this book as much as I enjoyed writing it. If you enjoyed reading this story, please consider leaving a review on Amazon and Goodreads, and please let other people know. A sentence is all it takes. Friend recommendations are the strongest catalyst for readers' purchase decisions! And I'd love to be able to continue bringing the characters and stories from My-Mind-to-the-Page.

Second, call or e-mail a friend and tell them about this book. If you really want them to read it, gift it to them. If you prefer digital friends, please use the "Recommend" feature of Goodreads to spread the word.

Or visit my blog https://elliemasters.com, where you can find out more about my writing process and personal life.

Come visit The EDGE: Dark Discussions where we'll have a chance to talk about my works, their creation, and maybe what the future has in store for my writing.

Facebook Reader Group: Ellz Bellz

Thank you so much for your support!

Love,
Ellie

Dedication

This book is dedicated to you, my reader. Thank you for spending a few hours of your time with me. I wouldn't be able to write without you to cheer me on. Your wonderful words, your support, and your willingness to join me on this journey is a gift beyond measure.

Whether this is the first book of mine you've read, or if you've been with me since the very beginning, thank you for believing in me as I bring these characters 'from my mind to the page and into your hearts.'

Love,
Ellie

THE END

www.ingramcontent.com/pod-product-compliance
Lightning Source LLC
Chambersburg PA
CBHW030137310726
48970CB00005B/1461